Why I Killed My Husband

Why I Killed My Husband

and other such Stories

ANITA NAIR

cntxt

Published by Context, an imprint of Westland Books, a division of Nasadiya Technologies Private Limited, in 2025

No. 269/2B, First Floor, 'Irai Arul', Vimalraj Street, Nethaji Nagar, Alapakkam Main Road, Maduravoyal, Chennai 600095

ISBN: 9789371977944

10 9 8 7 6 5 4 3 2 1

This is a work of fiction. Names, characters, organisations, places, events and incidents are either products of the author's imagination or used fictitiously.

Typeset by Jojy Philip

Printed at Manipal Technologies Limited, Manipal

Into my heart an air that kills
From yon far country blows:
What are those blue remembered hills,
What spires, what farms are those?

That is the land of lost content
I see it shining plain.
The happy highways where I went
And cannot come again.

—A.E. Housman
from *A Shropshire Lad*

CONTENTS

PREFACE

More than a decade ago, I heard the crime novelist Ian Rankin use the phrase 'state of the nation' in an interview. Something about the phrase grabbed me by the throat. While I had always found crime fiction a great platform for social commentary, I had just stumbled on a new way of seeing the world around us. A point of view that allowed me to meld the personal and the political. It stayed in my head rent free. Biding its time. Waiting for an opportune moment.

Sometime in mid-2019, Storytel commissioned me to write a set of original audio stories. It was a new medium for me and demanded a new way of writing. A voice narrating a story has a certain immediacy to it, and imprints itself on the mind in a way that the written word cannot. Exploring this medium was the most exciting thing I had done in a long time. There was the length of the story itself. At about forty-five minutes to an hour long, it was too long for it to be classified as a short story and too short to be a novel. But it was just right to capture a detailed slice of life. There were other challenges, of course. While the plot was within the purview of literary fiction, the pace had to lure the listener in within the first couple of minutes. Descriptions. Dialogues. How much was too much or too little? And the characters? How many were too many? While I speculated on the technicalities, the real issue became: what was I going to write about?

Then, one December morning in 2019, while visiting my ancestral village Mundakotukurussi in Kerala, I started on a story. It was set in the fictitious village of Kaikurussi which I had used in my first novel, *The Better Man*. As I wrote, the anti-CAA agitation which had begun at Shaheen Bagh on 15 December crept into the story and suddenly it was impacting the lives of my characters living in a tiny village 2,437 km away. What I had thought was going to be a pastoral tale turned pastoral-political. That was when I knew I had discovered my first state-of-the-nation story.

Most of us keep track of the news. International, national, regional, local. Except that we turn the page or scroll down and go on with our lives. We tell ourselves that it doesn't concern us. We convince ourselves that we can do nothing about it. We take refuge in apathy. All of us are guilty of this day after day. We forget that apathy, too, is a crime.

A couple of years after the Storytel stories went live, I revisited them and decided they needed a new lease of life. I set about recrafting the stories and drawing even more on the political, economic and societal tapestries of our time and their impact on the everyday. If a coupe in a train was what bound six women together in my second novel, *Ladies Coupe*, here, it is the state of the nation that binds the six stories together. Set within a span of a decade, all these stories are inspired by true life incidents.

As for the last story, 'The Land of Lost Content', all I will say is that it happened to me.

Anita Nair
21 October 2025

WHY I KILLED MY HUSBAND

I should have killed my husband on our wedding night.

It was a quarter past ten and I had been waiting in the bedroom for half an hour by then. My husband, how effortlessly my mouth shaped the word, my husband, my beloved, my soulmate, my everything was yet to come.

There had been some tittering from my relatives about the bride waiting in the bedroom for the groom. It was usually the other way round. But he froze them all with a look and said, 'She needs to rest.'

As if to make up for his abruptness, he added, 'It's been a long day and it's going to be a long night.' He winked, and they all tittered again. 'He is already smitten. Lucky thing!'

He had left to see a few colleagues off. Their car was parked at the end of the road. He had been gone a long time.

When I heard the door handle turn, I stood up and prepared myself. My heart thumped in my ears and I felt my legs tremble.

He looked at the jasmine festooned room, the fruit laden tray, and the incense sticks stuck into the side of a banana. He looked at me standing there, a silver tumbler of milk between my palms. I waited for him to speak.

'Seriously?' he snorted.

I was startled. Seriously what? I swallowed and said, 'I don't understand …'

'All of this, and that crazy old car the night before …'

Have you ever seen a gesture more dismissive than words? With a wave of his hand, he decimated my father's dream for me.

'It was like a Tamil movie from the seventies. Which rock were you people living under until now? It was embarrassing ... I can't imagine what my relatives and friends made of the wedding.' His voice was low and furious.

He looked at me for a long moment, then opened the balcony door and stepped out.

I didn't know what to do except sit on the satin-sheathed bed and pull apart a string of jasmine buds. I hadn't known how our first night would go. Some of my college friends had said that their husbands insisted on sex on the very first night, while some others said that theirs had preferred to wait.

I had imagined us talking into the night, holding hands and exchanging little kisses. I had imagined him drawing me to his chest and snuggling with him. I hadn't imagined this feeling of being abandoned.

It had been a beautiful wedding. Not as elaborate as a Marwadi wedding with marigolds and fireworks and a groom on a white horse. But it was grand enough. My appa was a traditional man, and he wanted his friends and relatives to see the prize catch he had found me.

The proposal had come via a marriage broker. B.S. Madhavan, aged twenty-nine years, medium height and build, with a high forehead and a straight nose, thick long hair swept back from his forehead, skin the colour of sandalwood paste, and a professional violinist. Amma asked, 'What is his job? Or is he just a fiddle player?'

Appa grinned. 'He is with the LIC. Life Insurance Corporation. Pension on retirement and full job security.'

'Do grooms like that grow on trees?' he demanded, turning to me, in case I still wasn't interested.

'What about the family?' My mother, ever pragmatic, persisted.

'The parents are dead. Madhavan has an older brother and sister. Both married and well settled. The sister is in Canada with her husband. So you don't have to worry about any in-laws,' Appa said, grinning at me.

'Appa, you don't have to sell him to me. You can ask them to come, but they may not like what they see.'

'Why?' my parents said in unison. 'What's wrong with you? You're well educated, you have a good job, and your mouth isn't where your nose is … why won't he like you?'

And so, Madhavan came. Madhavan saw. Madhavan conquered. Me as well as my parents and relatives. Apparently, Madhavan liked me too. I clung to the word 'like' and built my palace of dreams around it.

Like my father, who grew up on a diet of Tamil movies and continued to devour them, I too had a passion for films and watched all the Tamil and some of the English movies that came to town. My parents and I would go for the matinee show but first we would have lunch at a vegetarian restaurant before heading to either Shanthi or Safire or Casino or Plaza or Devi. Sometimes I went to watch Hindi films too, even if I didn't understand any of the dialogues.

I would look at Madhavan's photograph and play out all my favourite movie scenes in my head. I was Urvashi to his Kamal Haasan in *Michael Madana Kama Rajan*. I was Manisha Koirala to his Arvind Swami in *Bombay*. I was Julia Roberts to his Richard Gere in *Pretty Woman*. I was in love even though I knew next to nothing about him.

Sitting there on my nuptial bed, it slowly dawned on me that the man I had imagined Madhavan to be was probably nothing like the man I was married to. I started on one more string of jasmine buds, wondering what I had got into.

My father was nineteen when the MGR film *Nalla Neram* was released. He loved everything about it. He saw it twelve times, and on the twelfth viewing decided that for his jaana vaasam, he would demand an Impala convertible.

However, my mother's family could only get him a Standard. Middle-class Thanjavur households didn't go for Impalas. Appa didn't make a fuss, but he decided that if and when he had a daughter, there would be a red Impala convertible for the jaana vaasam.

Do you know what that is? On the evening before the wedding, the groom is seated in an open car decorated with flowers and driven at a snail's pace through the neighbourhood from a nearby temple to the wedding hall. The bride's parents accompany the car while a nadaswaram band leads the way, ostensibly for the groom to familiarise himself with the bride's family and surroundings.

Amma whispered, 'That's what they all say but really, he is being paraded for everyone to see.' She added with a giggle, 'In case he runs away, people will know who to look for.'

I asked, 'Do husbands run away?'

The thought had never occurred to me. Separations and divorces I knew about, but the thought of a husband running away was as amusing as it was appalling.

'It's been known to happen,' she said cryptically. 'It's in the wife's hands to keep her husband happy and at her side.'

The year was 1997, and the last Impala to ferry a groom through the city must have been from the late sixties when I wasn't even born. But that didn't deter my father. He wasn't rich but he was prudent.

My mother said that he had started saving money for my wedding from the day I was born. He started with a few rupees a day, and when I had my first period at twelve, he used up most of that for the ceremony. He had another twelve years to save for the wedding.

Meanwhile, I graduated and wrote all the bank tests and joined the State Bank of India. Appa and Amma said I was set for life. A well-paying job with a pension and benefits on retirement gave Appa the courage to find me a husband 'above our status', as he said.

Appa had wanted the wedding ceremony to be perfect. Once the date was fixed, he began organising every little thing himself. 'I don't want one whisper from the groom's side about what wasn't right about Anjali's wedding.'

He asked just about everyone he knew how to track down the man whose car 'MRZ2233' had featured in the film *Nalla Neram*. It was expensive to rent, but he was determined to show off his prize catch for his daughter. Except that the prize catch was furious rather than pleased with the car.

In retrospect, I wish Appa had spent as much time looking for a husband for me.

I should have killed my husband when he nicknamed me Bonda.

It was the fourth day after our wedding. I was at Madhavan's home. The hustle and bustle of the wedding was over and all his relatives had returned to their homes with their tamboolam bags, their share from the prodigious quantities of murukku, athirasam, laddoo and mysore pak, and seer bakshanam that had been made to accompany me to my married home. Not that this deterred them from grumbling in stage whispers: I think they used Dalda instead of ghee in the mysore pak; the murukku only has five varis in it, instead of seven; the diamond in the nose-pin could have been bigger; the girl looks like a brinjal—short, round and dark.

I didn't care about what the relatives said. I saw myself in the mirror every day and I knew what I looked like. As for the complaints, it was customary at every wedding. In fact, Amma said that if the groom's relatives didn't complain, there was something wrong with him.

The house still had a festive air. Madhavan's brother and wife lived there, and now so did I. His sister and her husband, and an aunt, all of whom lived in Canada, were to leave soon. The older children watched TV while the younger ones ran around. There was laughter and much chit-chat. It was exactly as I had imagined it would be.

Did I mention that our marriage was consummated? When what had to be done was done, I realised why the nuptial chambers had to be dressed up. Furtive and messy, accompanied by thrashing limbs and reined-in breath, the sharing of body fluids made me wonder what the fuss was all about. I had never had a boyfriend, but I had read up on sex and knew what it entailed. I even knew to expect some pain. But it was over even before I warmed up. And I was too shy to ask: what about me?

I thought of my mother making vadams. When I couldn't match her speed, she would say, you'll catch up once you get the hang of it. All you need is practise.

I don't suppose you know anything about vadams that are homemade. You probably eat those ghastly cardboard-like chips that come in a packet.

Come to think of it, sex and eating a vadam are pretty much the same. Vadams require elaborate preparation: mixing the dough, shaping it into coils with fingers or a press, spreading them out to dry while also safeguarding them from raiding ants and marauding crows. The oil has to be heated just right, so the vadams fluff out to a golden fullness and make everyone's mouth water when they are brought to the table. And what do we do then? We pop them into our mouths and in two bites, they are gone.

After all that build up in books and movies, and all the wink-wink from aunts and cousins about breaking the bedstead and making the earth move, etc., I had expected more from sex than the two-bites-and-gone experience.

But as everyone knows, vadams just add the crunch factor to a meal. They cannot be the meal itself.

Where was I? I was telling you that I had worn a double-shaded coffee-brown Kanjeevaram with a temple zari border in turquoise blue. The pallu was magnificent with elaborate zari work. I had fallen in love with the sari and bought it for myself after haggling with my conscience. I told everyone who asked that it cost just 5,000 rupees instead of the 10,000 I had paid for it. Even then, my mother had gasped a little. It was what my parents had run their household on till my job changed our circumstances.

As soon as I was eligible for it, I had taken a housing loan and bought us a small but brand-new apartment in Besant Nagar. It had a living-cum-dining room, two bedrooms with bath attached, a little study, two balconies that overlooked the quiet tree-lined street we were on and a fairly large kitchen.

My parents were ecstatic. We were a typical lower-middle-class Tam Brahm family for whom buying a house was a defining moment.

Custom and courtesy defined everything we did. It had held my parents and me in good stead, and I thought that was how it would always be. On the fourth day, I dressed in my new Kanjeevaram sari, changed my diamond studs for a pair of gold danglers with turquoise beads, added a string of jasmine to my waist-long braid and stepped out of our room. It was the first time we would be together as a family. Madhavan, his siblings and their spouses, and no relatives to deflect the attention from me.

I was both apprehensive and excited. New brides will understand this. You want so much to belong that you go the extra mile. You so want to make the right impression that you rush to do this and that. My husband watched me with an expression I couldn't read.

'Is anything wrong,' I asked.

'Those earrings don't suit you at all. That shade of blue makes you look darker.'

'Oh,' I said, not knowing how else to respond, my hand going to the dangler in my left ear.

'Danglers are for college students, not married women,' he added.

We were interrupted by his aunt. She wanted me in the kitchen. It turned out that Madhavan's older brother and wife had a wedding to attend, and had gone for the day to Kumbakonam.

I cooked alongside Madhavan's aunt. At one point, he popped into the kitchen to ask, 'Are you letting her cook, Athai? I don't know if she can.'

His aunt cocked an eyebrow, 'Of course she can. Look at this.' She pointed to the array of dishes I had made. Arachu uthiya sambar, beans paruppu usili, vatha kuzhambu, tomato rasam, fried arisi appalam.

He beamed, and I basked in his pride.

After the elaborate meal, which everyone praised, Athai suggested a game of Ludo. The board was pulled out and Madhavan's sister unearthed a pair of old brass dice from the sewing machine box. Madhavan, his sister, brother-in-law and aunt settled down to play. I wished they had included me, but I sat behind Madhavan as if to pledge my allegiance.

The brass dice fell on the floor with a clink. There was much talk and peals of laughter as family jokes were cracked and memories dredged out. The camaraderie in the room included me, or so I thought. I was the happiest bride under the sun.

Madhavan's brother-in-law was the first to lose the game. His wife mock frowned at him and said, 'Your mind is not on the game!' He grinned at her lasciviously and said, 'How can I concentrate on the game when you sit across from me? You look like a …' He groped for the words.

I supplied them in the spirit of the moment: 'In that yellow sari and your black pottu, you look like a laddoo with a raisin stuck in it.'

My laughter rang loud and clear. I failed to see my sister-in-law's face fall. I failed to realise that while her husband was allowed to rib her, I was the new bride. I should have said something appropriate like Akka looks like a goddess descended from the heavens to earth. Instead, I had called her a laddoo.

I failed to see the rage that striated my husband's brow. He turned to me and snapped. 'What are you laughing for? You look like a bonda. And in that sari, you look like a burnt bonda.'

I didn't know if it was the sari or me that was the colour of an overdone fried ball, but I heard the titter among the players and the audience. A couple of children took up the chant, 'Bonda, Bonda ... Burnt Bonda.' And just like that, I became Bonda.

No one ever called me by my name again. Not Anjali, my given name, nor Kalyani, which Madhavan's family had decided would be my married name. They just called me Bonda.

I gave the sari away to my mother, exchanged the turquoise danglers for a pair of nondescript gold studs, and learnt to zip my mouth when I was with Madhavan's family. On the weighing scales of matrimony, I had fallen short again.

I should have killed my husband when I first heard him play the violin.

I didn't grow up with music, not like Madhavan. My parents enjoyed listening to music, but it ended there. Despite this, when I was five years old, they decided to send me to a music teacher. I hid in the toilet that first evening, when it was time to go to class. The thought of having to open my mouth and sing in front of everyone petrified me.

It was my mother who dragged me out of the toilet. 'Who is going to marry you if you can't even sing sa pa sa?' she said as she thrust me into my father's arms. For the next five years, I endured a teacher whose method of teaching was to make us sing by rote. It was both tedious and dull. She would wind up a little alarm clock and place it next to the shruti box. Exactly when the hour was up, it would trill and she would stop.

Fortunately, when I was ten, I scored a mere 80 out of 100 in mathematics. My father couldn't have been more appalled if I had been expelled. The music lessons were replaced with maths tuition, and here I found comfort. The numbers were absolutes and much easier to grapple with than the whimsical musical notes that oscillated between microtones.

When Madhavan's marriage proposal arrived, my five years of music tutelage were trotted out. A classical musician like Madhavan needs a wife who understands the rigour that music demands—the broker said with a broad smile.

A week after we were married, the house guests returned to Toronto—to be said without the second 't', I was told by everyone, including the children—and Madhavan sat down early in the day with his violin.

For a moment, I wished he would gaze at me with the tenderness with which he looked at his violin. When he placed it in the sweet spot between his shoulder and chest and ran the bow over the strings almost without touching them, I felt bereft. There was passion, a deep sensuality that I had never seen in him. And I knew I would never be able to complete him the way his violin did.

He played a few notes, and it was as if he were speaking to the violin. Crooning to his beloved, persuading her to do his bidding. Then he played a Thyagaraja kriti, Mohana Rama in Mohanam raga. It was one of the few ragas I could recognise. I had heard it several times over the years, but Madhavan and his violin owned it.

He built it up phrase by phrase, and I felt my heart would burst with the love I felt for him. It was a moment unlike any

I had ever known, or ever would again. Thank you, O Gods, I murmured in my head. Thank you for bringing him to me.

The magnificence of his music overwhelmed me. When he finished, he looked at me, but I couldn't speak. Besides, I remembered what the marriage broker had said, that while Madhavan wanted a wife who understood music, he didn't want a wife with a musical opinion. So I sat there in silence, hoping he would read the admiration and respect in my eyes.

He put the bow down and shook his head in annoyance. 'Are you going to sit there without speaking a word? I may as well have played to a donkey.'

I should have killed my husband when our son was born.

Because we were not of our parents' generation, he wasn't born exactly ten months after the wedding. Instead, he was conceived a year after, and was born after our second wedding anniversary.

By the time I got pregnant, I had beguiled myself into thinking that I had found marital bliss. True, he didn't like how I cooked or how I dressed to work or my range of conversation. True, he spent more time with his violin than with me. But I was pregnant, right?

As my mother liked to say, there are no rose plants without thorns. I was married. I had a husband. We had a decent life. Everything was as it should be.

In the first trimester of my pregnancy, we had to attend a wedding at my father's ancestral home in Chidambaram. The old house was filled with people. I began to feel a little breathless, so we decided to step out into the backyard where the children were playing cricket. Madhavan watched them for a while, then muttered under his breath, 'I hope our child won't be like them.'

I said, 'Oh, don't be so hard on them. They are not ruffians. Just children having a good time.'

Madhavan raised an eyebrow. 'I wasn't referring to the noise. Look at them. Do you realise that almost everyone in your family is short, squat and almost black?'

I didn't say anything. How could I? It was the truth. I choked on my hurt—or was it rage?—and pressed my knuckles into my thighs. He saw the movement of my hand and said softly, 'It's the truth. Even you can see it. No need to get agitated.'

I didn't speak. I was never good with repartee. Mostly, a fitting retort would form in my head three days too late. I got up and went back inside to show my displeasure.

That night, and every night thereafter, I drank a glass of saffron milk. I would add strands of saffron to warmed-up milk and force myself to drink it. My child would not turn out with skin like mine. I knew that DNA determined such things. But when one is pregnant, sense and logic often fly out of the window.

In my seventh month, my parents celebrated my valaikappu ceremony. Relatives from my side and Madhavan's were invited. Women from our family and female friends gathered around me and there was much festivity. I wore a new nine yard sari. A cousin put a garland around my neck. The gathered women sang songs and my wrists were adorned with bangles. First, a bangle made of neem stem. Then a silver bangle and then a gold bangle and finally the glass bangles. Twenty on my left wrist and twenty-one on the right. When the baby was born, I would make an offering of these bangles at our family temple. Meanwhile, they would protect my baby's wellbeing.

I moved back to my parents' home in preparation for the birth. Madhavan joined me after a couple of weeks. It was more convenient for him to reach Anna Salai from Besant Nagar than from West Tambaram, he claimed. No one could fault that. And it didn't occur to me to ask: how come none of you thought about this when I was travelling to the Teynampet branch every day, morning sickness, fatigue and all?

Madhavan settled in easily. He laid claim to the study, with its enclosed balcony, which we had turned into a guest room. It became his room where he glanced through his files, practised the violin and did whatever he did behind a closed door. My parents spoilt him silly. He was the son they never had. He basked in their adulation and the last trimester went by quietly.

Once, when I felt the baby kicking, I asked him to feel my distended belly. 'Here, here,' I said, placing his hand on my baby bump. 'You can feel the baby move.'

It was the only time I saw him lost for words. His eyes became soft with the magic of the moment. Then he said with a laugh, 'It has to be a boy. Only a boy would kick so hard.'

My parents beamed. They, too, hoped it would be a boy.

When the pains began, I was rushed to the hospital by my parents. It didn't take long, and when the nurse placed my son in my hands, my first thought was thank god he isn't bonda-coloured like me. By the time Madhavan reached, the baby was swaddled and at my side.

I couldn't stop examining him. Madhavan smiled. 'You are looking at him as if he's a thousand-rupee note. Checking to see if he is the real thing and not fake currency.'

The baby gazed at me with equal caution. Then he blinked. I looked up to smile at Madhavan. 'He knows me … look how he blinked at me.'

Madhavan took the baby in his arms. 'Blinked? See how he smiles at me.'

And just like that, I was cast out of the magic circle. He made the baby his. I had merely been the carrier.

The baby was named Saranga. The name of a raga, he said. An offspring of the parent raga Kalyani, he laughed. My parents laughed too. So did my friends who came by to see the baby. Everyone thought he was witty. And so he was, as long as his witticisms were directed elsewhere. To me, his words were like hot coals singeing the skin, eating into the flesh.

I should have left my husband when we lived on the plateau of compromise.

Our lives had enmeshed with the arrival of Saranga. We continued to live with my parents. I was an only child. Once my maternity leave was over, my parents would care for Saranga while I resumed work. It made sense, everyone agreed. 'Besides, Bonda,' Madhavan said, 'the apartment is yours, and someday we will be living here for good.'

Our careers were dull but steady. Once a year, we went on holiday. We posted pictures of us in costumes on Facebook. We tagged each other on every post and planted little hearts.

Madhavan's musical career was taking flight finally. He had begun by accompanying the newer singers on the circuit. But now he was being called upon to be the accompanist for the near near greats. And he had begun playing solo concerts as well.

Once in a while he would say, 'I am considering VRS. That way I can give all of myself to music.' I pretended not to hear him. It was best, I had decided, to not encourage him.

The sameness of our daily life would have numbed anyone else, but not me. I found safety in routine. I didn't crave excitement or a surge of adrenaline. All I wanted was for each day to be like the next one, without any surprises.

I should have remembered that plateaus are formed as a result of subterranean tectonic shifts. And that plateaus almost always sit alongside fault lines that can heave and shift, changing the nature of everything else around it. I wouldn't have been caught unawares then.

My parents were returning from the Sai temple in Injambakkam when a bus rammed into their scooter. With that, the axis of my world shifted. On the day after the cremation, when all the relatives had left, the small apartment felt like a vast, desolate land. From then on, there would only be Madhavan, Saranga and me.

I should have left my husband on our thirteenth wedding anniversary.

A few months had passed since my parents' death. I hadn't been feeling well and had taken a couple of days off. Saranga had a school holiday as well. So I was not surprised to see Madhavan let himself into the flat at lunch time. I had expected him to take the afternoon off given that it was our wedding anniversary and both Saranga and I were at home. We would probably go for a movie in the evening followed by dinner. That was how we usually celebrated our anniversaries.

I served lunch. Madhavan pulled out a chair and seated himself at the dining table. He said, 'I have a surprise.'

I don't like surprises. They frighten me. I took a deep breath and exhaled, hoping it would be yet another pastel-coloured silk-cotton sari that he had bought on his way home.

He drummed his fingers on the table impatiently and asked, 'Aren't you going to ask me what it is?'

I said, pretending to be curious, 'What is it?'

'I've put my voluntary retirement scheme into motion.'

The frog inside my throat croaked, 'And?'

'And I'm going to do what I always wanted to. Work on my music and become a full-time musician,'

He helped himself to the kalyana-manga I had made for our anniversary meal. Chopped up mango with asafoetida and chilli powder tossed with mustard sautéed in sesame oil was one of his favourite dishes, but I knew him well enough to not make it more than a few times a year. He tired easily of things. How long would it be before he grew tired of being a full-time musician?

'How will we live? Saranga's school fees, the home loan, the car loan …' I rattled out the list of pay-outs for every month.

'Is that all you have to say?' he frowned.

'Money is money. You can't play a Bilahari kriti to the milkman or a Ragam Tanam Pallavi to the bank in place of an EMI,' I snapped and immediately wished I hadn't.

'I see. And I don't know that?'

'I meant …' I tried to make amends wondering if I had crossed a line. In my defence, I was petrified, and fear robs one of sensitivity.

He thrust an open palm at me, as if to say, enough!

'I know what you meant,' he said, rising from the table and shoving the chair aside. 'The VRS will be a tidy sum and there will be money from my music engagements.'

Really? I wanted to ask. He had worked for only fifteen years; the tidy sum would be not more than a few lakhs. He was forty-one years old and I was thirty-seven. I didn't think my salary was going to suffice for us once Saranga left school.

Madhavan paused to say, 'That mango thing you make, by the way, is terrible. You never get it right. I don't even know why you bother ...'

I took his plate and mine to the sink. From the study, I heard the violin come alive. P M P S D R S D S. The bow screeched and crashed. By now, I had learnt to identify the notes. The fury was unmistakable. P R ... S P S ... D. Musical phrases instead of hammer blows.

Saranga walked in with his eyebrows at his hairline. He had gone out to meet a classmate. 'Is Appa home? He sounds upset.'

'He's quit his job,' I said, cleaning the table.

'That's amazing, Amma.' He paused, reading my expression with the same intuitiveness with which he identified ragas. 'Did you bring up money? How could you, Amma? He's an artist, and artists need freedom and headspace to devote to their art. Appa should be allowed to concentrate on his music ...'

Saranga had started singing when he was three. At eleven, he had already mastered a great deal. And he often repeated things he heard his father and his friends say about music and musicians. I know that I should have sat him down and shown him the list of pay-outs. I should have asked if Madhavan's violin would pay for at least half of those. Instead, I asked him if he was planning to eat lunch or stand there glaring at me.

Saranga plonked himself in front of the TV with the plate I had made for him. I stared at the top of his head and mouthed silently, 'Next time you need money to go to the bowling alley with your friends, ask your appa to play the violin at the mall.'

I felt my rage rise as I slammed the dishes down in the sink. I opened the tap and let the water splash over the dirty vessels.

I let the water run as I went into the bedroom and took my handbag and phone. I let it run as I closed the door behind me. I was tired of being the practical one, always the villain of the story.

I would never be able to leave Madhavan. Not unless I was prepared to lose Saranga. Knowing this, I should have killed him the next day.

The fury with which I had stormed out of the house had vanished by the time I reached the main gate. The thought of all that wasted water made me go back.

Women can be such fools. I know. I was one too. I didn't address what was critical. The truth is, I didn't know how to. More importantly, I didn't have the courage to confront him. Instead I let the petty, insignificant details take precedence. Like our squabble over coffee decoction.

I was thrifty to begin with. My upbringing had been such. I tried to stretch everything as far as it would go. With leftover rice, I made lemon rice. With the lemon halves I had squeezed the juice out of, I made pickle. It was how people like me were wired. We made the last bits count.

I put the coffee on to steep first thing in the morning. Instead of tossing out the coffee grounds after the first press,

I got another half cup of decoction with a second press. There would be enough for a small but strong cup of coffee in the evening when I got home from work.

On the morning after Madhavan left his job for good, he hung around in the kitchen getting in my way as he made his grand plans. We had arrived at a truce by then. Saranga saw to that.

Madhavan said, 'Tell you what, Bonda, make some extra coffee decoction. Since I'm home, I'll need an occasional coffee.'

I didn't react to his calling me Bonda. I no longer did. It was just another word.

'How occasional a coffee?' I asked, trying not to let my mouth tighten.

He retorted, 'How would I know?' and took his cup of coffee into the hall. He switched the TV on to check the news.

I poured the first press into a container and added hot water to the filter for the second press.

He asked from the doorway, 'What are you doing?' I turned abruptly and felt my stomach descend to my knees at the look in his eyes.

'I ask for extra decoction and you give me the second press. Really? My mother used to give that to the maid. I didn't know I had married a pisi-nari.' His nostrils flared in anger.

I was annoyed at being called out as a tight-fisted woman and snapped back, 'All of us drank the second press in my home.'

He said, 'I can't help your upbringing but in my home you will do as I want.' He grabbed the coffee filter and tossed its contents down the sink.

'What's wrong with you?' I screamed. 'You've clogged the sink.' I wasn't sure if it was that or watching my evening decoction trickle down the drain that angered me more.

Madhavan shouted back, 'Deal with it. Just because I took VRS, are you going to treat me as a second-class citizen in my own house?'

I flung back, 'It was never your house to begin with. Besides, now that you've decided to quit and sit at home, I'll have to pay the home loan all on my own. And pay for everything else too, including the occasional coffee you want.'

He stared at me. Then he said in a whisper, 'You're sick in the head. That's what you are. Sick!'

I heard the door of the music room slam. I saw Saranga in the doorway, staring at me as if he had caught me slitting a kitten's throat. Appalled, disgusted, angry.

He said, 'What's wrong with you, Amma?' He went to his room, slamming the door after him.

I stood there in the middle of the kitchen, furious and strangely bereft. I didn't know if I was angry with them or with myself. Mechanically, I set about cleaning the sink.

You ask me why? Someone had to do it. And no one else would. The thing is, people who make grand exits seldom hang around to clean up afterwards. It's left to others, the not-so-brilliant, not-so-charming, not-so-dramatic ones, to pick up the pieces and restore some semblance of order.

I should have killed my husband three months later, when he decided to become an entrepreneur.

Once, when I was a child and we were in Chidambaram for a family function, my father decided to take me with him on a shopping expedition. Appa was very particular about the quality of things. Every year, he and my mother would go to Kancheepuram to buy the Deepawali saris. 'Straight from the weavers,' he would say. 'That way, we know it's pure Kancheepuram and not Arni silk.'

He would go all the way to a shop in Triplicane to buy best quality ghee. And now he was going to buy sesame oil. 'Wear your jeans,' he said. He usually insisted that I wear half-saris when we were visiting his family. Or 'Punjabi dress', as he called my churidar-kurtas.

He thrust a steel oil can into my hands. He started the Lambretta scooter he had borrowed from his cousin and said I should sit behind, legs astride, and place the can between us. We went through Chidambaram town and headed into a village. Appa seemed to know exactly where we were going. We stopped at the end of a dirt road. 'This is the best sesame oil you'll find,' he said.

It was an old-fashioned oil mill with grinding stones. A bull was tied to a rope attached to the grinding stones. It was made to walk in circles all day while the man sat on his bum chewing on tobacco and making conversation with anyone walking past. The bull was there to do his bidding and make his life comfortable, luxurious even. It belonged to him, and its destiny was to be yoked to the grinding stone. My situation, I realised now, was no different from that of the bull.

Madhavan decided to open a music store that would sell all things to do with Carnatic music. He had grand plans. The store was going to be a conduit to take music to the masses.

He sat cross-legged on the sofa and declaimed to the real-estate broker, 'Do you realise that music is where our people are? They study the music, they sing it and they listen to it.'

The top two buttons of the broker's shirt were open, so a bit of his yellowing cross thread was visible. He nodded and said, 'Well, that's how it is, anna...'

Madhavan slapped his thigh, a king setting out to conquer new territory. 'Unless we cultivate an audience, how will we have any? That's what I plan to do …'

After my parents died, I had broached the subject of hiring a maid. It would make my life easier if there was someone to do the top work, I told Madhavan.

'But will you find a Brahmin maid?'

'I don't think so. Not in this area, at least.'

'Are you actually considering bringing into the house someone who is not one of us? Are you out of your mind?'

And that was how the discussion had ended. So I was surprised to hear that Madhavan wanted to take Carnatic music to the masses. When the broker had left, I said, 'I'm really glad to hear you talk about opening up the music world. Music ought to belong to everyone and not just our people. Remember the film *Sankarabharnam*? Appa used to say that was the movie that changed how people perceived Carnatic music … stopped them from believing it was beyond their reach.'

Madhavan glared at me. 'You are a musician's wife. Hasn't anything rubbed off on you after all these years? I am talking about people getting serious about classical music. And you bring up *Sankarabharanam* … It's a movie that no real musician takes seriously.'

I glared back at him. 'That's what you think. I know countless people whose idea of Carnatic music changed after watching the film. They started appreciating it finally. Besides, it was a superhit. All those people can't be wrong.'

'People are fools, and I'm sorry to say you are one too.' With that, he walked into his music room and slammed the door.

To anyone else, it would have seemed we were arguing about music. The truth is, we were wrestling with the equilibrium of our marriage.

The music store in Avadi, far away from the music sabhas, was a disaster. In six months, he had to shut it down. He would have had better luck if he had started a shop selling pickles, chutney powders and appalam.

I hated seeing him fritter his life away doing nothing. The concerts were not frequent enough to keep him busy. So I suggested that he give music lessons.

'Musicians who are not sure about their abilities do that. Teach music to any fool.'

'But how do you know that a person has talent until you teach them?' I was chopping vegetables for the next day. I didn't have the time to do it all in the morning, so I did some of the prep work the night before.

I see the question in your eyes. Yes, Madhavan was home most of the day. He could have helped.

In all honesty, he did offer. And I let him take over the kitchen for a week. At the back of my mind, I saw the wheels of the cart we called a relationship turn in the same direction. We might be able to make this work, I thought with a flare of hope.

But I came home day after day to a mountain of dishes, a dirty kitchen and depleted groceries. His cooking was exemplary, I have to give him that. But it wasn't practical. Saranga, of course, loved it and stuffed his face. He would say, 'Amma, it's better that Appa cooks. His food is so yummy!'

I smiled and swallowed my indignation. Very soon, I took over the kitchen duties again.

Saranga complained that my cooking was dull. I ignored him. That was my new battle strategy. I ignored Madhavan when he spewed vitriol about the morons in sabhas, about vocalists getting paid more than accompanists, about nepotism when few solo engagements came his way, about artistic angst compounded by insensitive spouses and their constant nagging about money.

Saranga was now a teenager who realised that power came from playing one parent off the other. I saw how he talked to his father with a conviviality that was part indulgence and part awe. With me he was either scowling like a monkey that's bitten into a piece of ginger or wore an expression of irritation bordering on exasperation.

I was the one who questioned him about school and homework. I was the one who doled out a tiny allowance every week, unlike his father who did a song and dance routine about pressing a 1000-rupee note into his hand once in six months. Money that could have paid the milkman's bill, not that either Madhavan or Saranga wanted to acknowledge that. Instead, Saranga talked about the generosity of one parent while the other 'was a pisi-nari just like Appa always said'.

I ignored his sarcasm and surliness, which could be the result of his DNA or what he picked up from watching Madhavan with me, or a combination of both. The only way to not take a kitchen knife to father and son was by turning into an ostrich and keeping my head buried.

I should have killed my husband when he started encouraging Saranga to take up music full time.

Saranga had started singing at public concerts. Everyone spoke of him as a rising star. Just as they had about

Madhavan—and his star was still to ascend to any great height. The truth was, Madhavan had wrecked his own path to glory. It happened at a concert held at RNG Hall in T. Nagar. The vocalist, Giridhar Padmanabhan, was someone who drew crowds. People flocked to listen to him no matter where he sang. One of the committee members was Madhavan's relative and he persuaded the others to include Madhavan as an accompanist.

It was Madhavan's chance to shine on the big stage. It wasn't as though just about anyone would be invited to share the stage with Giridhar Padmanabhan, he told me and Saranga and everyone he knew.

I took the day off from work. Saranga carried a letter to school, requesting half-day leave for a doctor's appointment at 4 p.m. He was to appear for the boards that year and the school frowned on students asking for leave to attend family functions or other such flimsy reasons. Madhavan had, of course, wanted him to say that he had to attend his father's concert.

Madhavan was dressed in a bright blue silk kurta and a gold-edged veshti, which he had picked up just two days ago. His receding hair was slicked back. He had pierced his ears and wore tiny diamond studs that had belonged to my mother. Both Saranga and I had dressed up too. He looked at Saranga and said, 'Very good.'

Then he cleared his throat impatiently and asked, 'Bonda, where is that driver fellow?'

We had hired a driver for the evening so we could get to the venue early. Usually, I drove when we went out, but Madhavan didn't want to be driven to the venue by his wife. 'Your driving stresses me out and I don't want to lose focus before the concert. Call a driver, Bonda. Is that too much to ask?' he had said.

'The driver is in the basement,' I said, trying not to show how hurt I felt. I should have been used to it by now—the disdain and that dreadful name he called me—but sometimes it still drew blood.

'What is he doing downstairs? Who is going to carry my violin case?'

'I'll take it, Appa,' Saranga said dutifully.

The concert hall was filling up when we reached. Madhavan's eyes lit up. He had never played for such a large audience before. I don't know why, but I gave his arm a reassuring squeeze. He shrugged my hand off and pointed to seats in the second row. 'Sit there. And don't get up in the middle of the thani avarthanam,' he muttered as he took his violin case from Saranga and walked to the green room to join the other musicians.

We took our seats. Saranga didn't speak, but he threw me a look of concern. I smiled at him with some effort. I couldn't ignore the sense of injury that Madhavan's comment had left me with. Did he really think of me as a boorish ignoramus who would choose to go off to the washroom or the canteen in the middle of the concert while the accompanists displayed their prowess?

I may not be musical but when I listened to music, I felt my limbs turn fluid, a queer stillness seeped into me and a sense of—how shall I describe it—a searing happiness. I wished I could tell Madhavan what music did to me, but I was afraid of his scorn.

The musicians were seated and the sound checks were completed. The committee president made a speech and the introductions.

I clapped loudly when Madhavan's credentials were read out. He wasn't yet an AIR Grade Artist, I realised. I would tell him he ought to apply for it. I looked around the packed hall at the women in silks and jewellery accompanied by well-groomed men. All of them were here to listen to Madhavan as well. Perhaps he would finally have what had eluded him so far—success. Perhaps that would make him kinder, happier. For a moment, and for the last time ever, I felt hope that happiness would be mine someday. I wasn't asking for much. An uneventful life with no malice and no surprises. A husband who was a companion and partner. A son who would grow up to be a decent human being. A gentle sort of happiness was all I dreamt of.

Madhavan played a few phrases for a sound check. Giridhar Padmanabhan slipped into the Bhairavi varnam in ata talam. I clapped hard when the piece was over.

He moved to Vathapi Ganapathim next. A hint of what was to follow showed itself when Madhavan started playing rhythmic patterns where they were uncalled for. The vocalist looked at him in surprise as if to ask, you, what are you up to?

Giridhar Padmanabhan finished the piece briskly and started on a kriti in Pantuvarali. Madhavan joined in softly and I relaxed. When the vocalist was done with the anupallavi, Madhavan began. There is a norm for these things. A couple of minutes was what he should have played but Madhavan coaxed another phrase out of his violin and then another. A couple of times, the vocalist tried to cut in, but Madhavan wouldn't stop. The crowd grew restive. Someone sighed loudly. What was Madhavan doing? He was the accompanist and not the soloist. Eventually the vocalist found a gap and proceeded to sing.

The following ninety minutes were a nightmare. It started as a duel between the vocalist and violinist. People began leaving the hall. They had come to hear Giridhar Padmanabhan sing and instead they were being subjected to the violinist's drama.

The mridangam player, Ashwin Iyengar, glanced at his fingernails and looked at the dwindling audience. Then he proceeded to drown out Madhavan's playing. Once and for all. Each time Madhavan tried to show off his virtuosity beyond the expected time, the mridangam notes would thunder and overwhelm his playing.

No more invitations came to Madhavan from any of the prestigious sabhas. He had sabotaged a concert. The effect was like the stench from burnt milk. It refused to dislodge itself.

And now, it seemed that Madhavan wanted Saranga to know the ignominy of waiting for an opportunity to knock at his door instead of a secure future.

For once, I tried to reason with father and son. Saranga was a talented child; music was a part of him, and even his hard-to-please father would break into an occasional 'balle' when he listened to him. But was that enough? I didn't think so.

'Get an education, Kanna,' I cajoled him. Once you have a job, then you can devote yourself to music.'

Madhavan countered with one of his tired aphorisms: 'No man can stand with his legs in two boats.'

'I'm not asking him to give up his music. Just to have a Plan B.'

'Any fool with the necessary grades can become a doctor or an engineer—not everyone has music in them. But what would you know of that? They have a name for people like you: Gyanashunyam.'

Saranga looked enquiringly at his father. 'What's that?' he asked.

'Empty of knowledge. It's a polite word for idiot,' Madhavan explained with a sigh.

Saranga nodded in agreement. I wanted to reach out and box his ears.

Instead, I gave Saranga an ultimatum. 'It's up to you, Saranga,' I said. 'But henceforth, you'll have to fend for yourself. You have a roof over your head and food to eat, but you'll have to find the money to pay for everything else. Your phone bills, your outings with friends, your personal expenses ...'

Saranga's JEE ranking wasn't good enough for him to get into the top colleges. But there were colleges that would offer him an engineering seat for a hefty management fee. Madhavan shrugged and said, 'I don't have the money. And I don't believe in buying a seat. So you'd better find the money yourself, since you are the one who wants to turn him into a cog in the wheel. Just like you are.'

Ever since I joined work, I had made no attempt to climb the ladder. Any promotion came with the potential danger of a transfer and Madhavan had categorically shut me down when I broached the subject of appearing for a division test. 'Chennai is where the music is and I have no intention of leaving Chennai or letting you go to some godforsaken town for the sake of a promotion. Who is going to look after Saranga and me?'

Naturally, that meant that my cog-in-the-wheel salary didn't grow the way it should have. Now, as the single earning member, my savings had dwindled. So I sold the few pieces of gold jewellery I owned, including my grandmother's bangles, which I wore only for festive occasions. I cleaned out my savings and then took a loan for the rest of the amount required to secure Saranga's admission.

Madhavan and I went to Central Station to see Saranga off. He was on his way to Salem to study for an engineering degree. On our way home, Madhavan said, 'You have ruined his life.'

I was driving, so I continued to look ahead and said in an even tone, 'No one ruins another's life. We do it ourselves.'

He said, 'I suppose that's a dig at me,' and retreated into a resentful silence.

Once we were home, he locked himself in his room for the next few hours. He had announced earlier that he was composing an album which would take music to not just our people but the masses. It was going to make him famous and us rich.

As he flitted from one grand plan to another, I would put the food on the table, pay off the loans and Saranga's college fees and keep our bodies and souls together.

And that's how our lives would have continued but for two things.

The first thing that happened was an act of God.

I paid the last EMI on the home loan in July 2015. I was a homeowner for real now. It felt like a huge weight had been lifted off my shoulders. But I told no one about it. I was afraid Madhavan would find ways to spend the money that would otherwise have gone towards the EMI. Instead, I set the amount aside to get the house painted. By the time everything was in place, it was the first week of December.

Madhavan didn't ask me where the money was coming from or who was going to do the work. He just shrugged and said it was the wrong time of the year to be painting the house.

'It's raining, if you haven't noticed.'

Over the years, I had got used to his contrariness. I had learnt to either ignore him or snap back with my point of view. I glared at him now and said, 'You call that a rain? It's a drizzle and will stop soon. Besides, they are painting the interior.'

'The paint fumes will aggravate my allergies. The music season will start in two weeks and I don't want to be ill.'

He had exactly three morning concerts in random nondescript sabhas but Madhavan, of course, made it sound like it was the New Year's Day concert at the Music Academy.

I asked, 'Why don't you move in with your brother until it's done? It's just a matter of three or four days.'

He nodded. 'That's a good idea! What happened, Bonda? Are you getting smart—finally?'

He left soon afterwards, driving away with an impatient honk of the horn at the main gate. He knew how to drive. He just didn't like to.

It had been a very wet November, and it looked like December would be the same. I had taken the day off to sort things out and clear space before the painters arrived. By the time I was done, it was almost half past three. I stepped into the balcony to check if it was still raining.

It had drizzled all morning, but after lunch, a hard, relentless rain had begun to fall, each drop dense with purpose, and the skies were a slate-grey. There was something sinister about the afternoon.

I checked the weather reports online. There was no promise of clear bright days, as December days ought to be. I began having second thoughts and decided to postpone the painting. Once I let the painters know, I called Madhavan to tell him that he could return. He said, 'Bonda, I told you so. Anyway, good decision to postpone the painting. I'll be back tomorrow afternoon after lunch.'

I had just put the phone down when I heard a loud thud outside. A giant tree at the end of the road had fallen and a power line was down. I turned off all the lights except one, and put my phone on charge. There might be no power until the next morning, unless the rain stopped soon. The inverter would have to suffice for as long as possible.

The rain didn't stop falling and by night various parts of Chennai were flooded. I checked my phone for news reports and then went downstairs to caution the watchman and let everyone know in case they had missed the news.

My neighbour across the corridor asked, 'Is Madhavan home?' I shook my head.

'Call us if you need anything,' she said.

The apartment was dark and the floor wet. I had forgotten to shut a window. All the furniture had been dragged into one of the rooms and everything was in disarray. I sighed. I switched on a light to start tidying up and realised that, for the first time in my life, I was on my own.

I had never lived away from home. I had never ever been alone. For the first time, I knew what it was to be with myself. To be myself. Not watch myself all the time, not be afraid of saying something inappropriate, not be afraid of doing something wrong. To not be judged. To not have to hasten to fill awkward silences. To just be, on my own terms.

I stood in the middle of the room and stretched. I yawned loudly, not bothering to cover my mouth. I revelled in the sense of space I felt around me. I lit the tea lights left over from Deepawali and placed them on the dining table. The electric light suddenly seemed an intrusion. When I turned it off, the flames threw shadows on the wall. I watched them dance with an abandon that drummed within me.

I took a tea light into the bathroom and left the bathroom door wide open. My body became a play of light and shadow. In the soft glow of the tea light, my skin took on the hue of burnished teak. I felt beautiful. I poured several mugs of water on myself. Each drop of water teased a nerve end. The water was cold but a strange fiery warmth rushed through me and for the first time, I felt desire. I wanted to be touched. I wanted my body to know a million kisses. I wanted a finger caressing the back of my neck and my inner thigh. I wanted my body to be feasted on ... What on earth is happening to me? I asked aloud.

When I had dried myself, I didn't bother putting on clothes. Instead, I wrapped myself in a towel and went into the kitchen to make a cup of coffee. I drank it slowly, standing at the open window and watching the rain fall. A flurry of raindrops blew across my face and bare shoulders, and I shivered. I didn't know what to make of my brazenness. I had never done anything like this. But it felt good. It felt right.

I would have said I was at my happiest then. But happiness is too limited a word to describe how I felt in that moment.

Madhavan called in the morning to check on me. So did Saranga and a couple of colleagues. Chennai was a mess. The roads had turned into canals and low-lying areas had become lakes. I reassured them all. 'Our street is submerged in knee-high water but it's not as bad as in some other parts. Have you seen the news?'

I told Madhavan, 'It's best you stay where you are.' Not that he was offering to come and rescue me.

Anyway, I didn't need rescuing. I just wanted to be left alone. I wanted to celebrate my newfound freedom. To be able to choose what to eat, when to sleep or browse the net, without anyone hovering beside me. To play movie songs all day and not argue about opening the window or letting the rain come in. Briefly, I would be free from the constant scrutiny that had characterised my life until now. Amidst the death and destruction that Chennai was reeling under, I discovered a new me and I fell in love with her.

The neighbours popped in with offers of assistance and horror stories. Basements drownings. Families swept away when the Chembarambakkam reservoir was finally opened.

The toll kept rising. And every inch of Chennai seemed to be a potential death trap. I imagined how I would feel if Madhavan were to be sucked down an open manhole and disappeared. Appallingly, I felt nothing at all.

All through our married life, I had fasted and performed pujas for my husband's health and happiness. I realised now that I was tired of being a wife. Madhavan's wife.

I wondered if I should ask him to return. He would like that. Me admitting that I needed him. I wondered if hoping that the floods would swallow him made me guilty of murder. In the spirit of the moment, I planned his funeral. I had to be prepared for both: a funeral with his corpse and one without it.

The floods receded. Chennai limped back to some semblance of normalcy. Madhavan came home; my honeymoon with myself was over.

I couldn't stop thinking though about how to wrest my space back. A fortnight later, I called in the painters and Madhavan left again to his brother's home. I waited to see if I felt lonely. All I felt was relief.

Soon, I started looking for excuses to get Madhavan out of the apartment. I coaxed him to accept out-of-town engagements. He refused, saying that he preferred to sleep in his own bed.

Madhavan often jeered at my imagination or the lack of it, as though it made me sub-human. One Thursday in February, it began with an anecdote I shared about a colleague's house and somehow it ended as an argument about the furniture in the hall. He wanted to get rid of everything—the sofa set, the dining table and chairs—and instead hang a swing from hooks in the ceiling. 'I miss the swing in my house. Besides, it brings a traditional "feel",' he said, using a word that talent show judges spouted these days.

'What is a feel?' I asked.

'A good brahmin household must smell of coffee and sambrani. It must have a proper puja room and a swing ...' he began.

I sighed impatiently. 'And where will the rest of us sit? And what about mealtimes?' I didn't want to go back to sitting on the floor.

There was a caustic exchange of words. 'You are no better than a scurrying cockroach with not one creative cell in its body,' he said, his voice low but the words razor-edged. I didn't respond, just walked back into the kitchen saying I had work to do.

It was time, I decided, to give myself a holiday from him. In all honesty, he put the thought into my head.

That evening, I went down to the back of the building where the drains were. It was easy to trap a cockroach in a match box. I took it home. I let it loose in the living room while Madhavan was sitting there. He threw a tantrum, just as I expected him to. 'What's the point of painting the house when you can't keep it clean?'

I said, 'Don't blame me. It's the building. We have some new people who cook non-veg. Naturally, it will attract pests. The only thing to do is call in the pest control people. That way we can keep out the cockroaches as well as ants, spiders and lizards.'

We signed a year's contract. They would come once in three months. They offered us an option between the smelly kind and the non-intrusive, more expensive one. I chose the smelly kind. Since pesticide fumes didn't agree with Madhavan either, I knew I would get two nights and three days with myself every quarter.

Madhavan left for his brother's home as usual. The pesticide people came, and I left for work once they were done. I planned to get home early. The apartment would need to be swept and mopped. After that, I would have two days all to myself, to do as I wished.

Just as I was leaving, a colleague at the bank asked me to go with her to buy a violin for her daughter. The child would soon be starting classes. As Mrs Professional Musician, I was the resident expert.

I didn't let on that I had never been to a music store before. Not even into the 'erstwhile Saranga Musicals now in Avadi'. On the day of its inauguration, I had started my period. And then the time was never right.

So here I was in a music store, mesmerised by what I saw around me. The tamburas and violins, the flutes and the veenas. My colleague brought up Madhavan's name. The shop owner was a good businessman, so he pretended to recognise the name. But I could see through the pretence and quietly slid to the other side of the shop, where some of the Western instruments were. Guitars, an assembled drum kit, a line of clarinets. A tray with little boxes on which was written: Harmonica.

I stared. What was a harmonica? The shop assistant came towards me and said, 'Mouth organ, madam. A very good instrument for anyone. Here, try it ...'

'No, no ... I am just looking,' I mumbled. But then, something made me take it from him, hold it to my lips, and blow into it. Taking a cue from the movies, I slid it this way and that, and without knowing how it happened, I found I could make music too. Music that was all mine. Music that hadn't been composed or notated. Music no one had ever heard before. It was the most fulfilled I had ever felt.

It was a narrow piece of plastic with ten holes but what I saw was a friend. Someone who sat in a little box hidden from the world. A secret companion who already delighted me like nothing had ever before.

I smiled at the man.

My colleague and I left the shop. She with her violin, me with my harmonica.

In the evening, after I had cleaned the house, I sat on the floor in the middle of the living room and tried playing the harmonica. What I imagined playing in my head wasn't exactly what I produced. I went online and found a site that offered free harmonica lessons for beginners.

For the next few months, when Madhavan left for his evening walk, I played the harmonica. I refused to call it a mouth organ even to myself, it sounded so vulgar. I practised my lessons diligently and kept trying to play the song in my head.

October came, and with it Dussera. Every year for Navaratri, I set up the kolu. The marapachi bommai figurines that had been given to me at my wedding, as well as those I had inherited from my mother—gods and goddesses, people and animals—were stored in cardboard cartons in the loft in what was once my parents bedroom but was now Saranga's. The rack of steps were made of five planks kept in the kitchen loft and bricks that sat in the kitchen balcony.

As a girl, I had loved everything about the Navaratri festival. What I delighted in the most was the setting up of the display. The goddesses on the top step and scenes from the epics on the steps below.

Over the years, the festival had lost its sheen. Now it was just a ritual for which some of Madhavan's female relatives, some of mine and a few neighbours dropped in. Songs would be sung. Food eaten. And Madhavan, if he was home, would have something to gripe about when the door was shut after the last guest. I had learnt to switch off and make appropriate sounds. By now I knew it was enough to have just three responses at hand to get through my marriage: 'Is that so?', 'I didn't know' and 'Yes, it wasn't good enough'.

But that year, I wanted to celebrate Dussera. No one else needed to know it, but music was part of my life too. Navaratri wasn't about meaningless rituals anymore. I would be offering obeisance to the goddess of music.

A smile pulled at the corners of my lips as I made the rack of steps using planks and bricks and covered it with a cream-and-gold cloth I had bought on my way home. Madhavan sat cross-legged on the sofa and gave me instructions. I responded calmly: 'Is that so?' 'Yes, it wasn't good enough.' 'I didn't know.'

For the first time in the seven years after Madhavan had become a full-time musician, he had concerts almost every evening of the Navaratri festival. Various building societies were organising concerts as part of the Navaratri festivities and none of the big names would accept such invitations. But Madhavan did. He was always the senior musician there and he played the violin beautifully.

On the eighth evening, he brought his violin and bow to place on the puja platform. For a moment, I wondered if I should leave my harmonica in its secret home. But it was just as much an instrument of music as the violin. So I brought it out and tied a string of chrysanthemum around its gleaming body. I daubed a perfect round of turmeric and sandalwood paste on it and placed a kumkum dot right on its heart. My harmonica was resplendent as a bride and like the bride's mother, I smiled, my heart bursting with pride.

Madhavan asked, 'What's that?'

I swallowed. I had hoped he wouldn't notice it amidst all the figurines.

'It's something I picked up a few months ago ...'

I paused, unsure if I should say more. Then, unable to help myself, I added, 'I have been practising.'

'So you're the one who's been making all that noise.' He shook his head in amused exasperation. 'I thought it was one of the tone-deaf brats in the building.'

I said nothing, just tidied up the fallen petals. He continued to speak: 'What a waste of real estate. You may as well have kept the grinder on the puja platform. There's very little difference between that and the noise you make with the mouth organ ...'

Even when he stopped ranting, I kept hearing that one phrase: a waste of real estate. It echoed in my head.

Do you know what it's like to have a secret pulled out into the open and shown up as a foolish, worthless thing?

Later in the night, I heard him speak to Saranga. He chuckled into the phone, 'Your mother is having a mid-life crisis. She's got herself a mouth organ.' His laugh was the cruellest thing I had heard.

'I used to think one of the kids in the building was making the noise. Who knew?'

That laugh again. I looked down at my hands. They were clenched into fists.

It was Vijayadashmi day. After I finished the puja, Saranga, who had reached home the previous night, sang and his father accompanied him on the violin.

When the song came to an end, it felt as if the goddess was smiling on them. I smiled at Saranga. He smiled back and said, 'Amma, you should play your harmonica too.'

This was a Saranga I didn't recognise. Perhaps having to wash his own clothes in the hostel and go without the treats I periodically dished up had taught him to view me differently.

Madhavan rolled his eyes and asked, 'Why?'

Saranga snapped, 'It's Vijayadashmi day, Appa, and Amma is learning to play the harmonica. She is as much a student of music as you and I are.'

'Bonda, you must play the mouth organ then. But will you go to the balcony and play it there? It will keep the crows away at least.'

I looked steadfastly at the floor. When I raised my eyes again, Saranga was looking at me. I saw the pity on his face. And a question: Why do you let him do this to you?

I kept my own face blank even though I felt my eyes smart.

I heard those words again: 'waste of real estate'. It drummed in my temples. It whined in my ears. It itched in my throat. It raged in my heart. But it was Saranga's pity that broke and strengthened me at the same time.

A couple of days later, we had a bitter quarrel. Madhavan wanted me to speak to a distant cousin's husband, who had connections in the music world. He wouldn't listen when I told him that my cousin wouldn't take my calls. He worked himself into a state, spittle flecking the corners of his mouth. He flung his hands about and swept the new water glasses off the dining table. My heart wouldn't stop hammering.

The next evening, I let a cockroach loose in the music room and Madhavan found it. He did a tandavam about how the pest control people were all cheats.

I called the pest control helpline. They apologised and promised to send someone. Madhavan moved into his brother's home for two days till the fumes died down.

The earnest young man sprayed the rooms one by one. When we came to the music room, I shrugged helplessly at the locked door. 'My husband is a musician and this is his sacred space. He won't let anyone in unless he is with them.'

'What do we do, madam? Cockroaches don't know the difference between sacred rooms and regular rooms.' He looked at me.

I saw what he saw: A bonda of a woman with a mousey expression and stringy hair with grey at the temples. A respectable bank employee in an expensive-looking cotton sari with two slim gold bangles on either wrist and a decent-sized gold chain around my neck. I was a trope he was both familiar and comfortable with.

He said, 'Since you have no small children or pets, I could give you some of the chemicals. You can make little pellets of it and place it in there.' He added a little more to the mixture. 'If it doesn't work, we will have to spray the room, madam.'

I looked at it suspiciously.

'Madam, please wash your hands with soap after you touch the container. It's poisonous.'

When Madhavan returned the following morning, I told him about what I had had to do. He nodded. I showed him where I had left the pellets. He rolled his eyes. Later, I heard him tell Saranga over the phone, 'Your mother thinks I am three years old. She showed me the cockroach repellent and said I mustn't go near it.'

That night, Madhavan had his first bout of diarrhoea. Along with the asafoetida, I had added a tiny pellet to his rasam. I don't know what made me do it, I just wanted to punish him. To make him feel as helpless as he made me feel.

He complained in the morning, 'I don't know what it is I ate. I've been running to the toilet again and again.'

'Is that so?' I replied. 'Did you eat some rubbish from a street vendor?'

He flushed. I knew my husband's greed for oily snacks, especially milagai bajji.

He recovered in two days. A couple of days later, he had another bout of diarrhoea. I said, 'We should go to a doctor, maybe you have a stomach infection.'

He pooh-poohed me and asked me to make some kashayam. It seemed to help, and he said, 'It must be the weather.'

I knew I had been foolish. What if the doctor had suggested a blood test? The pesticide may have shown up. It was time I did some research.

The internet is a great tool for the amateur and the ignorant. There are YouTube videos on everything, from how to top up the water level in the UPS battery to how to kill an elephant with a sling shot and how to make manoharam. But I didn't find what I was looking for. I didn't want to get rid of him, just incapacitate him, so he would be easier to deal with. Madhavan was a hypochondriac and would take to bed at the slightest hint of a cold, rubbing copious amounts of Vicks on his temples, throat, chest and knees, and demanding Horlicks and rasam till he was sniffle free. Even a stomach ache would ensure he stayed in bed for a few days at least.

And thus, my search led me down my street.

At the corner was a small piece of land that belonged to the corporation. A couple of trees stood on it, and some shrubs, including the madar plant.

You would have seen it. It's a common enough plant with thick fleshy leaves and fat white flowers with a purple tip. The scientific name is *Calotropis gigantea* and it's also called milkweed, the internet tells me. I knew it as madar and I also knew that some of the milky sap would accomplish what I wanted it to.

The next time Madhavan lost his temper with me and sent a steel plate flying across the room, I mixed some of the madar sap into a glass of diluted milk and gave it to him instead of coffee. I said, 'Drink this. Coffee will give you heart burn and acidity.'

A little later, he complained that he was regurgitating bile. He threw up and had another bout of diarrhea. I called Saranga to tell him that his father was unwell. As expected, he demanded that Appa see a doctor. I said, 'Tell him that yourself. You know how your father is when I ask him to do something.'

So we went to the doctor who had been treating us for over a decade now. He listened as I told him about Madhavan's tummy trouble and prescribed some tests.

When we went back the next day, the doctor smiled at Madhavan and said, 'Nothing at all is wrong with you!'

The madar juice doesn't show up in bloodwork or basic tests unless it's taken in large quantities. As I said before, I wasn't seeking to kill Madhavan. I just wanted him to suffer.

The diagnosis was stress-related anxiety. As he wrote a prescription for anti-anxiety medication, the doctor said, 'Artists are always prone to bad stomachs.' He added a mild dose of antibiotics. 'Just in case there's some bacteria lurking in there.'

Madhavan gave me an I-told-you-so look. He was scheduled to play at a couple of small-ticket concerts. He was also going to be playing at a Shiva temple in Kerala. On our way home, he talked about the Kerala concert. 'It's a big deal for me, I guess that's why ...'

It was time for Deepawali. I started the preparations. Between Dussera and Deepawali, Madhavan had bouts of nausea and diarrhoea. He would recover and then it would begin again. He had to cancel all the performances and stay home.

Saranga was home for the Deepawali break. I decided to give Madhavan a small respite and let him recover.

On Deepawali day, after the pooja, Saranga and his father sat down to play together. Madhavan played a beautiful kriti in Sree raga. When he was done, I asked him to play Mohana Rama. He raised his eyebrows but complied. It filled me with a joy I couldn't explain. His recurring illness had taken the sting out of Madhavan. I almost felt sorry for him. And that I could live with.

That evening, I tried out a new recipe—my special kesari. I had learnt to make it from a colleague who was from Udupi. The semolina they used was finer, and they added cloves instead of cardamom. It was coloured yellow rather than orange and best of all, it had bits of pineapple in it. Madhavan tasted it and smiled in appreciation. He ate a few mouthfuls and looked at me thoughtfully.

'Next time I have my musician friends over, will you make this? Like MS amma's sukku-kaapi and Seshagopalan anna's coconut chutney, I think Madhavan's household will now be known for its kesari ... this is excellent!' he said, shovelling another spoonful into his mouth.

It was the first compliment I had received in all these years.

I said, 'I will.'

Saranga returned to college. Life went on. One evening, we had just started eating dinner, when the prime minister appeared on the television. It was the eighth of November and the time was 8.15 p.m.

Madhavan perked up at the sight of Modi. He had voted for the BJP in the elections and he thought of Modi's victory as a personal triumph.

Neither Madhavan nor I understood Hindi, but we let the man go on. Thirty-eight minutes into his speech, the prime minister began speaking in English. In the forty-seventh minute, he announced demonetisation. All 500- and 1000-rupee notes would be declared null and void at midnight, he said.

I felt my breath catch. Madhavan beamed. 'Exactly what is needed to put an end to black money. Politicians. Movie stars. Some musicians too,' he added. The PM went on to talk about how the 500- and 1000-rupee notes could be handed in at any bank across India. I thought of the chaos that awaited me the next morning. People would be queueing up to exchange notes.

I had about twenty-five thousand rupees in the Mahatma Gandhi series, and those weren't going to be difficult to exchange. But how could the government do this to us?

Madhavan got up and went to wash his hands.

I gathered up the plates and dishes and took them to the sink to wash and dry.

When I returned to the living room, panellists on a Newshour show were discussing the demonetisation. I picked up the remote to change channels.

The second thing that happened was an act of malice.

A week after the demonetisation announcement, we had finished dinner and I was shelling peanuts for a chutney I had planned on making for breakfast. The TV was on and I was watching a serial when Madhavan came into the room with a cloth shopping bag in his hands. He had a sheepish look which I didn't understand. So I went back to my serial where things were heating up between the mother-in-law and the daughter-in-law.

'I am going to need this exchanged,' he said.

With my eyes still on the screen, I said, 'How much is it?'

I turned at the sound of the thud on the coffee table. There were several bundles of 1000-rupee notes with yellow bands around them. And a few loose notes.

'What's this?' My voice dropped to a whisper.

'Fourteen and a half lakh,' he said, laying the money out on the table in neat rows.

'It's my share from the sale of the family home,' Madhavan said, as if it was a bag of tomatoes he was referring to. 'I was going to tell you,' he added as an afterthought.

'When did this happen?' I asked, my mind leaping back through the last few months, wondering what I had missed.

'About a year and a half ago,' Madhavan said.

'You had this the entire time I was scrounging to find the money for Saranga's admission,' I said, my voice rising. Within me, I felt something else too. Betrayal. Loneliness. Incomprehension about why he would do this. It took me by surprise, the hurt. I told myself that I would process it later.

Madhavan shrugged. 'It was your decision to turn him into an engineer. I never wanted that for him. And why would I put my money into something I didn't believe in?'

'It wasn't for me. He is as much your son as he is mine. And you don't think you ought to have told me, at least?'

Madhavan pulled out his phone to make a call. That was his answer. Don't ask questions you know the answers for.

I wanted to grab the phone from his hand and smash it on the ground. I wanted to break something on his head. I wanted to see him afraid and howling in pain.

Instead, I looked at the heap of money on the table, and the loose notes. 'How much was it in all?'

'Twenty-two lakh,' he said.

'Where's the rest?' I asked quietly.

'I spent it.'

'On what?'

'This and that ...' He shrugged.

'You don't even remember what you spent seven and a half lakh rupees on?' My voice rose, thinking of how I'd had to sell my jewellery, the scrimping and saving, the guilt I felt when splurging on a cab ride instead of taking the bus or a shared auto.

'You want to know what exactly I spent my money on, here, let me explain it to you. H A P P I N E S S. Happiness. Mine. My happiness. Satisfied?'

He walked into the music room and slammed the door.

I counted the bundles, put them into brown paper bags and put them away. I started making calls.

All through my marriage, I had made excuses for Madhavan. He was the sensitive, artistic type. He didn't have a practical bone in his body. Not everyone was meant to be grounded. The world needed paper kites soaring through the skies, just as trees needed roots to anchor them.

I said he was outspoken when I should have used the word savage. I told myself that he was callous when I should have said he had no empathy.

I had let myself hope all these years that one day Madhavan would become the man I had hoped he would be. That he would see me for who I had strived to be all these years. Not just as the Mrs Provider I had come to be. That he would love me for the woman I was.

That night, I gave up on him. And on hope.

The following weekend, Saranga came home. He had booked a train ticket online. I went to fetch him from the station. He didn't have the cash to pay for an auto.

Madhavan had woken up feeling unwell that day, but this time I had nothing to do with it.

On the way home, Saranga told me horror stories about the consequences of demonetisation. Of a classmate's father who had had a heart attack while queuing up outside an ATM. Of a peon who had sewn his earnings into a mattress and didn't know what to do with it. I nodded and added a few of mine, I was glad Saranga was here. It was time.

I told him about Madhavan's bag of money. I didn't say how it had made me feel or what he had said about having spent money on his 'happiness'. I made it sound like just another demonetisation story.

'You mean, he had the money and still made you take out a loan?' Saranga asked.

I shrugged. Done was done.

On Sunday morning, I asked Madhavan, 'What do you want me to make, payasam or kesari?'

Madhavan said, 'Kesari.'

Saranga asked no one in particular, 'Why am I not surprised?'

We had an enormous brunch and took the kesari in little bowls to eat as we watched a film on TV. Madhavan tasted it and said, 'Something isn't right. It has a metallic taste.'

Saranga glared at his father. 'Why do you have to complain about everything?'

Madhavan finished his bowl of kesari silently. A little later, he started sweating profusely.

'I'm not feeling well,' he said, and slumped onto the sofa.

Saranga and I took him to the hospital. The Emergency doctor examined him and didn't find anything wrong. He called our physician and I heard him say: His blood pressure is 120/80, pulse rate 76 beats per minute, lungs are clear, respiratory rate is normal, abdomen is soft to palpation and pupils are 4 mm in diameter. A random blood glucose test as well as the electrocardiogram demonstrated a normal rhythm. Clinically, there was nothing wrong with him.

We returned home. A few minutes later, Madhavan cried out for help. Saranga watched in horror as his father's limbs stretched and his neck and back contracted. His eyebrows rose to his hairline and his mouth spread in a crazy, mirthless grin. I thought he looked like an electrocuted cat.

It lasted only a few seconds. He came back to himself and said hoarsely, 'I am fine.'

Saranga rushed downstairs to start the car. He said, 'We are taking him to the hospital.'

As we rode down the lift, Madhavan had another bout of spasms. This time, as he struggled for breath, I whispered in his ear, 'You understand, don't you? I couldn't waste real estate anymore.'

I saw his eyes open wide. I saw the horror in them when he realised that he was going to die. There was something very satisfying in it, that he knew that I had engineered his death and there was nothing he could do about it.

Later, everyone would talk about how stoic I was in my grief. I didn't want to play the bereaved wife. But the world couldn't rest until it had me cast in one more of the roles women are expected to play from the moment we are born.

Madhavan's death went unquestioned. Besides, he left nothing for anyone that could rouse doubt. No savings, no real estate, not even a life insurance policy. He had no mistress either. It was just one of those things, was the conclusion. And everyone told me to find consolation in the thought that we had nineteen good years together. Now you must live for your Saranga, they said with neither pity nor irony. That is what middle-aged widows do, was left unsaid.

I see that look in your eyes. You think I used the pesticides and milkweed ... Really? You think I am that obvious? That's the problem with the young. You jump to conclusions too easily.

I did use them, and they ensured and established that Madhavan hadn't been himself for some time now.

Do you want to know who the assassin was? Let me tell you. It's one of the best kept secrets of Chennai. A botanical garden called Semmozhi Poonga.

Once upon a time, it was a drive-in restaurant called Woodlands. My colleagues and I went there a few times for their famous thayir semiya. I took my mother and father there once in a while for rava idlis, and if they were feeling adventurous, they would have the bhatura. I had wanted to go there with Madhavan and show him off to Mr Mani. But Madhavan scoffed when I asked him. 'I can't walk-in into a drive-in restaurant,' he said when I persisted.

We never went there after I bought the car. He said he didn't see anything special about sitting in a car and eating food from a tray.

The restaurant still exists, but without a parking area. Around it, Semmozhi Poonga remains a beautiful place to visit. Along with the vertical garden and the butterfly garden, it has many species of trees and plants. When you go, look for the nux vomica tree and say hello to it for me.

My colleagues and I had gone there a couple of years after it opened. But it was the internet that led me to the tree. Soon, I took to going by every week to look at the tree, and eventually, I found what I needed. For that final act, I powdered the seeds, added it to the sugar with which I flavoured Madhavan's bowl of special kesari. The internet told me it would do the job. The internet never lies. Not about these things. The internet also told me that it was almost undetectable.

Saranga went back to college. After his graduation three years from now, he will move to Canada. Madhavan's sister is going to make all the arrangements. I am not going to stop him from going. I want what is best for him.

These days, when I return home from work, I first have a strong cup of coffee. First press, I want you to know. Then I go to the music room which is now mine. I play the harmonica for as long as I want with the windows wide open.

Once you know what freedom means, it's hard to let it go. Once you know how serene a space your home can be, trust me, you'll do everything you can to safeguard it.

QUOTA GIRLS

It was exactly as Uma Shree had imagined it would be. The sweeping grounds and the pristine buildings set against rolling brown hillocks. The morning sun bathed the main building in a splash of golden light and within her, she heard her heart drum. That the Kanakadasa Government Medical College was in the middle of nowhere didn't bother her one bit. Or that she was several hours away from her home in Bengaluru. In all honesty, she was glad to put some distance between who she was and who she was going to be. This-is-it; this-is-it ...

Uma Shree's father lived as a framed photograph on a wall. He had worked as a manual scavenger until he disappeared down a manhole and never returned. There was some hue and cry about it until her mother was offered a job as a pourakarmika to shush her.

One day, when Uma Shree was nine years old, the class was learning the names of various professions. Doctor. Engineer. Lawyer. Accountant. Journalist. Designer. Deepa Miss listed the words on the blackboard. When she put down the chalk, Uma Shree put up her hand.

Deepa Miss frowned at her. 'Yes,' she said.

'There's one more, Miss.'

'Is that so? And what is it?'

Uma Shree beamed. 'Pourakarmika.'

Deepa Miss burst into laughter. 'That's a glorified word for road sweeper. And it isn't a profession.'

The class tittered. Uma Shree felt as if someone had peeled away strips of her skin. Her face almost crumpled, but she managed to stop the tears from escaping her eyes. She sat down and tried to shrink into herself. If no one saw her, no one would point fingers at her.

All her life. Uma Shree had been told that people like her would not be able to battle the system and survive. But here she was. She raised her head to the skies and smiled.

She climbed the four steps into the bustling lobby of the college building. A corridor wound towards the admissions office.

Amidst the hundred freshers there, Uma Shree's gaze snagged on a girl who was accompanied by a man wearing a white shirt and khaki-coloured pants. Just like Peter Anna. Savitha would later tell her that the man was a cousin who had been requested by her family to see her through the admission procedure.

Uma Shree's mother had thought it best that she be accompanied by someone who could speak English. Her brother Arun had said he was busy. Her uncles couldn't speak English. So it had been left to Peter Anna to go with her.

The other girl was across the hall. But in those first few minutes, their eyes met with the tacit knowledge that they were the odd ones out.

Uma Shree smiled at her; the other girl smiled back. Uma Shree walked towards her. As she went past a group of freshers, she felt their curious gaze. It was obvious that the magenta and white kurta she wore was new, as were the white palazzos. Uma Shree smiled at them. They smiled back. Tentative smiles, so she didn't stop to talk to them.

She continued towards the girl who was dressed almost exactly like her, except that her kurta was blue and white.

The smiles they exchanged signalled relief as much as recognition. Savitha was taller than Uma Shree, but their hesitant demeanour was identical. They were the most poorly dressed girls there, and they carried phones that were low-end versions. They could already sense that they were different from most others there.

Once the admission process was complete, they headed to the hostel to find out about their accommodation. Uma Shree hoped they would be allotted the same room. Peter Anna and Savitha's relative walked behind them, jabbering away like long-lost friends.

Savitha glanced at her as they walked towards the hostel. 'I've never stayed in a hostel before. Have you?'

'I was in the government SC hostel during my PU. Don't worry. It's not too bad. You'll get used to it.'

Savitha gave her a grateful smile.

Uma Shree had revealed her life story with that one piece of information. If she had stayed at the scheduled caste hostel, she must be a Dalit, like her. And poor, like her. Savitha suddenly felt less alone.

They were four girls to a room; by the time Uma Shree and Savitha got there, the other two had claimed the beds closest to the window, leaving them the ones by the wall. As Uma Shree unrolled her mattress and made the bed, she decided she would ask if they could swap after a month.

She didn't have to. Strangely, on the third day, the other two girls moved to another room.

'Why do you think they left?' Uma Shree asked.

'Isn't it obvious?' Savitha's smile was grim.

Uma Shree pretended not to understand. She said breezily, 'I'm not complaining. We have so much room now, and we can sleep by the window.'

'Are you really such a happy idiot? Or are you pretending to be one?' Savitha demanded after a while.

Uma Shree had been glancing through *Gray's Anatomy.* She had just bought the textbook from the college bookstore and couldn't stop looking through it. Each time, a queer elation bubbled up inside her. This is where it all began.

She looked up at Savitha. It wasn't the first time someone had accused her of pretending not to see. Or the first time she had been called out for choosing to see only what she wanted to.

She took a deep breath and said, 'Does this kind of behaviour still bother you? Haven't you experienced enough of it already? Didn't we survive it? Do you know at what age I realised that we would always be treated different? When I was six years old!'

We are different, is what Uma Shree's mother had said to her from the time she could remember. Uma Shree thought she meant that they were different from the others in the Sweeper Colony they lived in. Once in rural Bengaluru but now part of the city, the colony was a cluster of houses with tin roofs. There was a mango orchard in front and beyond that was the road that separated them from the village.

Her mother had a regular job which was almost as good as a government job. It meant that they had a steady income and that she never knew what it was to go hungry. Uma Shree thought that was what her mother meant when she said they were different.

One day, a few months after her fifth birthday, she picked up her mother's broom. She needed both her hands to lift it and even then she could barely clasp it around the handle. She pulled her brother's bottle-green shirt off the clothesline and wore it over her chemise. It looked almost like the uniform jacket her mother wore to sweep the roads. She remembered that her mother tied a kerchief over her hair, knotting it under her chin. She found a rag that did the job.

She made an attempt to move the dried leaves from the wild almond tree that were scattered outside their doorway. She wanted to sweep them all into a pile and move that to a corner of the alley. Across the dirt path were a few more leaves. She would sweep there as well, she decided.

Kamalamma, who lived diagonally opposite them, was sitting on a large stone outside her door, combing her hair with a lice comb. When she found one trapped between its teeth, she teased it out with the nail of her thumb and squashed it. It was a most satisfying thing to do, and whenever Uma Shree's mother combed her hair for lice, she demanded that she be the one to squash the little devils into a bloody mess. 'Why should you have all the fun?' she would demand. Amma would grin and let her.

Kamalamma watched her trying to sweep the leaves into a pile and laughed aloud. 'Look at your daughter, Pramila,' she called out. 'A pourakarmika in the making.'

The stinging slap on her back almost made her fall. Uma Shree's mother loomed over her, eyes blazing, mouth twisted into a snarl. 'Is this what you want to do, you piece of dog shit? You want to clean other people's shit and pee? You want to die like your father did, suffocated by the disgust he felt for himself?'

Uma Shree didn't understand any part of what her mother said. All she could do was bawl loudly as the blows fell on her. Her mother pulled out some of the coconut-leaf spines that made up her broom and began whipping Uma Shree with them. Again and again, she lashed her daughter's calves and arms. 'You want the broom? Here, take it … take it!'

It was only when Kamalamma and her grandmother pulled her back that her mother stopped. Ajji gathered Uma Shree in her arms and walked away muttering furiously, 'Who would beat a child like this? It's a good thing my son isn't here to see this …'

The next day, Uma Shree's mother dressed her in her best clothes and took her along when she went to work. 'She is too young to start school,' Ajji objected. 'And what is the point anyway? What is a school going to do for her? Or for any of us?'

Pramila ignored her mother-in-law and gave her daughter's hand a little tug to hurry her up. Who had told Pramila that her daughter's place was in the government school? What made her so courageous?

Uma Shree watched her mother talk to a lady whom everyone addressed as 'Head Miss'. Everything around her was new and strange, and she wanted to absorb it all so she could tell Ajji about it. It was a small building between the government hospital for animals and a free water-filling station. A giant tree stood in one corner and beneath it were three stone idols of snakes. Uma Shree would learn that once a week, a few women came to the tree to light a lamp. Otherwise, they left the tree alone and in its shade the children played.

It was almost the middle of the year, but Pramila convinced Head Miss to let Uma Shree join the school. Later, Uma Shree would wonder what her mother had said to convince Head Miss that she was ready for school. Or what favours her mother had to grant in return. But none of that occurred to her then. All she thought about was what it would feel like to be one of the girls there, wearing a sky-blue shirt and navy-blue skirt and with her hair braided into pigtails held in place by red ribbons. She wanted a school bag and a water bottle.

Lessons were held in five rooms. Each room held a batch and each class had forty children. There were only two or three benches in each classroom. Most of the children sat on the floor. A piece of metal was strung on a rope in the veranda and one of the teachers struck it with a metal rod to indicate the start and end of each period. There was a recess after two periods when they were given a cup of milk. Uma Shree didn't particularly like the taste of the reconstituted milk but people on television said that milk made the brain sharp. So she drank it as if it were medicine.

Lunch was at 12.30 p.m. A meal of rice, dal and vegetables all cooked into a mess. Uma Shree would be so hungry by then that it didn't bother her that the food tasted the same every day. There was a long recess afterwards, during which they slept or played.

At half past three, school would get over, but Uma Shree had to wait until 4.30 p.m., when her older brother came to pick her up on his bicycle. He was eleven and in middle school.

Uma Shree wasn't shy, so she made friends with everyone in her class on the first day itself. Most of the children left immediately after the last bell. Except for Rekha. Her father was responsible for treating the cows at the animal hospital, which was adjacent to the school. Soon the two girls became friends, and played hopscotch till Uma Shree's brother arrived. On days Rekha's father was busy with a cow, they would watch him wide-eyed.

A cow would be tethered within a metal pen, its hind legs tied to the back of the pen and its head bound tightly to the front of the pen. Rekha's father would shove his hand, wrapped in a plastic bag, up the cow's bum. Sometimes he removed balls of fresh dung before inserting a tube, and then the cow's head and legs would be untied and the cow and its owner would leave.

If Rekha's father was in a good mood, he would look at them speculatively and threaten to chase them with his hand still in the plastic bag. The thought of him touching them with his hand covered in dung made them squeal. Some days he would go across the road to a bakery and get the girls a samosa or a bun rich with cream and coconut shavings.

When Uma Shree's brother arrived, Rekha's father would smile and see them off. One day, he asked them, 'Where do you stay?'

'Gubbi Cross,' Arun said hurriedly before his sister could speak. She was going to add the exact street address when Arun started pedalling away.

For some reason, her brother always took the long route. 'I have chores to do and homework to finish,' she would complain. 'Why don't you take the short cut?' she asked one day. She was in a hurry to get home and show Kamalamma and everyone else on the street the five gold stars she had got in her Kannada copy book.

Arun shook his head and said, 'No, this way is best. You are too young to understand.'

When Uma Shree complained to her mother that evening, she saw her mother and brother exchange a look. 'Do as your anna asks you to,' Amma said, 'and come and help me feed the goats. Ajji didn't let them graze long enough. She isn't well.'

The goats bleated hungrily. Uma Shree trotted after her mother.

Uma Shree got the most gold stars in class that year. When the school year came to an end and summer vacation began, her mother sent her to stay with her grandparents. She didn't want to leave Uma Shree alone all day long, she said. And Ajji wasn't well enough to look after her on her own.

Uma Shree's grandfather had a job as a railway sweeper. All his sons and daughters, except for the last boy, had left home. And there was always a grandchild or two staying over.

One Sunday, her uncle Raju, a porter at Cantonment Railway Station, took Uma Shree on a train ride from Cantonment to Bangarpet. 'For getting the most gold stars,' he said, as they boarded the train.

'If you come first in your class next year, I'll take you to Mysuru. Do you know where Mysuru is? It has palaces and a zoo. And the Brindavan gardens.'

Uma Shree wasn't paying attention. All she could do was gaze at the moving world through the train window. It was nothing like she had seen before. Trees, houses, poles, people … everything went past even before she could take a good look at it. 'Can anyone travel by train?' she asked.

'Anyone. But you have to buy a ticket,' he said with a grin. 'Everyone has to buy a ticket.'

'Everyone?' she asked.

'Except the president of India probably,' her uncle laughed.

They reached Bangarpet, where they were to meet Peter Anna.

'Are you hungry?' he asked. Uma Shree nodded. And then she saw Peter Anna. 'There he is ...' she said, jumping up and down. Peter Anna was her uncle's best friend and his cousin. He worked as an attendant at an old-age home run by priests.

Peter Anna's smile greeted them first. Whenever he smiled, revealing gleaming white teeth, it was hard to look elsewhere.

Uma Shree hung from both their hands and skipped as they headed towards the exit.

'We have to feed this one first,' her uncle said, lighting a cigarette.

Peter Anna took them to a little pani-puri stall. 'I want an ice cream,' Uma Shree whined.

'Eat this first,' Peter Anna said, handing over a paper plate with crispy little puris, each with a hole in it. Inside lay dark-coloured water and odd bits of peas and onion and green leaves.

'What's this?' Uma Shree asked suspiciously, looking at what seemed to be a sliver of green chilli.

'Bangarpet pani-puri,' he said. 'Try it. You'll like it. You need to eat it whole, in one go.'

Uma Shree swallowed one mouthful, then reached for another. Her uncle burst out laughing at her expression. 'I have never seen anyone look so incredulously happy in my life,' he said, turning to Peter Anna.

'I can eat a hundred of these little puris. Actually, I can eat a thousand. I could eat more if I knew how to count beyond thousand,' Uma Shree said.

When she was done eating four, she announced that she was full. 'You still have to eat nine hundred and ninety-six more,' her uncle teased.

Uma Shree pretended not to hear him. She asked Peter Anna where they were going.

'We are going to meet my family, who are also your family,' Peter Anna said, hailing an autorickshaw.

The autorickshaw let them off near a cluster of shops beyond which there seemed to be just a vast tract of fields. 'This is as far as they'll come,' Peter Anna said as he paid the driver. Why did he sound so furious, Uma Shree wondered, as she looked around her curiously.

They went down a mud path between fields with tall plants in it. 'It's millet,' Peter Anna said.

They came to a group of houses with thatched roofs. Some of them had blue plastic sheets on the roof. A couple of dogs came running and a fat, black pig surrounded by plump piglets stood snuffling the earth.

A girl came out of the house and shrieked in delight when she saw them.

It was a hot day, and the heat from the hills that seemed more rock than mud pressed down. But none of that mattered to Uma Shree. For she was discovering that she had eight cousins, none of whom she had met before.

She told them all about the school she went to. Some of them went to a school that was nothing more than a thatched shed. She told them about roofs—the tin sheet over her home which played music when it rained; the concrete roof on the school building that they could stand on.

'Imagine that,' one of the boys said. 'We could fly a kite standing on a roof like that.'

Uma Shree recited the rhyme that had earned her five gold stars in school. She told them about what they did to cows at the hospital. She told them about her brother and his bicycle. She told them about Sharmila, their goat, and Pinky, their black dog with a pink tongue. She ate an enormous lunch of beef biryani. And by the time they left, she had decided that when she grew up, she would marry Peter Anna's brother Charlie, eat Bangarpet pani-puri three times a day, and become the president of India.

When they returned to her grandparents' house in the evening, her mother and brother were waiting. Uma Shree couldn't wait to tell them all about her day. Her mother listened absently at first, combing out Uma Shree's hair and braiding it. Then her ears perked up and a frown grew as she heard about the village in Bangarpet. Her hands stopped their work. 'You didn't finish my braid,' Uma Shree complained, but her mother was already up and stormed past without a word.

'How could Raju take Uma Shree to that colony? What's wrong with him?' Uma Shree's mother sounded more angry than exasperated.

It was Uma Shree's grandfather who answered. 'Why? What's wrong? They are our people. Or have you forgotten?'

Uma Shree's mother didn't speak. She gave her father an angry look and went into the kitchen where her mother was making dinner. The smell of meat cooking filled the small house.

Uma Shree sidled up to her grandfather. 'Nana, I want to ask you something. Who is our people?'

Her grandfather made her stand with her back to him and began braiding her hair. 'Madaru. We belong to the Madiga caste. We are the caste who descended from Jambavan. Do you know who he was? He was the king of bears, Jambavan, and he helped Rama in his fight against Ravana. His daughter Jambavati married Krishna.'

'So we are actually bears?' Uma Shree asked, turning around. She wasn't so sure that she liked the idea.

'Not really. We are humans now. We live in this world, so we can't be bears,' he smiled, tying a neat bow at the end of the braid.

'Long ago, one of our ancestors killed a divine cow,' he resumed.

'What is a divine cow?' Uma Shree asked, wondering if it was golden in colour.

'A cow that belonged to the gods,' he said. 'So we were cursed to become people who work in the nasty trade of skinning animals.'

'You forgot to tell her that Madaru are considered the lowest of the low, worthy only of cleaning human shit! Don't fill her head with your rubbish, Nana,' Uma Shree's mother said from the kitchen doorway.

Raju Mama, who had just come in from the back door, made funny faces behind her back. Uma Shree burst into laughter. Her mother glared at her and turned to look behind her. When she saw it was her brother, she shook her head, annoyed.

'You may be content living like this,' she said, arm flung out to indicate the room they were in. 'But I want her to find a way out. I want her to dream big.'

The two-room house had walls with plaster peeling from damp patches. The floor was cracked and there was only one window, overlooking the road, and a ventilator in the kitchen. A door in the rear wall led to a latrine that was shared by the row of houses. There was a makeshift bathroom beside the latrine for the women to bathe. The men bathed by the tap outside. This was exactly how they lived in the Sweepers' Colony. So Uma Shree didn't know what her mother was complaining about.

Uma Shree's grandmother, who had been silent until then, guffawed. 'So, is she going to become the mayor of Bengaluru?'

Uma Shree saw her mother turn her fiery gaze upon her grandmother. 'No, she is going to have an office job.'

'No, I want to be the president of India,' Uma Shree shouted.

There was a moment of quiet. Then her mother burst into laughter. Raju Mama guffawed, 'Would the president of India like to step out with me for some congress kadale?'

Uma Shree didn't understand what was so funny, but she didn't care. She ran to take her uncle's hand—the spicy peanuts were a great favourite.

When school reopened, Uma Shree went back eagerly. Two days later, she saw Rekha's father at the animal hospital. He gave her a wide smile.

'Where is Rekha?' Uma Shree asked.

'She will start school tomorrow,' he said as he shoved his hand up the cow's bum.

Uma Shree went close to him and whispered, 'You're lucky this isn't a divine cow. Or you might get cursed like us.'

'What are you talking about, girl?'

Uma Shree explained. He listened to her, a peculiar expression on his face.

From that day onwards, Uma Shree was not allowed to share a bench with Rekha or sit next to her during lunch.

She had to sit separately, with a few of the other children. Uma Shree told her mother about it that evening. Her mother was silent for a moment. Then she sighed. 'The truth eventually comes out. There is no escaping who we are. But you shouldn't have told anyone.'

Uma Shree had no idea what her mother meant then, but she did now. She looked at Savitha and repeated, 'There is no escaping who we are. But we don't have to remind them who we are by protesting. It's best we lie low and not make a fuss. I don't want to let any of this get in the way of our studies.'

Savitha nodded. 'Let's go to bed soon so we can wake up early.'

The college had a strict anti-ragging policy, but they knew it was best to stay below the seniors' radar. This meant eating their meals before anyone else or after everyone else. Once classes were over for the day, they stayed in their room.

Uma Shree switched off the light and lay on the bed on her back, arms crossed above her head. A thin bar of light from the streetlamp outside slipped through the window grilles and splashed onto the wall. Uma Shree stared at the moving shadows in front of her.

What would she have to do to be treated with some dignity and respect? She had believed that competing with everyone else would show them she was just as good. She had told herself that educated people could not be discriminatory. She had thought knowledge made everyone equal. She wasn't so certain anymore.

You can't shed your caste, she thought, just as you can't shed your skin. Even snakes don't become something else when they shrug off their old skin.

For a moment, Uma Shree wondered if there was a caste system among snakes too. The cobra with its elaborate naama must be a brahmin; kraits and vipers, kshatriyas. Was there a vaishya category of snakes? Was the harmless rat snake a shudra? And as for people like her and Savitha, was there even a snake that belonged with them? Perhaps not. They were the earthworms with their mouth and arsehole the same, buried deep in the mud. Out of sight, out of mind.

'Stop muttering and go to sleep,' Savitha grumbled from her side of the room.

Uma Shree turned on her side, tucked her arm around the pillow, and thought of her growing-up years.

The upper primary school was adjacent to the high school, and Uma Shree discovered that her caste had preceded her to the classroom. The only girls who would share the bench she sat on were girls like her.

In the new school, every section was responsible for keeping their classroom clean. Groups were formed, and each group was expected to clean the floor, tidy the benches, wipe the desks and the blackboard for a whole week. This was usually done in the lunch recess or after school.

When it was the turn of her group, it was decided that they would use the lunch recess for the task. It was also assumed that Uma Shree would be the one to sweep the classroom. 'She can probably clean the whole school in the time we take to do just this one classroom,' Ashwini Reddy said.

The others tittered. Uma Shree was furious, but didn't say anything. She went looking for her class teacher, who was also the social studies teacher.

Saraswati Miss wore her hair in a side parting and liked big earrings. She had the best collection of saris and her nose pin was supposed to be made of real diamonds. Her husband worked in a bank, and he dropped her to school in their car every morning.

'So?' she said, glaring at Uma Shree.

'But Miss, it's not fair that they always taunt me and call me names.'

'Stop making excuses to get out of cleaning the class,' Saraswati Miss snapped.

'Why are some of us different, Miss? Why does no one in the class want to do things with me? Or with Meena, Selvi, Priya, Chowrappa, Pratap, Joseph, Daniel?' Uma Shree persisted. 'It's not fair.'

Saraswati Miss studied her face. And then she said, 'Well, you are an untouchable.'

'Means what?'

'Means we can't touch you. It would pollute us.'

'Oh,' Uma Shree said. A thought occurred to her. 'So, Miss, that means you are an untouchable too. Because I can't touch you. That would pollute me.'

The slap stung, and though Uma Shree was almost as tall as the class teacher, the force of it made her reel.

'Get out,' Saraswati Miss screamed. Saliva sprayed from her mouth onto Uma Shree's face.

Uma Shree burst into tears and fled. No teacher had laid a finger on her before.

She went behind the girls' toilet building with its smell of piss and blocked drains, crying as quietly as she could. She didn't want anyone to see her. When the tears dried up, she went back to the class. She was late. The bell had already been rung and everyone else was in the classroom.

Saraswati Miss gestured for Uma Shree to go to her seat. When she was about to sit down, she asked her to kneel on the floor. 'That way, you'll remember never to be late again,' she said, turning back to the blackboard.

The next morning, there was a school assembly. Saraswati Miss walked up to Uma Shree and asked her to recite the national pledge. It was usually done by the class leader. All at once, the festering wound within her healed with the joy and pride of standing in front of the whole school and hollering into the mic: 'India is my country. All Indians are my brothers and sisters ...'

When Uma Shree told Arun about what had happened, he snorted. 'She must have been afraid you'd report her. Don't you see that they were buying your silence? I told you, there's no escaping who we are.'

In high school, nothing changed except the classrooms and the faces of the teachers. Uma Shree knew she should be used to the way things were by now. She should pretend that none of it bothered her. But it hurt. It was like having your skin cut in a million places into which someone rubbed salt. Yet, Uma Shree swallowed her rage and the humiliation. One day they would seek her out, she told herself like a mantra, day after day. She had begun to understand why Arun had dropped out. But she wasn't going to give up like her brother.

She studied harder than ever. She topped the class. She topped the school. She topped the district. The school put up flex boards with her photo on them. Her mother bought her a pair of gold earrings; Arun got her a new phone. The Ambedkar Sangham declared a cash reward.

She got a seat in the Government PU college and the Ambedkar Sangham helped her find accommodation at the Government SC hostel. This way, she would have time to attend a coaching class too, to prepare for the NEET entrance. She was going to be a doctor. No matter what.

'You are setting yourself up for heartbreak,' Arun said. She ignored him.

'Think of getting a BSc. BEd. You'll find a teaching job in a government school. You will be settled for life. And you'll get a pension when you retire,' he suggested.

'I am going to be a doctor,' Uma Shree said in her firmest voice.

'Leave her alone, Arun,' their mother said.

'Philip now, Amma,' he said. 'You need to remember I don't go by "Arun" anymore. And the two of you really should join the church as well.'

'Maybe we will,' Pramila said.

Uma Shree rearranged her books. Then, unable to hold it in anymore, she snapped, 'You're disgusting. We don't escape our caste by converting. We escape by bettering ourselves.'

She clung to this thought now, as she fell asleep in her hostel bed at Kanakadasa Medical College.

For a whole month, the first-year MBBS students went through an orientation process, including a rather solemn ritual called the coat ceremony, where each one of them was presented with a coat and a stethoscope. Uma Shree saw some of her batchmates take selfies. She did the same, and sent them to everyone she knew. She wanted everyone to be part of her new life.

Right at the end of the month-long orientation, there was a long weekend. Uma Shree went home and returned on Sunday night. Savitha would reach only on Monday. She had messaged: Wait for me before going to the dining hall.

The sounds of girls heading to the dining hall flooded their room as it did every morning. Uma Shree wondered where Savitha was. She was hungry. She glanced at her watch again.

The door opened and Savitha entered looking flustered. The muffled sounds from outside turned into shard-edged bits of conversation and peals of laughter.

'You are late,' Uma Shree said, rising from the desk where she had been trying to read an anatomy text with the help of an English–Kannada dictionary. 'Do you know that spleen is gulma? And that vrsana is testicles?'

'Ssh … don't use such words,' Savitha hissed.

For a girl who was studying to be a doctor, Savitha was priggish, Uma Shree thought. But she didn't say anything. 'Let's go for breakfast,' she said instead.

Savitha put her bag down. 'Are you sure? The seniors will be there.'

Uma Shree walked towards the door in response. No one had troubled them this whole month. Why would they start now?

The dining hall was bustling. Almost all the tables were occupied. Savitha paused at the doorway. 'C'mon,' Uma Shree said, giving her a little push.

'There are no tables.' Savitha sounded relieved.

'We're late. There won't be any free tables. We'll just share.'

'Come here,' a voice called out.

It was Rupa, a third-year student who excelled at everything. She gestured for them to approach the table where she was holding court.

'First-years?' she asked.

They nodded.

'What was your NEET rank?'

They told her. Rupa's eyes narrowed and she said in a dismissive voice, 'Oh, quota girls!'

They stood there for a few more minutes. When Rupa continued to ignore them, they walked towards a table that was littered with crumbs and puddles of water. Uma Shree stood there looking pointedly at the cleaning woman who pretended not to notice them or the mess on the table. 'Akka,' Uma Shree said, 'Deviakka, please clean the table.'

Someone said loudly, 'Look at that! The quota girls are now quota madams.'

Quota girl. There it was again. Before Uma Shree could say anything, the cleaning woman gave the table a cursory wipe with her rag, flicking the crumbs towards them. Uma Shree jumped back, but she was too late. Flecks of chutney splattered her kurta. The group of girls at the next table giggled.

'How can one quota madam look different from the other?' that same voice said. 'Her kurta needs some fancy work too.'

Rupa slid out of her chair and came bearing her plate with half-eaten idlis and a pool of chutney and sambhar. Deliberately, she emptied it on Savitha's feet. Drops of chutney and sambhar flecked Savitha's kurta. She stood there, unable to move or speak. 'There, now you look like proper quota madams,' Rupa said, surveying her handiwork with a tilt of her head.

Savitha burst into tears and fled. Uma Shree ran after her. 'It's just ragging,' she tried to console Savitha as much as herself.

But Savitha was inconsolable. 'Didn't you hear what they called us? Quota girls! Do you know what means? That we are here only because of the reservation quota ... They are never going to let us study here in peace.'

That night, as Uma Shree lay in bed, she replayed the scene from the dining hall repeatedly. She wished she had retaliated, said a few scathing words to Rupa and her coterie. Or, even better, slapped her hard. Tears of rage and humiliation ran down the corners of her eyes, wetting the pillow. She brushed them away and tried to think of something else. Her eyes burnt and the back of her throat stung with the unspoken words.

She had to think of something else. She had to, or she would do something terrible. Uma Shree turned her mind to the ten hours of dissection they were expected to do every week. Tomorrow would be their introduction to the dissection hall. It was probably best to eat breakfast early in case they were in the morning batch, she decided, pulling the sheet over her head.

The first hour was physiology. They were broken up into four batches thereafter. Batch A and C would head to the dissection hall and Batch B and D to the bio-chemistry lab.

Uma Shree and Savitha were in Batch A. They headed towards the dissection hall at one end of the anatomy wing. There was a senior batch already at a table inside the hall, waiting for the anatomy lab assistant to produce a body from the tank. When he pulled it out, a strong whiff of formaldehyde added to the stench peculiar to anatomy labs and meat markets.

One of the girls in the front retched and rushed outside. A few more followed. The rest of them waited to be directed to their tables.

Dr Rama Bai, the HOD, was waiting for them near the door. She usually greeted the first-years at the start of the programme, after which a tutor would take them through the dissection.

Their session was titled 'Respect to cadaver'. Savitha nudged Uma Shree. What is a cadaver?

Uma Shree shook her head. She didn't know either.

Dr Rama Bai led them into a hall which seemed like any other classroom. The session was about anatomical position, term and terminology. There was a sigh of relief. It seemed the inevitable had been postponed.

Everyone took notes diligently. As Dr Rama Bai reached the end of the introduction, she said, 'It's time now to take the Cadaveric oath.'

There were whispers: *What's the Cadaveric oath? Why do we need to take it?*

I think I am going to faint …

Dr Rama Bai must have heard them, but she pretended not to. Not many of her colleagues or peers followed the practice but she had always insisted that the Cadaveric Oath be taken. 'Raise your hands and repeat the pledge after me. I do solemnly pledge that I will always treat you with respect and dignity of highest order, as you are my first anatomy teacher. I will always respect your privacy and confidentiality. I will use this knowledge for the service of the society. In all my deeds from now onwards, I will do justice to your great sacrifice. My heart fills with gratitude, as I realise your kind and courageous act of donating your body for the purpose of our learning. I will be grateful to you and your family for this act of Living After Death.'

She led them towards a table where a dead man lay. That's how Uma Shree and Savitha discovered that a cadaver was a dead body. There was a gasp from some of the girls, while the boys stood ashen-faced. It occurred to Uma Shree that the rest of them had probably never seen a corpse this close. Or a naked man, ever. Which is why none of them heard a word of what Dr Rama Bai said. They were overwhelmed—death, nudity, the smell of the lab, and through it all, the thought that this would be their life as Doctor of Medicine, Doctor of Surgery.

Uma Shree drew closer to the table and looked at what had once been a man. The absence of life had turned him wooden. Who was he? Why was he a specimen for them to saw through and examine? Why had his family chosen to donate his body to the college? Or was he an abandoned corpse? She folded her palms and said the only prayer she knew, the one she had learnt in school: *Asatoma sadgamaya,* lead us from ignorance to knowledge, from darkness to light, from death to immortality. She touched the cadaver's feet and sought his blessing. She noticed nothing of what was happening around her. All she knew was that her dream was becoming a reality.

Dr Rama Bai watched her, looking surprised. 'How is it you are not afraid?'

Uma Shree wanted to tell her that she had seen death before. First her father, when she was barely four years old. Then her Ajji. Both had seemed peaceful at the end.

So it wasn't death she was afraid of, it was life. The words wouldn't form in English, though. All she could muster was, 'I am always wanting to be doctor.'

Dr Rama Bai looked at her for a long moment.

Later, Savitha said, 'Do you realise no one questioned the caste of the cadaver? Perhaps when we are dead, they will stop punishing us for who we are.'

'Let it go, Savitha. We are here to become doctors. Let's not think about anything else.'

Uma Shree didn't tell Savitha that she'd had the same thought, but she had quashed it before it could root itself in her mind.

Within two days, everyone grew accustomed to the cadaver and the stench of the lab. Some of the truly squeamish lurked behind those who drew a particular thrill from being at the dissection table.

When Dr Rama Bai came to the hall, she would usually stop beside Uma Shree and the tutor would move on to the rest of Batch A and C. Often, the HOD let Uma Shree lead the class. And that didn't go down well with the others.

The whispers began. 'These quota girls are used to the stench of beef and pork, not like us. Her mother works as a corporation sweeper … can you imagine?'

Savitha looked at Uma Shree's face when that last and particularly nasty comment was whispered loud enough for her to hear it.

'No, it doesn't bother me.' Uma Shree faked a nonchalance she didn't really feel. She was petrified someone would find out what her brother did for a living.

Arun had dropped out the year Uma Shree started high school. He refused to study further. Uma Shree tried to talk him out of it, but he only shook his head. 'You'll discover why, once you are there,' he told her.

'What will you do with a tenth-standard pass?' she demanded. 'You already lost a year when you failed in your ninth. You know the Ambedkar Sangham will help pay your fees if you join a PU college.'

'A tenth pass is enough to get the job I have in mind. In fact, I'm over qualified for it,' he said with a cryptic expression. 'And I have plans. I'll study privately.' That seemed to satisfy their mother.

'How can you work and study?' Uma Shree demanded.

'Easily,' he smiled, but wouldn't say more.

He had started work as a casual labourer at a construction site not too far from where they lived. Giant apartment blocks were coming up in the area. The new airport had suddenly made that part of Bengaluru very desirable. He was going to save up to pay the down payment on an autorickshaw, he told them.

A few months later, he began work at the Baiyappanahalli Protestant cemetery. He was a casual labourer there, digging graves, cleaning headstones when the family asked for it. There was plenty to be done.

'Amma, what is wrong with Peter Anna and Arun?' Uma Shree asked. 'Couldn't Peter Anna find him something better?'

'He wasn't really interested in studying,' her mother said, as she sewed a button on her neon orange jacket. The thread slipped out of the needle when she looked up. Uma Shree watched her struggle to insert the thread through the eye of the needle. Her mother was getting old. That was probably one reason why her brother had decided to start working. 'Here, let me,' she said, taking the needle from her mother.

'But to work in a cemetery?' she said again, as she began sewing on the button.

'Would you prefer that he goes down a manhole or cleans the railway tracks of shit?' Pramila demanded. 'With a tenth-standard pass, who will give him an office job? This is our lot. There is no escaping it. And you are foolish to think that it will be any different for you.'

Uma Shree stared at her mother. What had happened to the feisty woman who had insisted that she study? Something seemed to have died in her.

'No escaping what?' she asked.

'Who we are,' Arun answered. 'When I turn eighteen, I am going to convert. You may as well start calling me by the name I've chosen for myself. Philip.'

Uma Shree looked at her mother. Several of their family members had converted to Christianity, but her mother had remained a Hindu. She would say that it was no different whether you were Hindu, Christian or Muslim, people like them would always be treated differently.

Pramila merely smiled at him and asked, 'Are you hungry? I've cooked pork.' Her way of saying: end of discussion.

Uma Shree snapped the thread with her teeth and put the shirt down.

The nightmare continued. Rupa and her gang waited to pounce on Uma Shree and Savitha, no matter what time they went to the dining hall.

One evening, they waited until the dining hall had nearly emptied out. Uma Shree was ravenous. They had skipped lunch and eaten only a small pack of biscuits between them.

They hurried in when there were just a few minutes left. The hall was almost empty. Savitha went to collect the dinner trays while Uma Shree found them a table close to the door. There was just one chair there, so she went to grab one from the next table. But even before she could place her hand on it, a girl dragged the chair away to another table.

Uma Shree looked at the occupied table and felt her heart sink. It was Rupa and her gang. One by one, they dragged all the chairs in the room towards themselves until Savitha and Uma Shree were left with just the table. 'Oh look, the quota madams don't have chairs,' one of them said loudly. 'What will they do now?'

Amidst them was a girl who was fair as a movie star. She looked at them and crooked a finger. They went up quietly, Savitha behind Uma Shree. 'Were you born this black or did you become black over the years?' she asked them in a little-girl voice.

The group laughed loudly.

'Answer me,' she snapped, her tone hardening.

'We were born like this,' Uma Shree said.

'Even if we take a sandpaper to you, I doubt the black will come off,' Rupa piped up.

'Like the kadaknath fowl … even its bones are black,' one of the others giggled.

Rupa threw her a smile. 'You can always sit on the ground to eat, that is, if you need to sit,' she said in a most reasonable tone.

'But …' Uma Shree began.

'No ifs or buts. You'll do as we say.' Rupa took a bite of the carrot she was holding. She dropped the rest into Uma Shree's bowl of rice.

Uma Shree wanted to fling the plate of food at her face. But Savitha went quietly back to their table and began eating. Uma Shree didn't dare meet her eyes.

'I am going to complain,' Savitha said after they had managed to escape the dining hall. 'I am going to complain to the college union, to the principal, the human rights people ...'

'Don't,' Uma Shree said. 'There really is no point, and they'll make our lives even more unbearable.'

Two days later, they were told that the hostel matron wanted to see them.

'What's it about?' Savitha asked the helper who had brought the summons.

'Have you been smoking or drinking in your room?' the woman asked with a sly smile.

They shook their heads furiously.

'Have you been doing something you shouldn't?' she asked.

Uma Shree's face paled. A few days ago, she had been chatting with Riyaz, one of the Batch A boys and a day scholar. He was from Belgaum and couldn't stop talking about the mutton biriyani at Niyaz Hotel. 'Those fried onions on top of the biriyani, they make it extra special.' He had kissed the tips of his fingers and unfurled them like a flower.

Uma Shree had giggled. 'Mutton biriyani is great, but what I really want to eat is beef biriyani. Would you ...?' She had left the query open-ended.

'Are you sure?' he asked. 'Beef here is synonymous with undesirables. If they find out, you'll become one of the undesirables.'

'No one will know,' she said. 'We'll eat it in our room.'

He had turned up the next evening with a parcel for the girls. 'I wish we could eat in our room, every meal, every day,' Savitha said as Uma Shree divided the parcel between them. Riyaz had got them paper plates and two bottles of Bindu Soda. 'That's the combination,' he said.

The 'big-mutton', as Savitha called it, was succulent and plenty, and the girls had fallen on it hungrily. Savitha had eaten every grain of rice, spooned the salna into her mouth, and enjoyed it even more than Uma Shree did.

Except now, she was glaring at Uma Shree and whispering furiously, 'I told you we shouldn't have eaten the big-mutton biriyani. God knows what they'll do to us.'

The hostel matron suddenly emerged from one of the rooms on the ground floor. Uma Shree felt her fear subside when she saw the smile on her face.

The matron told them that they should move to a room on the ground floor. It was uncommon for first-years to have a ground-floor room. They were usually reserved for seniors. 'You'll be more comfortable there,' she said, not quite meeting their eye.

Had someone said something about what had happened to them in the dining hall? Had their absence at the dining hall the night before been noted? Or was it something else? Disquiet filled Uma Shree, but she brushed it aside, telling herself that she was reading covert meanings into what was probably a routine room change.

The girls collected all their things and their bed rolls and went down to the room they had been allotted. It wasn't big, and overlooked the back yard of the hostel. The kitchen and the dining hall were alongside.

'Because your room is closest to the dining hall, you can go last, after the others are done, and have a leisurely meal,' the matron said, walking into their room. She said it as if it was a special concession.

'And the food's unlimited,' she added, sizing up their skinny frames. What did she see in their faces, Uma Shree wondered. Perpetual hunger?

When she left, Savitha exploded. 'Do you know why we are here?'

'The warden probably heard we are being bullied. This is her way of protecting us,' Uma Shree said.

'And you think it's alright?' Savitha asked, her nostrils flaring. 'That we should be treated like this. That even someone in authority doesn't do anything about it, but herds us together for safety.'

'No, I don't think it's alright,' Uma Shree said softly. 'But I also know that there is nothing we can do to prevent it. Not until we raise ourselves above all this. And we can do that only through education.'

Savitha came from a small village somewhere near Tumkur. Her people lived on the edge of the village. They had a small piece of land which they had received as part of a government scheme. They grew millet on it. They also kept pigs, goats and chickens, and somehow managed to make a living without having to clean clogged sewers.

'But to this day, if there's something wrong with the sewage pipe or drains in one of the houses in the main village, they call my father or uncles. It's like they won't let us become anything else.'

'They should say no,' Uma Shree said.

'You have no idea what they can do to us,' Savitha retorted in a voice devoid of all emotion. 'We don't have the right to say no.'

Savitha's childhood was almost similar to Uma Shree's. Government schools and midday meals. Separate benches at first, and later, flex boards to celebrate her success.

But Uma Shree was a city girl and Savitha a village girl. Uma Shree often thought that was what made them different. Cities taught you to keep your emotions to yourselves. Cities taught resilience. Uma Shree had learnt it was easier to bend than be broken. She had learnt to numb her rage at insults and humiliation. Resilience is all, she told herself with every inhalation. Resilience will teach you to survive, she exhaled. Resilience. Resilience. Resilience. She drummed the word into every cell of her being.

'Let it go,' she told Savitha. 'I don't like what they are doing to us either, but its best to ignore them and concentrate on what we've come here to do.'

Uma Shree told herself that it was unfair to think everyone in the institution treated students like her as if they were the products of an unholy union of scum and slime. There were peers and seniors who were nice to them. Some of the faculty were supportive and encouraging. If only they could make themselves invisible, the others might leave them alone too.

A few of the students did dare to protest against the discrimination they faced. But it was as if they had a target on their back forever afterwards. They were always getting into trouble. Uma Shree and Savitha watched the others, the ones who never seemed to have any problems with batchmates or faculty. They decided to do as they did, behave exactly as they were meant to. They would be neither seen nor heard.

Then came the announcement. A new prize for physiology was being instituted, and it was for the first-years. This was almost unheard of. There were medals to be won from the fourth year onwards. But a prize in the first year would be a triumph. All of them wanted it.

Physiology itself was an insipid subject, but it was also vast and offered numerous opportunities for research. But when Uma Shree and Savitha went to the physiology department to enter their names, Prof. Ramakrishna Badugavi frowned. 'It's a prize. There's no reservation quota. You'll be competing with everyone else. Do you think you can match up to the rest of them?'

Uma Shree stared at him, wondering if the query was real or rhetorical. 'We want to try,' she said doggedly.

He dropped two forms on the table. 'You're wasting your time. State board girls, and quota girls at that ...'

He took one of the forms back and said, 'The two of you can make a joint presentation. I don't think you can do it on your own.'

'Maybe we shouldn't bother,' Savitha said on their way back to their room. 'How will we compete with the others? They are ahead of us in so many ways ...' The words trailed off when she saw Uma Shree's frown.

'We need to make a plan and see how to make time for the presentation,' Uma Shree said in a firm voice. 'We can't neglect our studies either.'

Uma Shree went to meet Dr Rama Bai. She would guide them, Dr Bai said. And she did. She told them how to research their topic and how to put it together. The prize would be based on the final presentation. Savitha worried they wouldn't stand a chance as Prof. Badugavi was to evaluate the presentation.

'He can't fault us if we do everything right,' Uma Shree retorted in a bright voice. 'Besides, Rama Bai Madam is guiding us.'

Savitha shrugged. 'I think you are trying to convince yourself.'

The PowerPoint presentation drew to an end. The overhead lights came on. Uma Shree blinked at the sudden brightness; her eyes had got used to the dark. It was the first presentation of the day. Uma Shree had wanted everyone to see for themselves that Savitha and she might be reservation quota students but they were no less than any of them. In fact, she knew with certainty that their presentation had been top-notch. They had chosen as their subject the cytoskeleton of a cell. Dr Rama Bai had been pleased with their presentation and said it would make a decided impact.

Uma Shree and Savitha waited for the applause. When none was forthcoming, Uma Shree turned to Prof. Badugavi with a hopeful look. She waited for him to say something. Words of faint praise or perhaps even criticism. Instead, he looked past them and said, 'Next.'

Should she have clamped down on her rage at that point and let it go? On hindsight, it was easy to rationalise. But in that moment, all she felt was a crippling frustration. They had worked for a whole month on the presentation. Uma Shree had insisted that they draw each diagram rather than scan and attach what was available. They had spent hours looking for the perfect template to cast the presentation from. They had asked one of their batchmates, Rachita, to lend them her laptop. They had made an effort and they wanted everyone in the room to acknowledge that they had made an effort.

'Sir,' Uma Shree said. Her voice sounded loud to her own ears. But it wasn't more than a whisper. She tried again. 'Sir ...'

Her voice rang loud and clear, and the question in it made him look at Uma Shree.

'Yes, what is it?' Through his black-rimmed glasses, his eyes crawled over her face without apology or a trace of kindness.

'What did you think about the presentation, sir? We tried to bring in a lot of extra information,' Uma Shree said in Kannada.

'Speak in English,' Prof. Badugavi barked.

In the classroom, a titter rose and fell. Uma Shree tried to form sentences in her head. But the English language failed her, and what emerged was a fragment: 'How it was?'

The class exploded into laughter.

The professor's sigh was dramatic. 'Repeat after me,' he said. 'How was the presentation, sir? Not, how it was?' His voice dripped sarcasm.

Uma Shree whispered, 'How it was, sir, the presentation?'

Prof. Badugavi leaned back against the table. Then he said, 'How do you expect me to believe that the two of you put this together when you can't speak a straight sentence in English? How does the government expect us to do anything with people like you whom they stuff professional colleges with? Go to your seats, please.'

'But wait, you wanted to know what I thought. Well, go back to the first slide.'

Uma Shree's hand trembled as she did what he asked. For a moment, she thought he was going to remark on the quote with which they had begun their presentation. Ernst Haeckel's words: 'The cell never acts; it reacts.' She had found it in a medical journal and had been most excited about using it.

'Stop,' he said, as she raised the clicker to move past the slide on which was written the title, their names and roll numbers. 'This is the most interesting part of your presentation. Your names. They explain why the two of you managed to find a place in this temple of learning. Reservation quota ...'

The professor's assistant caught Uma Shree's eye briefly and then he, too, looked away.

Uma Shree continued to stand there with a foolish grin on her face, unable to stop smiling, unable to take a step.

'You have wasted enough of our time. Please go back to your seats,' he said, moving away from the table and towards the edge of the dais. Then he stopped, bent at the waist, and with an exaggerated flourish gestured for Savitha and Uma Shree to return to their seats.

Uma Shree kept her eyes on the floor as she stumbled back to her chair. Savitha followed quietly.

The lights were turned off and one of the others started their presentation. Uma Shree didn't register a thing. She sat in the darkened room, biting down hard on her knuckles so she wouldn't howl, so no one would know that she didn't know what to do.

She should be used to it by now, she told herself. She should have known that this would happen. I am my caste, nothing else matters.

What was it like in Prof. Badugavi's home, she thought bitterly. What did he teach his children about caste rules? Were they told that in India, no one is equal even though the Constitution says otherwise? Were they made to feel that they had a moral right to superiority? Were they told that people like her were meant to be kept in their place?

When the presentations were over and the lights came on, everyone began leaving in a hurry. They had the afternoon off. Most of them avoided looking at the two shrinking girls. A few threw them a small smile of commiseration and a couple sniggered as they trooped past. Uma Shree sat still, waiting for everyone to leave.

When the hall had emptied, Savitha turned to her. 'You still think we have a chance?' Her voice was bitter, her eyes wet.

'This is just a prize. Our grades don't depend on it,' Uma Shree whispered.

Savitha didn't respond. She gathered up their papers while Uma Shree packed the laptop into its bag. It had to be returned to Rachita.

A week later, the prize winner was announced. Savitha and Uma Shree stared at the noticeboard, willing it to be different. A boy named Pranav had won. He had made a 3D presentation everyone had talked about endlessly. In comparison, what they had done seemed childish and inept.

Savitha turned on her heels and walked away. Uma Shree trotted after her. 'Where are you going?'

'Does it matter?' Savitha snapped. 'Why don't you go and pretend that everything is all right with the world we live in?'

That evening, they were waiting for them in the dining room.

'Come here,' Rupa drawled. She was sitting at her customary table, surrounded by her coterie.

Uma Shree and Savitha had managed to steer clear of Rupa for some weeks now. This was as unexpected as it was frightening.

'Don't let her see how we really feel,' Uma Shree murmured as they walked to the seniors' table.

'I hear that the two of you got disqualified,' Rupa said, watching for their reaction.

'That isn't true,' Savitha blurted out.

'So, quota girl, you think I am making it up?'

'How do you know?' Savitha retorted.

'She wants proof of how I found out?' Rupa said with an amused expression.

'Do you know Rupa is Professor Badugavi's niece? If she says it, then it's the truth,' one of the others joined in.

'Next time you do a presentation, try and find one original thought,' Rupa said. 'But quota girls like you, all you can do is jump the queue in the name of caste. You can get into a medical college on a reservation quota, but whether you can do anything after that is the big question.'

'Go now,' she said, suddenly losing interest. 'Go stuff your faces with all the food you can find. I suppose you have no mess fees to pay either. In my next birth, I hope I am born a quota girl. But not as black as you two.'

Neither of them responded. They picked at their meal and went back to their room.

'We were disqualified,' Savitha said, again and again. 'On what grounds?'

'Why do you believe what those girls said? They were just messing with us.'

'Do you think it's because we did a joint presentation? Maybe it was meant to be an individual presentation. But Professor said we should, so how can he disqualify us?'

Savitha was in a strange mood. She who normally slept earlier than Uma Shree was wide awake at midnight. She sat on her bed and shone a torch at the ceiling. On and off. On and off. Uma Shree pulled the sheet over her head and curled into a ball. That night, neither of them could find any false words of comfort for the other.

Something changed thereafter. Savitha stopped attending classes. Instead, she went to the library or sat in their hostel room. It was as if she couldn't face anyone anymore. Uma Shree tried to cajole her out of her sullen silence. But it was impossible to get through to her.

The first semester exams were soon upon them. It was only then that Savitha seemed to rouse herself from the near catatonic state she had fallen into. On the morning that the hall tickets were issued, she almost seemed herself. Like on that first day when they had met, Uma Shree thought as she watched Savitha getting ready. There was a sense of purpose and a compulsion to prove herself.

They were the first ones to reach the mess that morning. Savitha had insisted. 'I can't handle that Rupa and her bitches this morning,' she said as she plaited her hair into a long braid that reached almost mid-thigh. She rolled it up into a bun and pinned it. Uma Shree grinned at her. She preferred the foul-mouthed Savitha to the silent one.

They went to collect their hall tickets after the morning's lab-work. The clerk handed over Uma Shree's without a word, then stared at Savitha and said, 'You have an attendance shortage. I can't issue the hall ticket.'

When Savitha continued to stand there, the clerk sighed. 'There's nothing I can do … I am just following orders.'

'What if I ask the HODs to approve it?' Savitha said softly. 'Do you think they would, just this one time?'

'You could, but not everyone will comply. Professor Badugavi is a stickler for the rules.'

Savitha chewed on her lip for a bit and then decided to try her luck. Most of the tutors and HODs were willing to make an exception for her. Apart from the attendance shortage, she was a good student and caused no trouble.

But Prof. Badugavi would not budge. 'There are no exceptions even for quota students like you,' he said. 'Attend the classes next semester and you will get your hall ticket if you have the requisite attendance. End of discussion.'

There was a break before the exams, but neither Savitha nor Uma Shree went home. At first, Uma Shree studied and Savitha brooded. Then Savitha began preparing as well. Uma Shree wondered what she was planning to do. 'I might as well,' Savitha said. 'There's no way I can go home. They will be very upset if they discover that I can't appear for the exams.'

Uma Shree didn't know what worried Savitha more: the prospect of having to lose a semester or explaining to her family that the golden date marked in their diary would be delayed. Not to mention the shame of having failed her family.

'Don't tell them,' Uma Shree said. 'They won't know until you tell them.'

Savitha smiled at that. It was the first time she had smiled in weeks.

The rest of the study leave passed uneventfully. Some of the seniors who had stayed on in the hostel started talking to them. They introduced them to their friends. Savitha stayed resolutely in the background, but Uma Shree was more sociable and found herself spending more and more time with the older girls. It helped that many of them were quota students too.

For the first time, college life began to resemble the college movies the girls had watched. Jokes. Laughs. Teasing. Serious conversations. Uma Shree caught one of the senior boys gazing at her more than once. She was in a happy place, she thought.

Neither Savitha nor Uma Shree ever mentioned that they were Madaru. They knew better than to test the boundaries of these new friendships.

A week before the exams, the rest of the batch returned. Uma Shree caught up with the more friendly among them to discuss some problem areas in biochemistry. Savitha joined in as well. 'This way, Savitha, you are going to top the class when you repeat the first sem exams,' one of the boys said.

'Such a pity about the attendance,' someone else said.

Uma Shree looked at the group and felt the beginnings of a sense of kinship. One day they would all be doctors and all else could cease to matter.

'Look, I heard that if you get a medical certificate, they will have to issue a hall ticket,' Govardhan said. He was one of the smartest boys in their batch and was also in their dissection group.

Savitha frowned. 'Who will issue a medical certificate here?'

Govardhan looked nonplussed.

'Maybe we can get one from Bengaluru,' Uma Shree said, thinking Peter Anna might be able to help.

'It's too late now to get it from Bengaluru,' Savitha said.

'What about from a doctor near your home? You must have a family doctor?' Bindu asked.

Savitha flicked back her hair impatiently. 'Not really,' she said. 'We go to the PHC.'

That evening, Riyaz came up to them triumphantly bearing a certificate. For good measure, he'd had it certified by a government doctor. Savitha's face lit up. It was like watching the sun rise between the hills.

Savitha, the certificate said, had a slipped disc and had been advised bedrest for a month. The date on it matched the date around which Savitha had stopped attending classes.

'Thank you, thank you.' Savitha's voice wobbled with emotion as she clasped Riyaz's palm in hers.

'All the best,' he replied, equally stricken by emotion.

Uma Shree smiled to herself. This was probably Riyaz's idea of a love note to Savitha, she thought.

Next morning, Savitha went to meet each of the HODs. Dr Rama Bai looked at the certificate and nodded her acceptance. The bio-chemistry HOD said that she would accept it if all the others did. That left only the physiology department. Savitha asked Uma Shree to go with her.

Prof. Badugavi stared at the piece of paper and snorted. 'Do you really think this is the first time a student has tried to hoodwink me?'

'Sir, it won't happen again. I promise you. I won't miss a single class.' Savitha spoke in Kannada.

'What is the name of the doctor you met? Which hospital is this?' he asked.

Savitha stared at him. It hadn't occurred to either of them to find out.

Prof. Badugavi stared at her for a long time. 'The problem with you quota students is that you think you can bend the rules. You think because you entered through a quota, it's your passport to wilfulness. That you can do as you please. But this is beyond that. I am going to ask for an enquiry and disciplinary action.'

Neither Savitha nor Uma Shree understood precisely what he said, but they realised he was saying no. And that there would be consequences.

What was it, Uma Shree would ask herself later, over and over again, that pushed Savitha over the edge? Was it the fear of being suspended? The dread of a permanent taint on her CV? The routine humiliation she had endured? Or was it the call from her brother, telling her that their father would have to sell the little land they had to pay off the loan they had taken to pay for her education? Was it the guilt? Was it knowing that she had no more emotional muscle to fight the daily battles that came their way? Was it that one professor or the system that would always remind her that she would never be anything but a quota girl?

Or was it because of her?

Uma Shree's heart stilled at the thought. Was it because she had not stood up for Savitha and for them? Was it because she had failed to rally support for their cause? Was it because she had tried to convince Savitha that it was better to swallow their rage and humiliation than complain or protest?

Savitha jumped from the terrace of the hostel building. She waited until Uma Shree had left for the last exam. She waited until the exam was over.

The night before, she had given Uma Shree no sign that she was distraught. She had helped her revise for the exam. 'Promise me that you will score the highest in physiology, if nothing else,' she insisted. 'I want Professor Badugavi to see for himself that we may be quota girls but we are just as good as anyone else.'

'I'll try,' Uma Shree had replied, wondering why Savitha was being so melodramatic.

'Good, that's all I expect from you.'

Savitha left a note. It blamed no one but herself:

I don't have the strength to fight the system. I had no choice when it came to the caste I was born into. There are others who have the resilience to endure it. I don't. So I must leave. This is my choice and perhaps the only one allowed to a Dalit like me.

To survive is to resist. I only wish I knew how to.

Uma Shree would think of that note often. Each time her spirit crumbled and she wondered if Arun had been right to give up, she would think of Savitha. She would remember the line from her note: To survive is to resist.

It would become her beacon of strength. On days that were more unbearable than others, she would chant to herself: I survive. I resist. I will survive. I will resist.

THE LITTLE DUCK GIRL

As it happens every dawn, I wake up to trilling, whistling, cackling, hooting—the relentlessness of bird noises.

Over the years I have learnt to sleep through the amplified call of the muezzin followed by P. Leela's Narayaneeyam from the temple. But the birds are a wily lot. Their calls constantly change.

As I do every morning, I look at the copy of Induchoodan's *Birds of Kerala* on my bedside. For some years now, I have been meaning to identify each bird that won't let me sleep. Perhaps if I know who is making which note, I won't have to think about the kind of bird it is, its plumage, if it is a native or a migrant. As I do at each daybreak, I promise myself that I will do it the next morning, and then turn on my side and draw the sheet over my head.

There is really no need for me to rise at half past five in the morning, especially on a nippy December day in Kaikurussi. Especially as I had stayed up watching news hour debates on a new Act that the Indian Parliament has passed. While the CAA and the non-inclusion of Muslims don't really concern me, I like to watch the panellists snarl at each other, goaded on by a shrill anchor with floppy hair. News has never been so entertaining.

Then I hear a quack.

I turn back to face the window and prop myself on my elbow.

The quacks grow louder, and I feel a huge smile on my face. It is the wrong time of the year for them, but the ducks are finally here in Kaikurussi.

As my cousin Mukundan used to say when he moved back to Kaikurussi way back in the nineties, the thing about Kaikurussi is that there is nothing there to make anyone come looking for it. It is neither the birthplace of a Mahatma nor of a movement. There are no gods here that promise miracles. No craft form originated here. In fact, nothing of significance has ever happened and nothing much has changed over the years. So, when the ducks stopped coming some years ago, I had felt bereft.

Here is why the ducks make me happy:

One, they seem a purposeful lot even when they are doing nothing but splashing around in the mud. Nothing deters them—rain, sun, dirt, water, land or the back of the lorry they travel in till Kulapully junction.

Two, the ducks are a disciplined lot, unlike most young men and women of this generation. It takes the elderly to appreciate the joy of discipline. When something annoys me—not that much does—I watch videos of ducks crossing a road or ducks being herded across the backwaters. It's like watching the Republic Day parade minus the speeches and the drone of the commentary mouthed by imbeciles who seem to have overdosed on Kozhikodan halwa, for nothing else can explain the greasy, saccharine sweetness of their words.

Three, the ducks are good neighbours. They don't complain about my trees or the state of my garden. They don't ask for a loan every few months which they then fail to return. Their babies don't wail, and their young don't ride motorbikes that rev up outside my gate. There is a fair amount of quacking, but then you can't make an omelette without breaking eggs.

Four, the ducks bring me money by just being here. The duck keepers pay me a small sum for parking their ducks in my fields. They also gift me eggs for as long as they are here, and offer me a duck as a thank you gesture when they leave. A duck that's been killed, plucked, cleaned and chopped into pieces, ready to be cooked into a spicy duck curry.

And last but not the least, the ducks bring with them the little duck girl.

I first saw the little duck girl some years ago, when she came with one of the duck keepers. Every year, the ducks arrived after the harvest in August–September. Muthu, one of the duck keepers, had come the year before as well, and I liked to practise my rusty Tamizh on him. I used to be reasonably adept at it during my master's at Loyola College in Madras.

'Is this your daughter, Muthu?' I had asked. He smiled. 'No, no, she is part of our group,' he said. 'We found her by a roadside shack on the highway. Abandoned.'

'What is your name?' I asked her in Tamizh.

She looked at Muthu's face. He smiled at her and said, 'Her name is Asha.'

She didn't look like she was from Tamil Nadu. Her skin was a pale golden brown and her eyes were narrow and tilted at the edges. As for her nose, it was a little button. Her hair was cut short as though someone had upended a basin on her head and cut away everything that stuck out beneath it.

I tried to dredge from a long time ago the little Hindi I had studied. Meanwhile, she burst into a language that I recognised as Bangla from watching the films of Satyajit Ray and Mrinal Sen films. I presumed she was from Assam or Bangladesh. Or a Rohingya refugee, though I wasn't sure if they had ventured this far into the south. Not that it mattered either way.

I smiled at the animated child, patted her head, and gave her a packet of biscuits. She looked at it with eyes like light bulbs and cried, 'Biscoot!'

How easy it is to please the poor and hungry.

I look out of my window, which faces the canal. Beyond, the fields stretch as far as Pulmooth Hill and through it like a black snake winds the road to Cherpulassery. In the fields where once the paddy stood tall and green, the ducks have taken root. Though a little scrawny now, in a fortnight they will be plump and succulent and perfect for a Christmas duck roast.

The men are building corrals for the ducks while the women lead the birds towards the fields where the ground is rich with fat worms. I wonder where my little duck girl is. I keep hearing her high-pitched cry in my head as she races through the fields to me: Maashe …

That's how everyone addresses me.

My name is Shree Raman. I used to be called Raman Kutty. The elders of the family took with them to their afterlife their memories of me as a withdrawn child, a quiet young man and my childhood name. Now, at fifty-nine, all I can hope for are peers who remember me as I once was. My hair has several streaks of grey and my skin isn't as smooth as it once used to be. But not having a wife or children to be responsible for has kept the wrinkles away. I have most of my teeth, all of my hair and a little paunch. I like to think all my senses are intact. Cognitive decline is something I haven't considered yet.

A bird I haven't seen before, slightly larger than a sparrow, with a grey body and a yellow head, pecks at something on the low wall that girdles the canal. I almost reach out for the book of birds but I tell myself I will do it later. The bird will come back tomorrow. Shree Raman needs a cup of tea first. Everything else can wait.

I can hear Pushpa sweeping outside. Sometimes I think she announces her presence with the broom. In fact, her broom speaks a language of its own. This morning, it's a contemplative broom as it gathers twigs, leaves and dust with a languid but firm movement. I am quite certain she is going to ask for a loan, a few days off, or a favour of some sort.

I open the door of my bedroom and walk up the corridor to the main hall and throw open the top half of the stable doors. 'Pushpa, where's my tea?' I holler.

Pushpa raises her head and looks at me as if I have asked for her son's head on a plate. Then she sighs loudly, shifts her clasp on the broom to the top, above the string holding the bristles together, and gives it an angry tap on the tree trunk closest to her.

Then she sighs once more and walks round the side of the house while I go back in to open the kitchen door for her.

She walks in wordlessly and fills the long-handled vessel with water. I watch as she click-starts the gas stove and sets about adding sugar and milk to the water. She stirs in the tea dust and lets it boil while I wait for her to spit out whatever is simmering inside her.

'What's for breakfast?' I ask, my stomach rumbling.

'Don't ever ask me what's for breakfast,' she hisses.

'But why?' I am truly perplexed.

'You tell me what you want me to cook. I am your maid, not your wife, to plan your meal the night before.' She places the cup of tea on the kitchen table with an angry thud.

Whoa, someone is in a foul mood. But as is my nature, I pretend to not notice and take my cup of tea to the front veranda. I am not a confrontational sort of man. Never was.

When I finished my postgraduation, my mother had insisted that I live at home and teach at a college in one of the nearby towns. All I had to do was apply for a teaching post. But I shuddered at the thought of having to ask someone for a job. Besides, my mother had enough money for the two of us, and I had very few needs. So I pottered around pretending to work on my PhD.

Two years of living on my own during my MA had taught me that I was a solitary creature. A girl I was involved with at that point said I was confusing selfishness with solitude and being laid back was just laziness. I cut her out of my life. Shortly after that, I returned to Kaikurussi.

My mother brought up the subject of marriage when I turned twenty-eight, but I wanted to get my PhD, I said. She died when I was thirty-four, after which I abandoned all pretence of studying.

Meanwhile, my brothers decided to tear the old house down and sell it to people who bought old nalukettu houses and replicated them elsewhere for the rich and famous. With some of that money, they built me a little cottage. They also decided to manage my share of the rubber estate and the teak plantations and the two mills we owned. I was happy for them to do whatever they wanted as long as I received my payouts regularly.

I wanted for nothing. The truth is if I wanted something really badly, I would have had to put myself out for it, make an effort of some sort—and that wasn't in my nature.

The quacking of the ducks breaks my reverie. I take a last sip of my tea and go back to the kitchen.

As if ashamed of her outburst, Pushpa says, 'There's batter in the fridge. Will doshas do?'

'Yes,' I say meekly. Then, seizing the opportunity, I ask, 'Will you make appam tomorrow? And duck egg roast. They'll bring a few eggs in the evening. It's been so long since I ate duck eggs.'

She glares at me. 'What if they don't give you any eggs?'

'Why won't they? They need to keep me happy,' I laugh. 'Their ducks are in my paddy fields and they draw their electricity from our mills' mains.'

'You know that you can ask Kannan to buy you duck eggs when he goes to stock up his shop,' Pushpa says as she stirs the batter. 'You don't need to wait for the ducks to come to Kaikurussi.'

'I know that, but duck eggs are expensive and money doesn't grow on trees,' I say. The truth is, it's too much of an effort to ask Kannan and I can't be bothered.

I light a cigarette and settle down on the low wall. I really don't understand why everyone is so determined to make me push myself. Right from the time when I can remember, I've been content with what comes to me. I was never the kind who wanted what wasn't within my reach or anything at all that required me to raise a sweat, shed blood or twist my insides into a knot. I was content with low-hanging fruit, even if the fruit was tart and not as good as those higher up on the tree.

I take a deep drag and exhale the smoke in a perfect ring. I can do things like that but don't ask me to chase after labour to work the fields or man the rice or timber mill. I am just not interested. I know my brothers and nephews cheat me, that I only received a fraction of the actual earnings, but I can't be bothered to create a ruckus.

It requires so much more effort to provoke an argument. It's easier to be amiable. That way I am invited to their homes for an elaborate lunch every Sunday and on festive days. On my birthday, they make me gifts of shirts, a new phone, a heavy-duty flashlight or some such thing that I would have had to spend my own money on otherwise. And one or the other accompanies me to my doctor, whom I meet every six months for a general check-up. I don't have any of the ailments that are usually part of ageing. Both my blood pressure and sugar levels are well within the normal range. My cholesterol is a little above normal and once in a while, my knee twinges, but apart from that, I am as healthy as a man of my age can be.

I look at the field where the men are finishing the corrals for the ducks. I can hear the splash of the water pump from the timber mill across the fields. As I watch, two of the fields turn into a muddy pond. The women and the ducks are some distance away, but I can't see my little duck girl with them. Has she not come this year either?

I remember how she sidled up to me the morning after the day I saw her first. I was sitting on the low wall. She stood next to me silently and we watched the ducks together for some time.

'Tharavu,' I said in Malayalam, pointing at a duck.

I repeated the word again. She looked at me as if trying to understand. Then she pointed at the duck and said, 'Tharavu.'

I smiled at her. 'Now let's try the English word. D-U-C-K.'

She repeated, 'DOOK!'

'No, no, duck. D-U-C-K.' I made her say it again. Soon she got the hang of it, and she was a quick learner, I realised, for in a few minutes, she had learnt a dozen words in both Malayalam and English.

My mobile phone rings, and stops. It's Pushpa signalling that my breakfast is ready. I hoist myself up and go into the house.

I stop at the kitchen door and inhale the aroma of the dosha sizzling on the cast-iron griddle. Once upon a time, I used to write poetry. Now I see poetry in the making of a dosha. Sometimes I think there is more poetry in a lone dosha than there is in all of Shakespeare's sonnets. Allow me this:

The viscous fluidity of the batter as the ladle swirls it. The splattering of a few water drops on the oiled and heated cast-iron griddle. The kitchen filling with the aroma of heated iron, sesame oil and all the doshas that came before this one.

Over the years, I have watched so many doshas made that I could make one with my eyes closed. You don't just pour a dosha. There is a science to it. The ladle is filled to the brim and poured into the centre of the griddle. There is a restrained rhythm as the batter is spread in a circular movement till it coats the surface. A spoonful of sesame oil, nothing else will do because no oil loves the heat of the cast iron with as much intensity as the dense golden-brown sesame. A lid is placed on the griddle.

At first, hisses and splutters. Then a whiff of the batter cooking sneaks its way out. When you raise the lid, the edges are brown and crisp and the dosha will let the spatula slide under it uncomplainingly.

My mouth waters. Pushpa is about to flip the dosha the other way. 'No, don't,' I say hastily. 'That's not how you do it.'

Pushpa turns and glowers at me. 'Why don't you make it yourself then?'

I draw a chair out from beneath the kitchen table. 'And why should I, when you are here to do it? That's what I pay you for, no?'

I give Pushpa a long rope, but once in a while, I rein it in so she remembers that she works for me.

I know that Pushpa felt the tug when her expression changes to a more benign one. 'Would you like an egg?' she asks as she places the dosha on a plate and brings it to the table.

'Yes,' I say and walk towards the built-in loft in the kitchen. It's here that I keep the eggs so no one else can reach it. 'Yes, make me a bull's eye,' I say, standing on my toes and reaching for an egg.

When I am back at the dining table, I take the lid off the little bowl to see if she has made coconut chutney or the ulli samandhi I prefer but which she seldom makes, for I insist she use the grinding stone rather than the mixie to grind the shallots and dried red chillies to a fine paste. But it is the ulli samandhi, and she has sautéed it in coconut oil. I am certain now that something is afoot.

The fried egg and the instant coffee that I prefer to the boiled-up version arrive together. Anyone else would ask her if there is something on her mind. But I am not anyone. I break a piece of my dosha, dip it in the ulli samandhi and eat it slowly. The next piece is for the egg. The third piece will be eaten plain, with a sip of coffee.

Pushpa watches me eat for a while. Then she clears her throat. I pretend not to sense the change in the atmosphere. When you spend as much time with yourself as I do, you learn to gauge the quality of silence. You learn to sense how expectation weighs the air around you with a peculiar but definite tensile strength. Lesser mortals succumb to it by asking: Is there something you want?

Instead, I continue to eat my dosha and drink my coffee until Pushpa blurts, 'I need a week off.'

'Why?'

'I want to go with my son to Sabarimala,' she says.

That's when I noticed that she is wearing a black sari and has a string of thulsi beads around her neck. 'Do they let women of your age in?'

'Don't you know, Maashe, the Supreme Court has said women of any age can enter now,' she retorts.

'Do you know that Sabarimala hasn't let young women enter all these years? Are the priests stupid? Not at all. That is the belief Sabarimala is built on, no? What is the Supreme Court thinking, letting young women enter the temple premises?' I am repeating what I've heard my brothers say. I don't particularly care, anyway.

'I am fifty-three years old. I don't think even the priests will have a problem with my entering the temple,' Pushpa laughs, dismissing my objections easily.

'Why do you want to go where every Chathan and Pothan will be?' I shudder at the imagined stench of damp clothes and sweat.

'Please don't call them names. They are swamis. Like me, each one of them would have taken a vow of abstinence for forty-one days. I may cook your fish and meat, but I haven't touched anything for three weeks now. So please don't call them what you just did,' she says in a fierce voice.

Why is she so rattled by my using a common Malayalam phrase?

It's time to change tactics. Does she actually expect me to cook and clean on my own for a whole week? I take a sip of coffee and gave her a stern look. 'Have you found someone to take over while you are gone?' I ask as I tear a piece off the last dosha and wipe the bits of yolk that cling to the plate before popping it into my mouth.

'You do know that it isn't easy to find a temporary replacement,' Pushpa says in a placatory manner.

'So, here's your choice: you can take off for two days Or you find someone who will fill your place while you are gone. Or, I find someone to replace you for good.'

'But ...' Pushpa begins.

'It's entirely up to you,' I say as I rise from the table. 'Very nice ulli samandhi, by the way,' I add, feeling very much like Al Pacino in *Scent of a Woman*. It was the last Hollywood movie I saw in a theatre before I left Chennai for good.

I walk to the gate where the newspaper lies pushed into a piece of PVC tube. Once upon a time, I couldn't start the day without the newspaper, but now the news alerts on my phone keep me informed all the time. I only read the newspaper to know about local goings–on and check the obituary pages. In fact, those are the pages I read first. After a certain age, photos of your peers, family, friends and acquaintances start appearing in the little black-edged boxes. Not that I attend any of the funerals, but I still want to know who is dead.

I open out the obituary pages and discover that my cousin Mukundan has passed. He had moved away from the village several years ago after taking up with a married woman. I had forgotten her name, but it's there beneath his photograph. His loving wife Anjana. I didn't know they were married. My mother and brothers would often say that if I didn't get a job and have a family of my own, I would end up like him—a ratty and sad old man. Then, Mukundan started living with Anjana and the resulting scandal rocked the village. People my mother hadn't seen for years took to dropping in bringing tidbits about Mukundan and Anjana. But, as is the nature of scandals, it died out soon enough and my family switched to saying, there is no fool like an old fool.

I toss the paper down and gaze out at the vegetable garden. The pumpkin plants have flowered, and I can see bees droning around them. There is something very fulfilling about looking at vegetables that grow on your land as if by magic. Each day there is something new: a leaf or a bud, a vegetable that had grown bigger or changed a shade ...

It's Mukundan who gave a small piece of his land to the house painter Bhasi; Bhasi is now a neighbour. I remember there was a discussion about it those many years ago. About Mukundan being as touched in the head as the house painter, whom everyone called One Screw Loose Bhasi.

A few months ago, Bhasi had asked if he could grow vegetables on a piece of my land.

'What do I have to do?' I asked Bhasi, wondering if he expected me to water the plants and watch out for troupes of wild boars and peacocks coming down from Pulmooth Hill.

'Nothing at all. Just let me use the land and some water. At the most, you might need to switch on the water pump,' Bhasi said.

I tried to read his eyes for mockery. But he was being earnest. So I agreed, and now at the bottom of my acreage, I have pumpkins and cucumber, bitter gourd and brinjal, spinach and ladies' fingers growing.

Most mornings, one of my brothers drops by. The oldest comes to enquire on my well-being. The second one comes to shoot the breeze with the misguided notion that I may be lonely. The last one comes to complain about our older brothers, their wives, and how he doesn't think we are getting our fair share of whatever money came into the family coffer. Thus, the morning goes past punctuated by an occasional smoke and cups of tea.

By noon I know that the little duck girl hasn't come this year. And I feel a sense of loss I don't understand.

It's been a while, but I cannot forget how the little duck girl tagged after me that first year. She would come to my house in the mornings and accompany me on my evening walks. In the one month the ducks were in the fields of Kaikurussi, I taught the little duck girl the English alphabet and the numerals. It began with me helping her create a pictogram for a signature.

I was signing a cheque when she asked me what it was. I told her about signatures. 'I want a signature too,' she said.

'Tell you what,' I said as I led her into the garden. 'Push your thumb into some wet mud.'

She did as I asked.

'Now press it on this paper.'

She looked up from the paper and said, 'It looks like a duck's foot.'

'Exactly. Now draw a line around it.'

I watched her, and when it was done, I said, 'That's your signature. It means Little Duck Girl!'

She ran to the ducks, clutching the paper to her chest, to show them her signature. The next day, I started on the English alphabet. There was no point in teaching her Malayalam. Her people spoke Tamizh. At least, this would help her read road signs and place names.

When they left, I gave the little girl a bag with an ABC primer, a notebook and a few pencils. 'Don't stop practising your letters and numbers,' I said, tugging at a strand of her hair. She hasn't lost her sense of wonder, I thought, as I saw her peer into the bag. Her eyes gleamed with excitement.

'You should have given her a biscuit packet instead,' my third brother said. 'What will she do with an ABC book? Teach English to the ducks?' He laughed, vastly amused at his own joke.

I said nothing, and opened the little basket she had brought for me. In it were fourteen duck's eggs and on each one of them I could see the letters of the English alphabet, two to an egg. On the fourteenth egg was a smear of mud encased in an outline to suggest the footprint of a duck.

I don't know if I was touched by her gesture or if it was a teacher's sense of gratification for having done his job well, but I couldn't stop smiling.

It occurred to me then that I should have asked what Muthu was going to do with the little duck girl. He had a young wife, and there was an old man and woman with them. A little girl would be a nuisance. But it really was none of my business. I couldn't be responsible for every orphan who crossed my path. So I put the niggling thought out of my mind and picked up my newspaper to point out a news item to my brother.

That evening, I had eaten the signature. For a week, I boiled, scrambled and fried the English alphabet, till I couldn't bear the smell of duck's eggs anymore. And then I gave away O-P-Q-R-S-T-U-V-W-Y and Z to Pushpa and her brood of children.

Where could the little duck girl be now? I hope she survived the floods from two years ago. I have an address for her. Maybe I will write her a letter. It will have to wait though, for it's time for lunch.

Pushpa has left the food in hot cases on the kitchen table. All I have to do is eat and put everything away. I take the dirty dishes to the outdoor sink and leave them there after running some water on them. Pushpa will deal with them when she returns in the morning.

My kitchen is spick and span, just as I like it.

I go into my room and lie down on the bed. Idly, I check Facebook. There's much frothing at the mouth about the Citizenship Amendment Act. I read a couple of posts and grow weary of the rant. How does it concern us or our lives? If you ask me, in an over-populated country like ours, why do we need to give asylum to any refugees?

I decide to watch a Ted Talk instead. But why are all the speakers dressed in black or navy blue? I listen to a woman talk about the Me Too movement only because she is wearing a red dress. She gets agitated about predators at the workplace. Does she think any of this waving of hands will make men behave differently? Men will be men. That goes without saying.

I fold my hands over my chest and drift into sleep.

Most evenings, I go for a walk. I have a route for each day of the week, but this evening I decide to break with routine and visit the ducks. No one has come yet to pay their respects with a few eggs for an offering. Perhaps seeing me will remind them. I can also check with them about the little duck girl. It's quite possible they don't know who she is. But if they do, I won't have to search for the inland form or write the letter.

The year after I first met the little duck girl, Muthu had come with a new brace of ducks. The lorry had arrived late in the evening, so I didn't know until the next morning, when the little duck girl came racing across the field. I was on my habitual perch on the low wall. 'Maashe, Maashe,' she called as she drew closer. She had grown a little taller and looked less hungry. She also had her hair in pigtails.

I smiled at her. In the course of a year, she had picked up the Malayali affectation of calling men 'maashe' and women 'teachere'.

'I was looking for you,' she prattled, her face stretched in a giant grin. I tugged at her pigtail and asked, 'How are you, little duck girl?'

'Don't call me that, Maashe … my name is Asha. See, I know how to write it.' She took a twig and scratched on the mud: A S H A.

'Excellent. So have you been practising the alphabet and numerals?' I asked, watching her prance after a yellow butterfly.

She let the butterfly go and came running back. 'I am going to school now.'

I saw Muthu walking towards me. He took off the towel wrapped around his head and looked at the little duck girl. 'Did she tell you that she goes to school now?'

The old man and woman worked at a plantation near Thrissur, he said. The little duck girl stayed with them and went to a government school nearby.

'Do you like school?' I asked.

She nodded furiously. 'I get lunch at the school. Everyday.'

'Let me see what you've learnt,' I said, and watched as she read the newspaper I thrust in front of her. When she couldn't fathom a word, her eyes screwed up and she bit on her lip.

That year, they didn't stay very long. 'My school will reopen in a week's time,' the little girl told me as she sat doing some simple addition. She spoke Malayalam fluently and always had a lot to say.

So did my brothers. My oldest brother called her my new toy. The second one said, 'If you had married and had a family, you wouldn't be so lonely.'

My third brother mumbled, 'How come you never showed so much interest in your nephews and nieces?'

I ignored their mockery, as I always did.

There is neither logic nor reason for why we like some people more than we do others. The little duck girl lifted my spirits and it made me happy to have her around.

When Muthu and she came to say goodbye, I gave her some money in a little envelope and told her to buy herself an umbrella. 'Don't get wet in the rain and catch a fever,' I said.

'Nothing will happen to me, Maashe,' she said. 'I am used to the rain. I like water.' She grinned, 'I live with ducks, remember!'

'Indeed!' I tugged at her pigtail. I didn't know why I liked doing that, but I did.

'But you are not a duck, and water won't slide off your back. So, buy that umbrella.'

The following year, the ducks came back, but the little duck girl wasn't with them. The people who came with the ducks didn't know anything about her or Muthu.

Then the ducks stopped coming. More and more people had taken to growing bananas in the paddy fields, while some others left theirs fallow.

Has it been six or seven years since the ducks were here last? It is only now I realise that I had missed them. The monotone of my days will acquire a new hue, a new sound. The thought makes me smile.

On the way back home from my walk, I stop at the village square, which everyone refers to as City. The conductor who came on the first bus ever to Kaikurissi was something of a wag. He had looked at the huddle of shops and called out, 'City, City, Kaikurussi City.' I had been on that bus and laughed as well, but the name stuck, and now everyone refers to the place as City.

Once upon a time, a few shops and Shankar's tea club had constituted the city. Now, a long row of shops stretches on either side: a branch office of the Kayiliad Service Co-operative Bank, a hardware shop and even a beauty salon for men and women. I go into Kannan's shop and pick up a pack of cigarettes.

A few men are standing around discussing the Citizenship Amendment Act and what its implementation might lead to. 'Anyone without papers will be sent to the detention centre, especially if they are Muslim. We must protest against the CAA,' Yusuf says. He is a youth leader, and an integral part of the local Islamic Party.

I shake my head in baffled amusement. Here in Kaikurussi, everyone has enough proof to show that they belong. What happens in other parts of the country doesn't really affect us, and yet this fool wants to hold a protest march. It reminds me of the time when Bill Clinton came to India and all the compound walls in Kaikurussi were plastered with 'Go back Clinton'.

'You'll join us, won't you, Maashe?' Yusuf asks.

'Of course,' I say, though I have no intention of doing so.

'It's when people like you join the protest that the political statement we are making acquires gravitas,' he says. 'That's when it gets noticed.'

'I'll be there. Just let me know when and where,' I say. On the day of the protest, I will suddenly take ill.

As I leave, I hear someone mutter, 'Why waste your breath asking him to join the protest? You know he won't; he's a sugiyan.'

I blink and stop mid-stride. Why does he think I'm a fried dumpling stuffed with green gram, jaggery and coconut? Then I understand. Sugiyan is an old-fashioned word for a lazy so-and-so who can't be bothered to put himself out. I walk away briskly so the others can't tell I've heard them.

Sometimes it's best to pretend that one can't hear or see or know ... Awareness isn't what it's touted to be. It's mostly a burden that weighs you down and makes you want to change yourself or the world around you. I was inclined to do neither.

I start walking towards the fields but stop when I see how dark it has become. A few emergency lamps light up the shack and the area around the duck corral. I don't think it's prudent to visit them now. The men will be in the toddy shop and the women busy with their chores.

All evening, I wait for someone to come by with duck's eggs. At eight, I swallow my disappointment and lock the gate. The night sounds creep into the house. The crickets hiding in the undergrowth sharpen their knives. Leaves rustle with the swish of a whip. The devil bird shrieks poo-ah, poo-ah. If my mother were alive, she would have rushed to put an iron ladle over the embers of the wood fire. That's how you keep death at bay, she would have said.

I used to look at my mother's swollen joints and toothless mouth and wonder why she was reluctant to die. Now I know. No matter what, I want to live a few more days. If nothing else, I want to eat duck's eggs one last time, I tell myself with a laugh as I put on Sreevalsan Menon's album, *Sringaram*. In a little while, my eyes shut on their own, lulled into a state of splendid calm. I cannot sleep until I hear him sing. And my last thought usually is, I want to hear him sing one more time.

Early next morning, I walk to the wall and sit on it, waiting to see who is at the duck camp.

Pushpa has a key of her own to open the gate. I hear its creak, and her voice speaking to someone. Pushpa is wedded to her phone. She dusts, sweeps, mops, washes dishes and clothes, cooks and waters the plants, all with the phone perennially attached to her ear. Who does she talk to all day? And what does she talk about?

'Here he is,' I hear Pushpa say. I turn to look towards the gate. A young, fresh-faced woman in a kurta and churidar stands there. Her hair is in a loose ponytail, and a small, round, maroon pottu is stuck on her forehead. She carries a shopping bag in her hand.

'Who is this?' I ask, wondering how Pushpa has found a replacement so quickly.

'Don't you recognise me, Maashe?' The young woman says, stepping forward. The voice is different, but the intonation is the same. I look at the narrow eyes tilted at the end, the high cheekbones, and feel a thud of surprise. My little duck girl. But how can this young woman be her?

Pushpa sniggers at my expression. 'When did you see Asha last?'

'I'm not sure. Four or five years ago?' I say.

'Nine years,' the little duck girl says. 'I am eighteen years old now, Maashe.'

'Nine years, is it? In my mind, you are still the little girl in pigtails ...' I say, as much to myself as to the two women.

'I waved to you yesterday morning, but you looked through me,' the girl giggles.

'Obviously ... I don't wave back at young women who wave at me. What would people say?'

Pushpa clears her throat. 'I met Asha on the way here. She was bringing you some duck's eggs. So, anyway, she says she will step in for a week until I return.'

'Are you sure, Asha?' I ask. Pushpa is an emotional bully who knows how to switch on the tear tap when necessary. I don't want her luring the girl into doing something she doesn't want to do.

'Yes, I am sure, Maashe,' she smiles. 'Pushpa chechi will show me what needs to be done, and tomorrow I'll take over.'

I feel ridiculously happy. To be honest, I don't know if it's because of the egg roast I am going to have for breakfast, just as I want it, or because the little duck girl is back in my life.

Asha fills me in on the last nine years. She had lived with Muthu and his wife at a plantation in Munnar. She was at a school camp when Muthu and his wife were swept away in a landslide during the floods of 2018. Muthu's brother, who lived nearby, took her in. When she turned eighteen, he put up her name at the labour recruitment department at the plantation. 'They are good people, but they have their own problems to deal with. Once I get the job, Maashe, I won't have to depend on anyone,' she says with the self-assurance she possessed even as a child.

When Muthu's brother mentioned that someone he knew would be taking the ducks to Nilambur, Asha had asked to go along. 'Until the job comes through, I need to earn some money. I was the one who told them about Kaikurussi. I told them it's on the way to Nilambur. I knew that you would be here. And that you might be able to find me a job till such time as they put me on the rolls at the plantation,' she said.

A lot has been happening in the country. The television news is all about the anti-CAA protests and how they had erupted one by one in various places, from Assam to Delhi to Lucknow to Bombay to Kolkata to Bengaluru. On 17 December, all of Kerala was to go on a dawn-to-dusk hartal. Political parties, including the ruling party, would stay away, but a group of thirty Islamic and political outfits would make it happen. Shop shutters would be down, schools and colleges closed, the roads would be empty since no one would want to risk being pelted by stones or attacked. Most people would stay home glued to their mobiles. Who doesn't enjoy an unexpected holiday?

The CAA has half the village worried. Kaikurussi has a mixed population of Hindus and Muslims: fifty-fifty. The Hindus, of course, swagger around as though they own the village and the world. Not the Muslims, though. Even I can sense the reining in of steps and movement. It's as if they are consciously trying to become inconspicuous. They have even stopped selling beef in the village, I hear. It's not surprising then, that the local chapter of the Muslim League in Kaikurussi are taking out a protest march.

I stand on the verandah as an SUV fitted with speakers cruises past, calling out to everyone in the village to join the protest. A few bikes speed by, muffling the words.

'Hooligans!' I say to the little duck girl who is sitting there and cleaning rice.

Three days have gone past since she arrived. We have fallen into a routine. The big difference is that Asha does her work as though she enjoys it, while Pushpa always behaves as if she is doing me a favour. I've begun to dread her return.

Asha hates being in the kitchen, preferring to do all her chores in the backyard or in the front veranda.

'The wall seems to close in on me when I sit in a room,' she said on the first day, laughing in embarrassment. 'I am like a duck,' she added. 'You can't keep a duck in a cage. I guess I spent too many years with them, I've acquired some of their behaviour.'

We laughed together. I wondered which animal I had learnt from. But I quickly deflected the thought with a frown.

'Jobless fools!' I grumble aloud, as the jeep continues down the road blaring its message of protest. 'What do they think will happen because of a protest march? Just like those women in Delhi. Apparently, some ten or fifteen housewives blocked the road or some such thing. You think an Act is going to be repealed because a few jobless idiots here and there took out a protest march?'

Asha raises her eyes from the rice and looks at me as if she is seeing me for the first time. Like she has spotted a weevil. For a moment, I am startled. Then I realise that it's a trick of the light. My little duck girl who thinks the sun rises and sets with her Maash would never look at me with disgust.

The morning of the hartal dawns. The bird who sounds like a dying UPS had disturbed my sleep. I had got up in the middle of the night and put off all the security lights and gate lights, not wanting the battery to die out. Then I saw the streetlights were on and turned all the lights back on and went to sleep. I am still a little groggy when the Indian tree magpie starts its annoying whickering call. Honestly, the bird needs a tranquiliser. I sigh and begin my stretches.

A day like any other day, I think, when I hear the brisk scratching sound of the broom in the front yard. I lie in bed waiting for the familiar sounds and smells to make their way to me. The smoke from the wood fire as it heats my bath water. The creak of the pulley as water is drawn from the well. The clanging of vessels from the kitchen as water is put on the gas hob for my tea. The little duck girl is in my home, God is in heaven, and all is well with the world. I stretch my toes in contentment.

When I enter the veranda, Asha appears with a cup of tea and the newspaper. As I sip the tea, I make up my mind to ask Asha to stay on if she is willing. It will be a relief to let Pushpa and her tardiness go.

After breakfast, I walk to the back of the property. I had watched a video on how to protect roses from aphids. The principle can't be very different. A plant is a plant. I tell Bhasi what to do about aphids and root rot. He looks at me, stupefied. I know what he is thinking. I haven't even grown a chilli plant in my life and here I am advising him on yard-long beans and pumpkins. Like an expert. It feels good.

The first twinge of unease comes when I discover that Asha has left the premises without telling me. It's my oldest brother's turn to have me over for lunch. Before leaving, I try calling her on the mobile phone I had given her; an old one I had kept. But it's switched off. I don't know what to make of it. Where could she have gone?

I had asked Asha to move into my house. She occupied the servant's room alongside the kitchen. The room is a comfortable one. It even has an attached bathroom. She only has to step out of the back door to access it.

When I had questioned the building contractor about the servant's room, saying it was unnecessary, he had scratched his head for a moment and said, 'Let's call it a storeroom.' Now, I am glad that I didn't fight too hard with him about it.

Asha is still not around when I come back from lunch. I feel a twinge of irritation, or is it anger? I can't be bothered to examine my own feelings; I am replete with ghee rice and mutton curry and semiya payasam and want my siesta more than ever.

As I wake up from my nap I hear the gate open. I get up when I hear noises in the kitchen. I go to sit in the veranda. Asha comes there with a little smile and a query: would I like pappada vada with my tea?

My mouth waters at the thought of the crunchy pappadam coated with gram flour and fried to a crisp, punctuated by sips of hot tea. 'Yes, yes,' I say. 'Don't forget to add chilli powder and asafoetida in the gram flour. And a pinch of rice flour. That will make it crisp.'

She nods with a strange expression on her face.

'Where did you go?' I ask her.

'I had some personal work,' she says.

'On a hartal day?'

She pretends to not hear the disbelief in my voice. 'Yes, it was something I had to do today.'

I let it rest. I don't want to annoy her by probing. I just hope it isn't some hooligan who lured her out. There are many young men in the village. And why does he have to be young, even? He could be an older man, a married man. I am rattled by the very thought of it.

I hear the gate open. It's my second brother. He is ten years older than me, but has the energy of a twenty-five-year-old. He strides towards me. I am surprised to see him look agitated. 'Is everything alright?' I ask.

'Yes, yes but an idiot raced past on a motorbike and almost knocked me off my scooty,' he says, dropping into a chair and wiping his brow.

My brother taught himself to ride a two-wheeler six months ago and is still a little wobbly.

'Have some tea,' I say, and call out to Asha to make another cup.

'Is she back?' he asks.

'Yes, she came in at four,' I explain.

'Did she tell you about the protest march in Pattambi?'

'What protest march?' I frown.

My brother rolls his eyes. 'Rama, you can't be so removed from what's happening around us. Don't you know that there have been rallies all over the country, protesting against the CAA? There was one in Palakkad, and Malappuram. Massive ones. And also in smaller towns like Pattambi. This one was at the Government Sanskrit College.'

'I didn't know she had joined the march. Why would she?' I look at my brother disbelievingly. 'Are you sure?'

My brother shoots me a dirty look. 'Ask her yourself,' he says.

Asha comes into the hall just then, with two cups of tea and a plate piled high with pappada vada.

'Asha, were you in Pattambi?' I ask, quite certain that my brother had mistaken someone else for her. 'Ettan says he saw you. I said it couldn't be you.'

Asha places the tray on the little table. Then she turns to me and says, 'Yes, Maashe. I was there. I joined the protest march against the CAA.'

I am nonplussed. When she leaves the room, I turn to my brother. 'Why would she go on the march? How does this CAA thing matter to her?'

'Your little duck girl is a revolutionary ...' my brother says, biting into a pappada vada. His teeth are his own and make a loud crunching sound. 'None of our business, you'll soon be rid of her. When is Pushpa coming back?'

'I am thinking of replacing Pushpa with Asha.'

'I know it's easier to find a grain of gold in the field than to find a maid in Kaikurussi, but keeping a young girl at home ... That's inviting trouble, and people will talk.'

I swiftly change the subject. My brother has a wife and children. His sons are married and live at home. I have no one to take care of my needs. I know I have to do what is best for me.

The next morning, I broach the subject with Asha. 'Would you like to stay on and work for me?'

Her eyes light up, but I sense her hesitation. She goes back to grating the coconut.

I've already thought of what to say if she doesn't agree right away. 'You could attend a college in Ottapalam or Pattambi and get your degree. Or you can join a tailoring class. I'll pay for the books, fees and bus, and also pay you a salary for the work you do. Whatever I eat, you will too. Fair?'

Asha looks up from the little heap of grated coconut. 'Maashe, there is something you must know. My name isn't Asha; it's Ayesha. Do you still want me as your live-in help?'

I stare more in surprise than shock. 'How is that possible?'

'When Muthu Uncle found me, he said it's best that I be known as Asha. It would lead to all sorts of complications otherwise. I have no papers to prove that I am Ayesha, except for my SSLC certificate. But that's the truth.'

'I see.' I can't find the words to say any more.

In Kaikurussi, we are not divided by religion. However, we are governed by tradition and old, unwritten rules. My barber and coconut picker are Muslim. But when it comes to entering the house and the kitchen, it's another matter altogether. Muslims don't work in Hindu households and vice versa.

I shrug. 'It doesn't matter to me. Just don't tell anyone your real name is Ayesha. And no one will come asking you for ID papers here.'

In my head, it's clear: Asha, Ayesha, or whatever she wants to be known as, is too good a worker for me to let her go. And I do feel some affection for the little duck girl.

A week goes past. Pushpa does not return. The ducks and their keepers leave. The CAA protests don't stop, and the little duck girl goes to a few, including a massive one at Malappuram which was led by the Kazi. Apparently, there were no spectators; everyone joined the procession.

I let her know my displeasure each time. My brothers mutter under their breath about the girl living under my roof. I ignore them, like I do the repeated entreaties from various people who want me to participate in the protest meetings in Kaikurussi.

Things come to a head when, one afternoon, a scuffle breaks out near my gate. Personal enmity camouflaged as political enmity erupts and there is some kicking and slapping. The little duck girl is very quiet that evening.

The next morning, her face is wan and drawn. I wonder if she is on her period.

As she serves me breakfast, I ask her what is wrong.

'I am afraid, Maashe,' she says.

'But why? Because of those fools fighting at our doorstep?' Note the "our". I want her to feel she belongs in my home.

'I've seen worse brawls than that. But I overheard something one of the men said later. The one in the saffron mundu, with an orange string around his wrist. He shook his fist, looking at this house, and said, 'One of them has moved in here already. Before you know it, they'll be taking away our temples from us.'

I close my eyes. Did I make a serious error of judgment by keeping the little duck girl here? Then something strikes me. 'How did he know you are a Muslim?'

She flushes. 'I should have told you earlier, but I really thought he wouldn't tell anyone.'

'Who is this "he"?' I frown. My brother was right to caution me about the foolishness of letting a young girl live under my roof. I wonder where she met him, and when. Is that why she came to Kaikurissi?

'The Ustad,' she says softly.

'What does an Arabic teacher have to do with you?' My voice rises.

'There is this little girl, Bipathu. She used to come to look at the ducks and we became friends. She told me that Balkies Umma has an Ustad come to their house to teach Arabic to her grandkids. Apparently, they don't like attending the madarsa. I went to see Balkies Umma with her and asked if I could join the class. The Ustad didn't agree at first. He said the Quran is a holy text and not a storybook. That's when I told him my real name is Ayesha. He agreed then, and I thought he would understand when I said I wanted to keep it quiet.'

'How long has this been going on?' I ask.

'Just three days,' she says in a small voice.

'Why this desire to study the Quran now?'

'Maashe, do you know what it's like to not belong to any religion? Even though I was born a Muslim, I know nothing about my religion. And Muthu Uncle wouldn't teach me about his either.

'Muthu Uncle wouldn't let me light a lamp or take me to the temple with him. He always made some excuse. I could see that even he, kind as he was, couldn't get himself to flout the rules. So, who do I pray to when I need God? Who is going to watch over me? Muruga or Allah? Who am I? Asha or Ayesha?'

'Is that all?' I ask, leaning forward. 'I'll tell you. You are the little duck girl.' I laugh, amused at my own quick repartee.

'Maashe, you don't get it, do you?' she says in a tone I have never heard her use before.

'What is it that I don't get?'

I notice then the two dishes she has placed before me: pongal and chutney. I can't remember when I ate pongal last. Not after I left Chennai, perhaps. 'You made pongal?' I chirp.

'Paati taught me,' she says after a long moment of silence.

'Paati? I didn't know you had a grandmother.'

'Muthu Uncle's mother,' she says.

I can see that she wants to resume our conversation on religion and belonging and all that nonsense. When she sees that I had no intention of doing so, she serves herself some of the pongal and sits down on the floor. I wonder if I should ask her to sit at the table with me. But I can't bring myself to do it.

Kaikurussi turns into a hotbed of rumours. There wasn't as much speculation when Bhama sneaked away one dawn with a very unsuitable boy and, being the new-gen girl she is, announced her elopement on Facebook.

Now the little duck girl and I are the subject of gossip. I think it might die a natural death as with Bhama, but it turns into something else.

First my brothers drop in, all three together, bringing their indignation with them like an extra brother. Indignation sits on the chair alongside them. I am dragging the family name through slush, they say. Their granddaughters won't find good alliances if the word gets around.

'What did I do wrong?' I ask my brothers, trying to understand what has made them so tetchy.

'You are living with a young girl,' the oldest one says.

'And she is a Muslim,' the second one adds.

'What is bothering you?' I demand, careful to hide the anger seething in me. 'That she is young or that she is Muslim?'

'Both,' the last one says, glaring at me.

'What if I adopt her?' I say, trying to inject some levity.

'She is an adult. You can't adopt her,' they say in unison.

'Well then, I'll have to marry her,' I say, the words tumbling out of my mouth with careless abandon.

My brothers leave in a huff. I don't know what worries them more. That I might marry a Muslim girl or that someone else will inherit all that I own.

I watch the little duck girl as she goes about her chores. She will take care of me, and I will be her protector. I am a lot older than her, but she will never find an educated, well-settled husband like me. The more I consider it, the more I am convinced.

When my mother died, we divided the jewellery between us. I open the cupboard and pull out the pouch. I still have the two bangles, her padakkam and two pairs of earrings that were put aside as my share. I take out the padakkam. A diamond shaped pendant of rubies and white sapphires strung on a choker chain. It's an older woman's ornament. But it will suit my little duck girl, make her slender neck look even more slender. I'll give her this and tell her that I am going to marry her.

In the evening, some of the elders from the nearby mosque call on me. Among the men in their impeccable white full-sleeved shirts and white mundus, with their heads encased in pristine white turbans, I recognise the Arabic teacher, and also my school friend Hassan Ali Haji. They are polite but firm. A Muslim girl should not live in a Hindu man's home. Especially when he is unmarried.

'Look at her ... she doesn't even cover her head,' the Arabic teacher mutters. 'The child has lost her way.'

'She can live in one of our homes where she will be able to live as a good Muslim,' Hassan Ali Haji says. None of the usual camaraderie shows in his tone or expression.

I don't tell them of my plan. I am afraid things will get out of hand. Instead, I placate them by saying that I will talk to her.

'We take care of our own,' the group leader Suleiman Haji says with an imperiousness that is hard to counter.

'I understand, but she must decide. It's her decision,' I say in my most sincere voice. I wonder how long it will take to register our marriage. There is a lawyer I know in Ottapalam. I'll call him as soon as these men leave.

When the little duck girl returns from her Arabic lesson, it's almost dusk. I don't like the thought of her walking on the road in twilight, so I am a little curt with her. 'You are very late this evening. Where were you?'

'The Arabic teacher had a meeting to go to, Balkies Umma said.' She frowns at the rasp in my voice. 'She said I should wait till he returns, so I did. What's wrong, Maashe?'

I had intended to lead up to my plan of marrying her by offering the padakkam first. Instead, I tell her that our living arrangements seem to be troubling both my family and the village. I also tell her about Hassan Ali's offer. She listens quietly. 'What should I do?'

I smile at her. 'I will marry you,' I say.

'Are you serious?' she asks softly, almost disbelievingly. I suppose she can't believe her good fortune. One day you are a homeless migrant, the next day you are to be the mistress of a house and two acres of land.

'Of course.' I go to my bedroom and bring her the padakkam. 'This was my mother's. As my wife-to-be, I want you to have it. Wear it. It will make me happy.'

She takes it in her hands and looks at the pendant studded with rubies and white sapphires. 'Is this very valuable?' she asks.

'It is. The rubies are from Burma. They are more than a hundred years old,' I say. For a moment, I wonder if I should have waited till we were married. What if she scoots with it?

'I have never seen gold this close,' she says, looking up. 'The pendant is beautiful, but I don't understand why a yellow metal is considered so valuable.'

'Wear it,' I say.

She does as I ask. Against the pale skin of her throat, the pendant is luminously large. I detail my plans to her. 'I'll start the registration process for the wedding. I suppose I'll need some ID for you. I'm sure the lawyer will find a way. I have already spoken to him. You will need to convert to Hinduism, which will make it easier all around. But don't worry about any of it. I'll send you to stay with Hassan Ali's family in the meantime. The whole process will take little more than a month. On the appointed day, we'll take a taxi to Ottapalam. Until then, no one needs to know about it. Once we are man and wife, all will be fine.'

She listens without interrupting me. Then she says, 'Maashe ...'

'I've made up my mind. End of discussion,' I say, picking up my phone.

I eat my dinner with great relish. I am beginning to feel as though I am shedding years, hour by hour.

I switch on the TV and find a news channel. She comes and sits on the floor. 'Come, sit here on the sofa,' I say.

We both watch the news quietly: the former ISRO scientist Nambi Narayan, who had been accused of espionage, is to receive 1.3 crore rupees in settlement from the state. Railway fares will go up. It is the coldest winter in Delhi in 119 years. And the women's protest at Shaheen Bagh is almost a kilometre long as more and more people join in.

'Why are these women protesting, Maashe?' the little duck girl asks.

I shrug. 'I am not entirely sure.' We watch the women of all ages in burqas and hijabs. The stoic expression on their faces unsettles me.

'I suppose like you, they are afraid. Once the CAA act is passed, if you are not a Hindu and don't have the requisite papers, you will be sent to a detention centre.'

'So, none of these women have papers—they are like me, Maashe?'

'Who knows? But you don't have to worry about any of that. Once you convert and our marriage is registered, you will be my wife. And that's all you need for an ID card. Go to sleep, my little duck girl,' I say, leaning towards her and caressing her cheek with my fingertips. Her skin is like satin.

I wake up as dawn creases the sky with a runnel of red. The birds have begun chirping. The first prayers from the mosque echo through the village. Soon, the music from the temple begins. I feel a glow of satisfaction as one set of prayers blends into another. Everything is possible if there is understanding between two parties. I go back to sleep.

When I wake up next, it's a little past six. I wait for the sound of the broom. Ever since the little duck girl became my live-in maid, I have been getting out of bed as soon as I hear movements in the front yard.

Soon, she will be my wife. I wonder what it will be like to share a bed with another person. I'll have to buy a new bed. I should dye my hair, I decide. I don't look my age, nevertheless, I didn't want anyone asking if she is my granddaughter. At fifty-nine, I am starting to live my life, and I can't wait for it to begin.

I glance at the clock again. Has she overslept? I rise from my bed and go to her room. It's empty. I feel my stomach go hollow. I look for her bag. That's gone too.

Has she run away with my mother's padakkam? Were my brothers right to caution me? What was it they said—if you take a leech into your bed, it will bleed you dry eventually.

My legs are trembling as I stumble into the dining room. There, on the table, is the phone I had given her. The padakkam rests beside it, on a piece of paper.

'Dear Maashe,' she had written. 'I do not want to bring strife into your home or to Kaikurussi. I have only affection for you. But, you see, I have had no control over my life all these years. And now you, too, want to take away my right to decide. Who I worship or who I marry must be my choice. What I am trying to tell you is that I cannot be your wife.

'I am going where there are others like me. People who don't know what their place is and hence must fight for it. I belong with them.'

She had signed it with the duck print, like I had taught her.

I hear the sound of sweeping and rush to the door, certain that she has changed her mind and come back. It's Pushpa. She straightens when she sees me and offers a sheepish smile, 'I am sorry I am late by a few days. Asha has left, has she? Anyway, everything will be fine now that I am back. Shall I make your tea?'

'Yes,' I hear myself say. 'Tea would be good.'

I sit on my chair in the veranda and stare at the horizon. A strange sense of emptiness fills me. Is this loss, I wonder for a moment.

Then I realise I am just hungry.

FIELD OF FLOWERS

Four months have passed since that day. No one talks about it anymore. The furore on social media and television has died down. In this new India, there is a new crisis each day that sanctions forgetting. Perhaps it's only in Balram's mind that the early hours of 15 September continue to be an open wound, a festering laceration that refuses to heal.

Farmers are laying siege to Delhi. They want the government to repeal the new farm laws. 'The greatest organised revolt by farmers in the history of mankind' is how someone referred to it. Balram knows that he should be with them now. But he is no longer the man he once was. He is a hollowed-out shell. A broken creature who cannot face water cannons or walk through teargas or leap over the barricades that the police are using to push the farmers back.

Balram knows a million ways to forget what was done to the girl. But he forces himself to remember. Again and again, all through the day, every day.

When Balram left his farm by the Yamuna, he had wanted to flee as far as he could from everything that was familiar and could remind him of what had happened in the field of flowers. He rode his Bullet west to Dwaraka in Gujarat and then east to Puri in Orissa. Krishna and Subhadra flew down there to convince him to return. He waved to them as he started his Bullet once again.

He decided to head south-west to Udupi in Karnataka and then east again to Srirangam in Tamil Nadu. As long as he was on the road and moving, he felt better.

Stopping in Kerala happened on a whim. They say that after Parasurama went around the world twenty-one times and slaughtered all the kshatriyas and filled five large lakes with their blood, he decided to throw his axe into the sea, from which emerged a narrow strip of land. Perhaps in this very same narrow strip of land that is called Kerala, the rage and guilt in him would be tempered. Perhaps here he could absolve himself and become who he once was.

Balram had seen several photographs of Kerala: the backwaters and beaches, the houseboats and toddy shops. But he wasn't a tourist. He wasn't a pilgrim either. He avoided all the well-known temples and went down whichever road beckoned. Until, one day, he rode through the small town of Angadipuram and saw, to his left, a temple that stood on a gentle hillock. Something about it made him want to pause.

He parked his Bullet in the parking area alongside the temple and went seeking the deity.

The granite stairs were smooth and worn out with time, and the rise of each step was higher than usual. It must require some effort for older pilgrims in particular to climb these steps. He liked that. The gods should not be easily accessible.

There weren't too many pilgrims at that hour, and those he passed ignored him. A security guard peeled himself off a bench near the steps and gestured to him to take his shirt off. 'No pants. Only dhoti,' he said.

Balram frowned. Within the akhada, with his students, he thought nothing of stripping down and strutting around in a langot, but this was something else. He disliked the thought of having to walk bare-bodied with a strip of cloth around his waist. He turned to leave. As he went down the steps, a thought struck him, and he stumbled. A girl had been stripped naked and left for the world to find her, and here he was, baulking at having to bare his chest. His eyes welled with shame and guilt. How long could he run from what he didn't want to confront—his part in what had happened to the girl?

Adjacent to the temple was a shop where he could buy a dhoti. The shopkeeper showed him how to tie it around his waist. He refused the offer of an upper cloth.

When the man at the shop mentioned that the deity was a goddess, it seemed like divine ordination that he should bare himself to her. This would be his first penance. He prayed that she would find it in her heart to forgive him.

Balram walked bare-bodied into the temple, feeling naked and vulnerable.

In the past few months, Balram hadn't stayed in one place for more than three days. But something about this temple made him want to linger. His new best friend, the man at the shop, recommended a lodge nearby. And just like that, a month has passed, and he is still at Durga Boarding & Lodging.

Every morning, when he wakes up, he sees the girl sitting on the turtle-shaped stone. She stares at him, fear and sorrow in her eyes. 'Bhaiyaji, where were you? Why did they do this to me? Why did you let them do this to me?' she asks.

Each day, Balram tries a new penance. He rolls around the temple. He walks around it, one foot measure after another. He hops on one leg. He fasts for days together. He doesn't touch a drop of alcohol. Eventually, he runs out of penances, but the goddess will not relent.

Each day, when he stands with folded hands and closed eyes before the glistening black deity he waits for a voice to comfort him. 'You didn't do anything wrong, Balram. What is this crime you accuse yourself of?'

He goes to sit under the peepul tree on the northern side of the temple. Under it is an idol of Ganapathy. A breeze blows through the trees. He will wait here until noon when the uccha puja begins. When the temple closes, he will return to his room at the lodge. Even the gods need time to recover and heal, he tells himself with a wry smile.

When Balram's brother Krishna, or Kanhaiya as he was called, had come to Puri to dissuade him from travelling any further, he kept saying that what had happened was unfortunate—a tragedy—that a girl had been raped. 'You do know the statistics, don't you?' he said, to comfort his older brother. 'According to the 2019 report of the National Crime Records Bureau, 32,033 rape cases were registered across the country. Do the math. That makes it an average of eighty-eight cases every day. Of these, 94.2 per cent of rapes were committed by perpetrators known to the victim. Such is the state of our land.'

Balram had listened quietly without responding. There was no point in arguing with Kanhaiya on the point of their culpability. Kanhaiya didn't see it as he did. Kanhaiya had chosen to accept what had happened as an unfortunate incident. His sin was that of denial.

But Balram couldn't resign himself to what had occurred on his watch. His sin was that of apathy, it weighed even heavier. How could he not have seen it coming a long time before it did?

Bhim, the girl's fiancé, and Duri, one of the men who raped her, were both his students and he had seen, again and again, how their rivalry and mutual dislike had goaded them into a senseless rage. In the end, the girl had become collateral damage in the battle of their egos.

But why did he keep referring to her as girl and woman? Why couldn't he say her name, at least in his head? Shyama. All of nineteen years old.

Kanhaiya, always a great one for applying salves on bruises, was the one who had named her Shyama.

Her people were Dholis. The brothers had inherited them along with the land, and whenever anything significant happened in their lives, they came to Balram and Kanhaiya, seeking their blessings. One day, they came to ask them to bless their son. It was Kanhaiya who noticed the other baby in Lajju's arms and asked, 'Who is that?'

Ramu shrugged. 'That's Kaali, the girl. His twin.'

Shyama had emerged two minutes after her brother was born, the hue of a jamun fruit, purplish black. Among her people, dark skin was the norm, but she was darker than dark, while her twin was a few shades lighter. Her parents had decided on a name for the child, assuming it was a boy. Satyajit. No one had expected her or thought of a name for her. So, they just called her Kaali.

When Kanhaiya heard her being referred to as Kaali, he decreed that she be called Shyama. Kanhaiya himself was as dark as his brother was fair, and Balram knew that it was a sore point with him. Which is why he never mentioned the tube of Fair & Lovely he had once seen on Kanhaiya's bathroom counter.

Which is also why he told Kanhaiya that Shyama was just a pretty synonym for Kaali. He knew that Kanhaiya was trying to protect her from a lifetime of ridicule and constant colour-shaming, but now that he had the time to retrospect, he realised that Kanhaiya was always a bit of a do-gooder, rushing around doing things that were probably best left undone.

Had Shyama's destiny changed with the new name? Balram would ask himself this again and again.

Balram ran his akhada alongside his sugarcane fields. The boys he trained there were chosen for their strength and skill, and most of them belonged to the Yadav caste like him. So, when two Baheliya boys from Jhansi came to the akhada, it irked everyone.

Kanhaiya brought the murmurs among the villagers to Balram. Their grouse was that he was disregarding all the caste rules. 'They are too afraid of you to grumble openly,' he said with that beatific smile of his. That's how he dressed up any unpleasantness, so you couldn't help but forgive him for the message he brought.

Balram was working on his tractor's engine. 'Ignore them,' he said. Kanhaiya shook his head as if to say, what am I going to do with you, and sauntered away.

Balram glanced at the sky to check the time, and then at his watch. It was 3.30 in the afternoon. He smiled. It was a little conceit of his, to read the time by the light and then confirm it. Kanhaiya probably had an assignation somewhere with one of his married women lovers.

'When will you be back?' he hollered after him.

'I'll see you when I see you.' Kanhaiya's words floated back from the fields.

Balram whistled under his breath as he went back to repairing the tie rod end. They no longer used a plough, now that the tractor had replaced it; his workers had all learnt how to drive the vehicle. But he still kept two bullocks and a plough. Each season, that's how he started the furrowing of the land, in preparation for the sowing. After an hour, he would stop and the tractor would take over.

The villagers would come to watch him while he completed the ritual as though he were a circus animal, but he didn't mind. Every man who builds his body must delight in his rippling muscles and their effect on those watching him. Why else would he put himself through the rigours of relentless exercise?

Balram liked it when people stopped to eye his biceps and pectorals, visible through the blue banian he wore over blue track pants as he ploughed the land. Kanhaiya would shoot a few pictures and post them on Facebook and Instagram. He was a great one for networking. And Balram was happy for his brother to show off his muscles to the world.

But he wasn't entirely happy about the photos Kanhaiya posted of Subhadra. He scolded Kanhaiya each time he posted a picture of Subhadra. He told him about the importance of decorum and honour. He talked to Kanhaiya about the male gaze that stripped clothes off a woman and turned her into an object to be leered at. And yet, Kanhaiya continued with his Insta posts unperturbed. 'Don't be so old-fashioned, Bhaiyaji,' he would laugh, dismissing Balram's objections.

Yet, each time, the thought of strange men looking at his sister filled Balram with a rage that he could only douse with

Varuni. He would get half a dozen quarter bottles and drink them back to back. Straight from the bottle and in one single swallow, almost. Then, for the rest of the evening, he would be at peace.

For several years now, Balram had held a sizeable stake in Varun Distilleries. Varuni, its flagship brand, was a great favourite, and the government-owned liquor stores told them that Varuni Whisky sold almost as much as Fighter, if not Bunti Bubly and Miss India.

One of the salesmen mentioned to Balram that they would sell a lot more if the brand name was catchier. Something like Hawaldar or Dabang. But Balram wouldn't budge, nor would Varun Yadav. For Varuni was the name of Varun's daughter. And she had been Balram's secret love, a fire in his blood, whom he could never have enough of.

Even now, sixteen years after the Yamuna had swept her away, he saw her everywhere—in the fields and the skies, and in his dreams. As vibrant as when she was alive.

Balram wipes his brow with the back of his hand. The day is warmer than usual. He gets up and goes towards the temple office. It is halfway up the hill and cool all through the day.

He hears someone say that there is to be an annadanam that day. People will soon gather for lunch. The devotee who has paid to feed people as an offering to the goddess will be present as well. What sin is the devotee trying to erase? What kind of blessing does he seek?

He would have liked to place some of the blame for all that happened at his wife Revati's feet. But then, he was the one who had turned her into the woman she was. Once upon a time, Revati—tall and statuesque, educated, and with strong opinions—would have pointed things out to him without mincing her words but he had cut her down to size as a new bride and continued to do so until she became the kind of woman his mother was: soft spoken with no opinions of her own, content with her lot.

Ever so often, he had wondered why Revati had chosen him as her husband. When he asked her, all she would say was that only he was man enough for her. Once, while they were in bed, he asked her if she was referring to his sexual prowess. 'I am not Kanhaiya,' he told her, trying not to sound downcast.

'I am glad you are not him. I know who you are, and that's exactly what I like about you,' she had retorted, cupping his chin, holding his gaze. 'I won't have to keep looking over my shoulder all the time or second guess you ...'

He had loved her sassiness at first, but then he noticed how his mother looked at him each time Revati spoke out of turn or interrupted him mid-speech. She thought nothing of attacking his opinions, and he could see that it irked his mother to no end. So he began to chisel away at her confidence with the occasional cutting remark or snide barb, often just ignoring her or talking over her about something inconsequential, drowning out her words with his disregard.

The only time he glimpsed the old Revati now was when he offered her a drink. He knew people who drank for courage or oblivion—it amused him that Revati drank because she liked the taste of alcohol. He liked to get her drunk and see her transform into the tigress she had been before he tamed her. And he was almost certain that both their boys had been conceived on such drunken nights.

He was careful not to do it often, lest it turn into a habit. But he never had to seriously worry about that because the morning after, Revati was always back to being the good wife and dutiful daughter-in-law whose life revolved around the children, the farm, petty squabbles with his mother and endless recriminations about the servants. She had learnt to not come between the siblings or question their decisions. It was not a woman's work to do so.

The siblings had always been close to one another. Kanhaiya and Subhadra in particular had a special relationship. He was more than her brother; he was also her best friend. So it was inevitable that he should look out for her, Balram told himself, when Arjun erupted on the scene.

Subhadra and Arjun first met at a mall in Agra. Kanhaiya had taken Subhadra and her friends there for the day. While they giggled and shopped and ate burgers, popcorn and ice cream, he met with Arjun, who was also in Agra on some work. It was like a village fair, that mall, teeming with people, but amidst all the kerfuffle, Subhadra spotted Arjun. And he, her. A few weeks later, they eloped.

Balram had come home furious. Revati had called him to say that Subhadra had run away with a boy named Arjun. She had left a note asking them to not worry about her.

Balram had wanted to take his Scorpio out and chase after them. He would haul her home, and he swore he would break Arjun's back.

'You encouraged this, Kanhaiya,' he shouted, a vein throbbing in his temple.

Kanhaiya glared at him. He had told Arjun that a suitable boy had been found for Subhadra, and he should forget all about her. 'What more could I do, Bhaiyaji?' he said, raising his shoulders to his ears in a theatrical shrug. Kanhaiya was a great one for effects.

'Arjun is not a Yadav. He is not one of us,' Balram snapped.

'But his caste is on the same level as ours ... Besides, your favourite student, Duri, who you wanted Subhadra to marry, isn't one of us either. He is the same caste as Arjun,' Kanhaiya argued. 'Listen, it isn't as if she has run away with a low-caste fellow. So it would be best to accept her decision. Also, you do know that he works for the government? And his family, they are well off and decent people. Nothing to worry about there. So what are you objecting to?'

Balram stared at Kanhaiya, baffled by the way he had thought it through. Had he set up this whole thing?

'How do you know him?' he asked.

'We met at the collector's office.'

'What is his job?' he demanded.

'He's the collector's PA. For now,' Kanhaiya grinned. 'But as long as he is there, he has the ear of every officer who occupies that seat in the collectorate. We need someone like that in our family, Bhaiyaji. Plus, he himself told me he is preparing for the Civil Services.'

Balram would have hated to admit it, but he felt a tiny twinge of relief. They had a running feud with the government fellows. One of their own in their midst would make life easier.

'What do I tell Duri?' he asked, still unable to approve of what Subhadra had done. 'His father and I had an understanding that next year we would wed her to him.'

Balram saw Kanhaiya repress a shudder. Or perhaps he imagined it. He could never be certain with Kanhaiya.

'Tell me, Bhaiyaji, do you think Subhadra would be happy with Duri? Do you think they will respect her in that household when they know she eloped and we brought her back? Do you think Duri will ever let her forget it?' Kanhaiya asked.

Balram rubbed his forehead as if to clarify his thoughts. Kanhaiya had a point. Duri was the best wrestler he had trained. He had that rare combination of genius talent honed by the severity of discipline. His father was a landowner with immense political clout who, despite being blind, was one of the most ruthless men Balram had ever met. He knew how to use his blindness to his advantage, and things always went his way, whether legally or not. When it was time, Duri would take over the reign of his father's empire. And Subhadra, their sister, would have been mistress of it all.

Duri was smitten by Subhadra. He treated her like she was an exquisite piece of glass and always brought her expensive gifts to coax a smile to her face. But Balram also knew that Duri was a stubborn creature who refused to see reason once a notion lodged itself in his head. He was also quick to take offense. He could make Subhadra's life either heaven or hell on earth. And that was not a chance he could take, Balram realised.

He nodded. 'I'll talk to them.'

'Bhaiyaji,' Kanhaiya said, twirling a paperweight, 'Let's welcome Subhadra and Arjun into our home, not grudgingly but happily ...'

'Of course,' Balram said, hiding his disappointment as best he could.

The akhada was closed for a couple of months. They had a wedding to organise, and it would be the best wedding ever. They even brought in a wedding planner.

Like in the movies, garlands of chrysanthemums and marigolds were hung everywhere; white tents were raised with gauzy, billowing curtains and plush carpets on the floor; white takhiyas and white satin-clad chairs were laid out for those who couldn't sit on the floor. Fairy lights twinkled in the trees and lit diyas edged every path and step. Balram had never seen Subhadra so happy and radiant, and his grudging acceptance of Arjun was replaced with a certain affection.

Arjun was a decent sort. Good-looking, and educated, which was something neither Kanhaiya nor Balram could claim to be. The two brothers had been sent to a boarding school near Ujjain when they were not yet into their teens. They lasted exactly sixty-four days, after which they were packed off home. The other boys at the boarding school were like privileged infants compared to them, and they had thought it necessary to tell them as much, just as they had protested at every rule and regulation at the school.

They left quite happily, of course. The only two people they had built up any sort of friendship with were Sudama Matuka, a boy from Gujarat, and Sandipan Pani, their housemaster.

Sudama was so timid, they had taken him under their wing to protect him from the school bullies. As for Sandipan Pani, he was a harmless creature who liked to listen to old English songs. Every Friday he would assemble all the boarders and make them listen to Ann Murray and Cliff Richard, Dean Martin and Doris Day, and a few others whose names Balram no longer remembered. He himself couldn't hold a tune to save his life, but Kanhaiya was very musical and picked up a few songs. To this day, when he wanted to make a point about men fighting destiny, he warbled in a fair approximation of Doris Day's voice: *whatever will be, will be*.

All in all, Arjun was a good catch. And Balram could see why Subhadra had risked incurring her brothers' wrath for his sake.

When all the fuss had died down over the elopement and the subsequent wedding, Duri came to visit. He hadn't attended the wedding. A sudden business trip to Macao had been his excuse.

Balram saw him pull up in his SUV. He jumped out of the vehicle and came towards him. He touched Balram's feet, and Balram tried to catch his gaze and apologise as he pulled him up. But Duri brushed it aside with a dignified response. 'It was not meant to be. Besides, Subhadra's happiness is the most important thing ...'

Balram knew Duri was pretending to be unmoved. Over the next few weeks, he observed his anguish at losing Subhadra to another man. But he kept it well hidden from everyone else. Watching him, Balram's regard for him grew.

One day, Balram suggested Duri move to Lucknow and train at an akhada there. Duri readily agreed—his loyalty and trust in Balram were unshakeable.

Later, Balram would tell himself that was where it all began. A teacher is meant to have the impartial gaze of a judge. Someone who can tell right from wrong. His vision, on the other hand, was increasingly clouded by an almost fatherly love. He saw in Duri only what he wanted to see and pretended the rest didn't matter. He failed to notice his sense of entitlement, which turned into aggression when he couldn't have his way. He failed to see the streak of vicious ruthlessness in him, and how full of pride he was. Would

Shyama's destiny have been different if Balram hadn't been so blind?

It was time to reopen the akhada. Two of Shyama's cousins and Satyajit, her brother, arrived to help Balram. He was surprised when she turned up as well. The akhada was no place for a young woman.

'I am taking a break from my books,' she said, grinning.

Balram nodded. Her twelfth-standard boards were going on. 'You know you shouldn't be here,' he said.

'There are no pehelwans here, Bhaiyaji. What is the harm?' she retorted.

Balram grunted and turned to watch the young men who were working the soil. He had seen some of them grow up before his eyes. As they dug and smoothened the mud, their muscles undulated in the early morning light. It pleased him no end to see them in such good shape.

'You should have taught them to wrestle, Bhaiyaji,' Shyama said.

'Wrestling is not for everyone,' he laughed.

'Why?' she demanded. 'Because we are Dalits? And we would pollute your akhada ...?'

He turned and pinned her with his gaze. 'Don't talk rubbish,' he snapped, remembering to keep his voice low. Her father would slap her silly if he discovered that she had been questioning him. But Kanhaiya and he were fond of her, loved her even, and let her take liberties that didn't extend to the rest of her family.

'If it was about caste, would I let them into the akhada?' he said, feeling the need to explain. 'You have to follow the kind of diet wrestlers need, and have the time to build your body and stamina ... would your brother and cousins give up their jobs to do that?'

'That's true,' Shyama said. She looked at him with a smile he couldn't quite decipher. 'So, if there's someone with talent, you won't let the fact that they are Dalit stop you from teaching them?'

Should he have said something then? Would things have been different?

Instead, he nodded and said, 'That's exactly what I mean.'

Later that day, he told Kanhaiya that he was opening the akhada to anyone with talent, and if he knew someone who deserved to be there, he should send them over.

'Aren't you eating, Bhaiyaji?' Kanhaiya asked. He lived in the farmhouse attached to his dairy farm, but they ate one meal together every day. Balram insisted on that. When brothers stopped eating together, their paths seldom met again, and he didn't want that happening with them.

'In case I wasn't clear, I meant I'm thinking of opening it up to anyone, no matter what caste or religion,' Balram said. The more times he said it, the more real it felt.

Kanhaiya was busy tearing up the last roti into shreds. He paused to look at his brother. Then he popped a piece of roti into his mouth and muttered indistinctly, 'A good idea.'

In retrospect, Balram would wonder if he said, 'Not a good idea'.

From when he was a little boy, Kanhaiya had liked to add sugar (from their fields) to a bowl of dahi (from his cows) and use a piece of roti (from their fields), still warm to the touch and glistening with ghee (from his cows) to scoop out a bit of the curd. It made Balram sick to watch him. A grown man eating like a child. His need to sprinkle sugar on everything, be it word, deed or curd.

Kanhaiya wiped the bowl of dahi clean and crunched the last bit of sugar. Then he got up and declared that he was off to the capital city.

Subhadra and Arjun lived there now. The district collector, who was fond of Arjun, had taken him along to the capital when he was transferred. Now that Arjun had got his law degree and was preparing for the Civil Services, he had been happy to move as well.

Balram went up to his room. He wanted to watch some wrestling online. He found a video of a master who talked about malla-yuddha from which the more contemporary kushti had emerged. Duri needs to see this, he thought, and forwarded him the link.

Balram was often asked why he himself had not taken up wrestling professionally; he was talented enough to have made it to the national team. The truth was, he loved wrestling. He loved it more than life itself, but he wasn't the competitive sort. Halfway through a competition, it would get to him. The crowds, the bestiality, the need to win … And he would switch off. For him wrestling was about the moment, the rush that came from knowing his own body and how best to plan his moves in order to weaken the opponent.

That was what made wrestling exciting. It wasn't about providing entertainment to the gallery. Or humiliating the opponent. Or even for medals and trophies. Ever since he started the akhada, his reward has been seeing one of his students understand what wrestling was truly about.

The temple watchman saunters towards Balram and gestures for him to join him. 'There is an annadanam today with payasam,' he says.

Balram hasn't eaten all morning. The watchman leads him into the hall and finds them places next to each other. 'Good food today,' he says, pointing to the banana leaf and making a thumbs up sign.

Rice is served on their banana leaves. Various curries follow.

Balram looks around. Some of the people gathered here are from the neighbourhood adjoining the temple. There are a few devotees from elsewhere. The rest are all beggars who line the temple steps every day. No one asks what another's caste is. In the goddess's presence, all are equal.

How had he been he so oblivious to the injustices he perpetuated? Balram feels his hunger dissipate.

Once the monsoon set in, Balram became busy. He was in the fields all day. They had a new project lined up: growing flowers. Revati had said she wanted to try her hand at floriculture, and he had agreed. He had learnt a long time ago that it was best to agree to the smaller demands. That way, he could take control of the bigger issues without having to raise his voice or retreating into a sullen silence.

Revati spent all her time poring over articles about gladioli cultivation. One night, he said, 'Revatiji, just tell me what you want me to do, and I will …'

She smiled as she always did when he added the suffix to her name.

It had begun as a private joke between them, then grew into a term of endearment he used when he was feeling amorous. That's how it is between husbands and wives. A code evolves which only the two of them are privy to. You look beautiful; something different about your hair? I could tell the palak paneer didn't have your touch. Pretty much all leading to: let's fuck tonight ...

Revati, who was never in the mood these days, was a tigress in bed that night. If this was what gladioli could do to her, he was happy to give her more land to grow tuberoses, marigolds, cauliflowers or whatever else she wanted to grow.

He hitched the tiller to the tractor. The land was going to have to be turned with care. Which was why he had decided to do it himself.

He started the tractor. The tiller lines broke the soil. Their last crop here had been soyabean. It was a lucrative crop, but Kanhaiya hated that he grew soyabean. 'You are aiding my competition,' he would say, waving his phone in Balram's face. 'Soya milk is the worst thing known to mankind after landmines.'

Kanhaiya would be pleased with this field of flowers. Balram could see him stop to snip flowers with his Swiss army knife to offer to his various lady friends. His cheeks would dimple, and the mischief would set ablaze little lights in his eyes. 'Which woman can resist flowers?' he would say. Kanhaiya was predictable, but strangely, that was his strength. To do the appropriate thing with a flourish so that it seemed unique.

Balram loved his brother, but sometimes he wasn't sure he liked him.

He didn't need to go deeper than twenty centimetres, so he tilled the soil with a light touch. The soyabean is a fragile plant that buckles and buries itself in the soil.

'We want residue in the soil,' Revati had said.

It was an experiment, so he let her have her way. If the experiment succeeded, he would need to do a soil test and take over, he told himself as he drove the tractor up and down the fields.

That was when he realised that he was being watched. He turned his head to see Shyama standing at the edge of the field. Her father and brother were in the field beyond this one, turning the soil with a hoe. That, too, was an experiment. He needed to know what would work best for the flowers. He thought Shyama was here to talk to her father and brother. But she stood on the path, seemingly waiting for him. He waved to her. 'Give me a few minutes.'

Shyama went to sit on the rock that had once been a kind of boundary. Balram was not entirely sure what it separated their land from. The place where Shyama's people had their jhuggi-jhopris or the point to which they were allowed to come.

For as long as he was alive, that was how he would remember her: a slender girl sitting on a turtle-shaped rock, fiddling with her phone. But that day, as he looked at her, he only wondered where the device had come from. Revati had once given her an old phone, but this one seemed to have a touch screen.

Shyama's results had come out last week. She had topped the district in the boards while Satyajit had merely scraped through. There was talk of her going to college. One of her school teachers had apparently put the idea in her head.

He looked at her again. Her skin glistened like the skin of a jamun in the morning light. Kanhaiya had named her well.

It struck him then that he wasn't entirely happy about Shyama trying to leave the farm to find her place in the world. Slowly, an idea began to form. He would ask Shyama to assist Revati with her field of flowers. It wasn't like he was asking her to take the cattle out to graze or work alongside her family in the fields. She would protest at that, he knew. She was, after all, more educated than some of his own relatives.

While they prepared the fields to put in the gladioli corms, he would send her for a part-time accountancy course so she could help Revati with the orders when not helping the flowers grow. Kanhaiya and he shared a munshi who did all the paperwork, and he often complained that it was getting too much for him. Shyama could help him as well. Hard work never killed anyone. This way, the natural order of things wouldn't change. Nor would Shyama get any ideas above her station in life. When people did that, disaster was sure to follow.

Balram stopped the tractor. Shyama stood up and came towards him. Her smile was hesitant and her eyes didn't quite meet his. He groaned under his breath. This was exactly how her father shuffled his feet when he came to ask for yet another loan.

'Bolo Shyama, what is it?' His voice was brusque to his own ears. He saw her face fall. He forced a smile and asked in a more even tone, 'Is everything alright?'

Relief replaced fear in her eyes. Balram was startled by the transformation. He didn't think he wanted to evoke fear in people. Kanhaiya had said that he did that. 'It may be unconscious. But your expression … It's like you look at people and find them wanting.'

'Bhaiyaji … I was wondering if you know anyone at the Dwarkanath Munshi College. They have a scholarship for Dalit students. I'm eligible, but I need a recommendation letter.'

Balram looked at her with a steady gaze and remembered to keep his voice cordial when he spoke. 'Shyama, the scholarship will pay for the tuition fees, but where will you stay and eat?'

'The college has a hostel, Bhaiyaji,' she said.

He nodded. 'Yes, of course. But I am not sure the college hostel will have room for you.'

Her mouth tightened. He had seen Revati and his mother do it as well. That little upward twitch of the mouth to show displeasure. Subtle but sharp.

'There's a Dalit hostel where I can stay.'

'I see that you've done your homework well. But have you seen the place yet? Kanhaiya keeps his cows in better sheds. As for the toilets ...' He shuddered. He had built toilets for his workers long before the government declared that every citizen deserved one.

'Do you want to leave all this to go bury yourself in a dirty little hole?' he said. As if on cue, a breeze blew through the tops of the mango trees, rippled the sugarcane leaves and hummed through the maize fields. A koel called from somewhere nearby. It was as if they had stepped into a painting.

'What would you have me do, Bhaiyaji? Work in the fields till they marry me off to a drunken wife-beater?' She didn't mince her words.

He laughed out loud. 'I have a better plan,' he said.

She listened. He saw the anger dissolve, her shoulders relaxed. 'When can I start the course?' she asked.

'Let me make a few calls and find out,' he said, pulling out his phone.

'And where will I stay?'

The girl was sharp as a pin.

'It's a part-time course, so you only have to go for a couple of hours every morning,' he said. 'I'll arrange with Kanhaiya to have his dairy van take you there and fetch you back after the morning delivery. Or you can take the bus back.'

Shyama nodded. She knew when she was defeated.

Shyama registered for the course. Balram converted one of the outhouses into an office. Two of the men were sent to town to buy a table and three chairs, and Shyama and a computer were soon installed in the room.

The gladioli corms were procured from a wholesaler. Kanhaiya knew someone who knew someone. When they arrived, all of them looked at the corms speechlessly. Balram didn't know what he had expected, but it wasn't this. For a moment he wondered if they had been cheated. Revati spoke for all of them when she said, 'Do you think they sent us onions?'

Shyama grinned. 'No, this is how they are meant to be.'

'And you know this how?' Kanhaiya asked.

Shyama switched on the computer. 'I was reading up on gladioli, Bhaiyaji,' she said, opening a page. They looked at the image. 'In fact, we could have chosen the variety of gladioli we wanted and bought it online.'

Revati moved closer to the screen. 'Next time, we'll do it properly. This time is an experiment, Shyama.'

'And it's in your hands to make it a success,' Balram said in his gravest head-of-the-family voice.

'I don't understand, Bhaiyaji.' Shyama's face showed her consternation. Revati and Kanhaiya looked just as perturbed, he noticed.

'Bhabhi and I will tell you what to do. You get it done,' he said.

'On my own?'

'On her own?'

The voices rose to a crescendo.

He nodded. 'On your own. Your father and brother will prepare the furrows. You can ask your mother and two other women to help you plant the onions. Revati Bhabhi will, of course, supervise what's going on, but she can't be there all the time. The home and children take up a great deal of her time. So, you are in charge.'

Later that night, Revati said, 'Shyama is an educated girl. She won't like getting her hands dirty.'

'I get my hands dirty, Revatiji,' he said, giving her his look. She pretended not to see it. When he moved closer to her, she inched away. 'What's wrong?' he asked.

Revati propped herself up on her elbow. 'You're disrupting the order of things as we know it,' she said.

'How?' he asked, running a finger along her arm.

'She's a girl, a Dholi. Her family has worked our lands forever. Why would you suddenly elevate her?' Revati had been thinking about this for a while, he realised at her carefully worded question.

'Because the alternative could be worse for us,' he confessed.

'What do you mean?' Revati sat up.

'She asked me for help to join a college. God knows what she would have chosen to do after that. She's smart enough to become a government officer, even without a reservation quota. Now that would really change the natural order of things,' he said, twirling a lock of Revati's hair around his forefinger. 'Her family wouldn't be beholden to us anymore. And where would we be without them? Worse, imagine Kanhaiya and I having to stand in front of her, waiting for a signature, while she sits at the table pretending not to see us.'

Revati didn't look convinced. He tried to read her expression.

She sighed and then burst out, 'Shyama is not a child anymore.'

'Why are you stating the obvious?' he frowned.

'Because you don't see what's right in front of you,' she retorted.

'And what is it that I'm not seeing?'.

'That she is a woman, and by giving her this responsibility, you are opening the door to speculation—about your interest in her.'

She was jealous! He tried to hide his grin. 'Kanhaiya and I have known her since she was a baby. Besides, she's not my type. She's too scrawny.'

'What is your type?'

'I like my women tall like you. I like my women buxom like you. I like my women with a mole on their chin like you,' he said, pushing her back onto the pillows.

Revati looked into his eyes. His tall, statuesque wife who could stop a raging buffalo in mid-stride with one tug of the halter around its neck, was suddenly like well-tilled alluvial soil, soft and crumbly, subservient to his will and needy in a way that set his heart racing.

Before dawn broke, he slid out of bed and pulled on his pyjama. Then he went down to the kitchen where the cook gave him a tumbler of milk and a handful of soaked almonds.

The sky was still a dense grey with streaks of light.

Summer was here and this was the only time of day when the heat didn't press down on man, beast and soil. Balram flexed his shoulders as he walked towards the fields, chewing on the almonds. In the distance, he spotted a lone, slight figure. Shyama.

She was seated on the turtle-shaped rock. Her dupatta was wrapped around her like a shawl. As he watched, she rose and walked into the field.

She bent down and took a fist full of soil. She opened her fingers slowly and looked at it as if seeing it for the first time. Then, as though it were a pet squirrel, she caressed the lump of soil. When she'd had her fill of whatever sensation it evoked in her, she let it trickle through her fingers. Soil rained on soil.

'How does it feel?' he asked, going to stand at her side.

She turned, startled. What had she been thinking about? Then she smiled. 'Incredible.'

He stared at her. 'I mean, does it need to be tilled again? We can't have soil with clods in it.'

'It's fine. The soil is fine,' she said hastily.

'What did you mean by incredible?' he asked, curious at the choice of word.

'Bhaiyaji, all these years, every time I looked at a field, I saw a lifetime of servitude. But this morning, I saw and felt something else. As though I could smell freedom. Like the soil was telling me I could be whoever I want to be, that it would be my ally.'

Balram stared at her in surprise. No one had ever voiced the way he felt each time he stood barefoot in the mud. How could a wisp of a girl feel as he did?

Kanhaiya drove up to the house in the morning in a Canter truck. A man sat in the back supporting what looked like a small tree. Balram watched in surprise as the vehicle stopped and Kanhaiya jumped out. 'Look what I've brought,' he grinned, unhitching the metal flap at the back of the truck.

Balram didn't know whether he meant the man or the tree, so he said nothing.

'What's this, Bhaiyaji?' Shyama asked. Revati and she were in the front yard, discussing the planting.

'A parijat tree. When it blooms, the flowers are white with orange stalks. And the fragrance is heavenly,' Kanhaiya said, helping the man unload the tree.

'Where did you find it?' Balram asked.

'I stole it,' Kanhaiya grinned. 'Satya Bhama and I were invited for dinner two nights ago at District Collector Divaspathi's home. The party was held in the garden. I didn't think the collector would let me take it if I asked for it, so, last night, I stole it.'

'Are you mad, Kanhaiya? This isn't like stealing butter from a neighbour's house. Do you want the police landing up here?'

'Chill, Bhaiyaji.' Kanhaiya smiled without the faintest trace of worry. 'I may be reckless but I am not foolish. Bhim here will transport it to Dwaraka for me.' Satya Bhama was from Dwaraka, and she had persuaded Kanhaiya to build a house there. 'Do you think the cops are going to follow us to Dwaraka for a tree?' Kanhaiya laughed.

The young man smiled. Shyama grinned. Balram shook his head. Kanhaiya was a law unto himself.

Bhim had a job as a cook in a highway dhaba, but all he wanted to do was wrestle. Kanhaiya had persuaded him to be part of the tree-heist by promising to introduce him to Balram.

Balram sized up the sturdy young man as he lifted the tree and placed it in Kanhaiya's pick-up truck. He wore floppy track pants and a t-shirt that fitted him like a second skin. Under the morning sun, his biceps tightened and his belly caved in with the effort, but only a tiny line of sweat gleamed on his forehead.

'Walk the talk, Bhaiyaji,' Kanhaiya muttered.

'Walk the talk, how?' he demanded.

'The boy is a Dholi. Didn't you say you would open the akhada to anyone as long as they had talent? Bhim is good. I've seen him.'

When Bhim returned from Dwaraka, he began working for Balram. In the fields, at the distillery, pretty much wherever he needed an extra pair of arms to do his bidding.

Then, one evening, Revati twisted her ankle and had to rest her foot. And Shyama became the de facto supervisor of the field of flowers. The compost had been worked in and the planting ridges were ready. On the day of the planting, she was in the field at the crack of dawn.

September is never a pleasant month in the northern plains. It is either very hot or very wet. But Shyama was young and possessed by a manic energy. She was ready by the time her mother and two other women reached the field.

The gladioli corms would need to be planted at a depth of about 8 cm with a gap of 30 cm between them. Shyama gave each of the women a twig cut to size and insisted that they go only as deep as the notch marked on it and maintain a distance of its length between two corms. The women burst out laughing. They thought she was joking.

Bhim stood alongside Balram watching her. 'That was a smart thing to do,' he said.

'She's an amazing girl,' Balram replied, watching Bhim's eyes follow her every move. 'Smart and hardworking. She'll make someone a wonderful wife.'

Perhaps he planted the little corm in Bhim's head. As any farmer will tell you, ideas are like seeds, they need to be left alone to germinate.

'You can start at the akhada tomorrow,' Balram said.

Bhim was the first one to walk into the akhada each morning. By the time the others appeared, he would have taken a hoe to the sandpit. While the others stripped down to their langot and stood there shivering in the light of dawn, his thin, wiry body would already be gleaming with oil and sweat except where the loincloth covered his privates. Balram heard some of the other pehelwans chortle about Chota Bhim not being so chota after all. But he pretended not to hear. Boys will be boys. He was just relieved at their camaraderie.

Balram's boys often went to practise in other akhadas. The yellow earth which was the akhada's essence—a mixture of soil, mustard oil, turmeric powder, ghee and curd—symbolised equality, that all men come from the same earth. But there weren't many akhadas that let lower-caste men in. And Balram had worried that Bhim wouldn't be welcome. So, these jokes were good. They might never fight him in a dangal, but in his akhada, the spirit of the yellow earth rang true.

Bhim was eager to learn, and the akhada he had attended before had trained him well in the basics. In a few days, everyone could see that he was a natural-born pehelwan. All he needed was guidance to move to the next level.

Meanwhile, the gladioli corms threw up shoots and leaves. Revati's ankle healed, but she couldn't put too much weight on it. So Shyama started making video calls from the field to show her what was going on.

Shyama was as fierce as a new mother. Any weed that dared sprout was ruthlessly yanked out. She shooed away stray dogs and birds.

Bhim had to walk past the field to get to the akhada. If, at first, he and Shyama ran into each other by sheer chance, soon they were finding reasons to run into each other.

Young love is as innocent as it is predictable, Balram thought as he watched them almost wistfully. Once, Varuni and he had been like them. If it were in his hands, he would wish that all lovers be blessed with an early death or an abrupt mutual severance.

As their romance played out, Balram felt like the god of love. Like Kama, he had made things happen. 'Who would have thought that of me?' he asked Revati, as he got into bed.

She was daubing cream on her hands. She wiped some off her palm onto her elbows and snorted, 'You and Kama Deva? From which angle? The truth, my dear husband, is that you can be sure there will be a fire when you throw a lit match into a heap of dry kindling.'

Balram turned on his side and went to sleep. No matter what Revati said, he was certain he had made it happen.

The gladioli plants grew. Shyama was forever checking on them. She needed help weeding and mulching the soil. Balram saw to it that her mother and the older women couldn't be spared from their other work. Eventually she turned to Bhim, as he had known she would. When Bhim came to Balram to ask permission, he agreed instantly.

Over the next few days, as the saplings grew taller, Bhim worked almost exclusively on the field of flowers. The ends of each sapling had to be covered with soil so the plants would grow straight.

'Don't let anyone tell you that flowers are an easy crop,' Balram grumbled to Kanhaiya. 'I know no crop is. But flowers are like babies. They need a constant eye on them.'

By the time the stakes had been put in to help each plant bear the weight of the buds once they appeared, Bhim and Shyama had taken to brushing against each other. Revati noticed it and said, 'I think we need to get those two married before they have half a dozen children out there in the field of flowers.'

Balram laughed and agreed to talk to Bhim and Shyama's parents.

Everyone was delighted. Bhim went around with the hint of a smile on his face. Shyama's parents looked vastly relieved. Her twin brother Satyajit became Bhim's shadow. Balram had given Bhim his old Hero Honda and Satyajit, who was a quiet boy otherwise, whooped with delight each time he rode pillion on the 100cc bike.

It was Shyama who insisted that she would marry only when she was ready.

'Ready for what?' Revati asked her.

'Ready to be a wife, Bhabhiji,' Shyama said.

Kanhaiya pried the truth out of her. She first wanted twenty-thousand rupees in her bank account, and she was only a quarter way there. 'One more harvest and I'll be ready,' she said. She had been saving part of her wages. 'Or if Bhim wins the akhada contest, we'll have fifteen thousand to add to it, and then we can get married.'

Balram walks back to the lodge. The sun is blazing. The clerk at the front desk looks up as he enters the lobby. 'Very hot,' he says in Hindi.

Balram throws him a small smile. 'Yes,' he responds as he collects his keys.

The room is cool. He is glad that he didn't choose one on the second floor; there is another floor above his. He goes into the bathroom and stands under the cold shower that turns tepid in a few moments. He dries himself, winds a fresh dhoti around his waist and lies down on the bed. Above his head, the fan whirs, and within him the questions that taunted him as he walked back to the lodge continue to whirl.

Why didn't Kanhaiya or he just offer her the money? Why didn't Revati?

It wasn't because they were worried about denting her self-respect. They just didn't think. Had they offered, had she accepted, would things have turned out differently?

The buds appeared. Tight little fists on the sword-like stalks. One half of the field was covered with red buds and the other half was a bright yellow.

Kanhaiya shared pictures of the field on Instagram. Bhim took pictures of Shyama amidst the flowers. The villagers came to see too. Shyama told Balram and Revati about the videos that some of them made. Soon, tourist buses on the way to Mathura and Agra took to stopping so passengers could get down to admire the flowers and take selfies.

Balram began to wonder if he should fence the field. But as Shyama pointed out, they were nearing the end of the season and Holi was nearly upon them.

Winter was almost over, but the sun still rose late. The air had a razor-sharp edge to it. Balram stood at the window and stretched. He felt a great happiness course through him. Holi was here. And it came under his purview, while Kanhaiya handled the Diwali celebrations.

He had started on the bhaang thandai the night before. The almond paste needed to cook in the milk for a long while. Now all he had to do was cook the cannabis leaves and flowers in a little water. When it was ready, he would add it to the almond milk with sugar.

Balram usually made the thandai in an open kitchen near the akhada. As he kept an eye on the caudron, he saw the pehelwans come in and rub themselves with oil.

Balram drank the first glass. The thandai was creamy and sweet. He wiped his mouth with the back of his hand and downed another glass.

The pehelwans in their langots were already throwing colour on each other. Balram laughed aloud. His little boys had come to the akhada to join the fun. Balloons filled with coloured water were flung around.

Revati suddenly appeared with a water piston. Balram laughed some more as she sprayed the pehelwans with it. Then she turned and sprayed her husband on his laughing face. He growled and lunged at her with hands full of coloured powder. Revati ran towards Kanhaiya, who urged her to come closer and then, laughing, doused her with green and pink. Laughter. Colours on the skin. A woolly lightness. How much he loved Holi, Balram thought. Like wrestling, it was all in the moment.

Bhim and Shyama stood to one side, watching the fun from the sidelines. No one asked them to join, nor did they show any inclination to. There were some boundaries you didn't cross.

It was mid-morning when Duri pulled up in a spanking new SUV. It was more than a year since he had left the akhada. There was a ripple of excitement as he leapt out. He was a great favourite at the akhada and it was his absence that Bhim had filled.

'Bhaiyaji,' Duri said, bending to touch Balram's feet. Everyone else called Balram Guruji or Ustad. Duri called him big brother.

Balram raised him by his shoulders and enveloped him in a hug. They smiled at each other. Balram hadn't realised how much he had missed him. 'It's so good to see you, my boy,' he said, reaching into the pots of colour and smearing some on his face.

Duri grinned, then grabbed a fistful of colours and painted Balram green and yellow.

Balram offered him a glass of thandai. 'Shuru karo,' he said. He took the glass and drank it in one gulp, as if he had been thirsting for it.

Two of the house servants came bearing baskets filled with gujiya and kachori. One sweet and one savoury, to keep the balance while bhang reigned.

Bhim and Shyama came up to them. 'Bhaiyaji,' Bhim

said. Balram saw Duri's eyes dart towards him. Was it then that he first saw him as a usurper?

Shyama gave Duri a stiff smile and turned to address Balram and Kanhaiya, 'We have to get back.'

Duri's eyes followed her and Bhim as they rode away on the bike which he recognised as Balram's.

Would their lives have turned out differently if a virus hadn't swept through the world decimating lives and throwing their days off track?

On 22 March 2020, all of India went into a lockdown. Balram shut down the akhada. He wasn't afraid of the virus and they didn't get many strangers here. But he had no way of knowing what the pehelwans did when they went back home. Also, how could they ensure social distancing when grappling in the akhada?

So, he decided to follow the government's orders. Everyone who was not part of the household left. Follow the rules on your own, he advised as he sent them away. Only Bhim remained to keep the spirit of the akhada alive.

The field of flowers was wilting. The markets were shut and the flower vendors had disappeared. Shyama thought they should let the land rest. 'Bhaiyaji, we'll stop watering the field for some days. The stalks will dry up, and then we'll remove the corms from the earth.'

At the akhada, Balram began teaching Bhim some of his best moves.

Duri drove up one morning. He had moved back to Hathras. He saw the Bullet parked near the outhouse and came looking for Balram. That was how he walked into the office room and saw the flowers on the computer table. Shyama had converted an old glass jar into a vase. Inside it, forty stalks of gladioli stood tall. Buds, flowers, leaves, each one perfectly formed.

Shyama was standing by the steel almirah, her body half concealed by the open door, putting away some papers. She saw him look at the gladioli. She could see he was puzzled by the flowers. She saw him touch them, as though to check if they were real or plastic. She watched him bend his head to smell the flowers. She laughed aloud.

Balram had followed Duri into the office room and heard her laugh.

Duri was a sensitive man. Quick to love and quick to take offence. Balram tried to smooth things over by saying, 'Our flowers are so perfect that they look more artificial than real.'

Duri turned, erasing the fury on his face. Lords don't get ruffled by ants, do they?

He bent to touch Balram's feet. As he pulled him up for an embrace, Balram felt the familiar tug at his heart. Then Shyama called out, 'Bhaiyaji ... social distancing.'

He pulled back. Duri's jaw clenched. 'Yes, yes ... we must be careful,' Balram said.

It occurred to Balram that in a span of a few minutes, Duri had endured more indignities than he probably had in his entire life. To assuage his feelings, more than anything else, he said, 'Duri, come to the akhada and tell me what's been happening with you. How are your parents?'

Duri took a deep breath. He looked at the flowers, then at Shyama's face, her mouth still split in a grin. He turned on his heel and walked away towards the akhada.

Balram followed him, Shyama's laughter still hanging in the air between them. Balram was wondering how to appease Duri when he saw the young man staring at Bhim, who was weight training with a gar-nal.

Bhim had wielded the danda with such ease that Balram had thought he needed to try something more difficult. The wooden clubs weren't enough of a challenge for him. So he had started Bhim on the gar-nal, something he didn't let any of the other pehelwans do.

It was an impressive sight, the man in his blue langot, with the massive circular stone ring around his neck, doing squats. The muscles of his thighs flexed and tightened; his well-oiled skin gleamed. Sweat dripped from his forehead. In the last eight months, Bhim's body had filled out. His shoulders had widened and his chest broadened. His biceps and hamstrings were like cannon balls. Only his belly remained sunken like it always had.

Duri couldn't believe his eyes. 'Bhaiyaji, why are you letting him use the gar-nal? You never let me do it. I had to use the truck tyre. Who is he? I saw him earlier too, with that Dholi girl, when I came here for Holi.'

Balram saw his hands curl into fists, that clenched jaw again, but ignored the warning signs.

'Bhim. One of Kanhaiya's finds,' he said. He wondered if he could get the two of them to wrestle. Duri hadn't been training for a while now, so they would be evenly matched and would improve each other's technique. More importantly, both were fiercely competitive and that would egg them on to perform better.

'Is he one of us?' Duri asked.

Balram shrugged. 'How does it matter? Inside the askhada, all men are the same.'

Later, he would ask himself why he didn't use the word 'equal'. Same isn't equal. The man he was then would have dismissed the thought, but he knew better now.

'So, he isn't!' The voice came from behind. Balram turned on his heel to see a younger and cruder version of Duri emerge from behind the SUV. There was something of a makebate about him; he looked like he enjoyed exciting quarrels.

'Bhaiyaji, this is my younger brother Dush,' Duri said.

Balram nodded at him. Dush grinned back. It was a malicious sort of grin. He disliked him at first sight.

Dush bent to touch his feet only after Duri gestured for him to do so.

'Bhim works for me. A very good boy,' he said.

'A Dholi?' Duri asked.

'Yes, Duri, and in an akhada, what does the yellow mud signify?' he said in an even voice.

'That all men are the same,' Duri muttered, the expression on his face suggesting otherwise.

'So then ...?' Balram shrugged. If he could see it, so should Duri.

The lockdown continued. The news was all about deaths caused by the virus and of migrant workers plodding their way home. Stories of hunger and deprivation. Balram debated whether he should offer refuge to some of those dead-eyed, hollow-cheeked creatures, then decided he had enough workers already. The black gram crop was faring well and they were ready to clean the irrigation ditches in time for the monsoon.

Duri came to the akhada every morning. He had resumed training. Bhim and he exercised separately, although Balram could see that they were constantly trying to outdo each other. If one did fifty squats, the other did seventy-five. He thought it was healthy how they egged each other on to do better.

One day, Shyama came to the akhada while they were training. Munshi had sent her with some papers for Balram to sign. She stood with her hands crossed over her chest and asked, 'If they wrestle each other, who do you think will win?'

'Hard to say when they haven't even grappled,' he replied.

'Is that what you think?' Dush asked, emerging from the shadows.

Shyama was startled, as was Balram.

'You think my brother can be defeated by the likes of him?' Dush snorted.

'Likes of whom?' Shyama snapped.

'Low-caste vermin,' Dush drawled.

'Mind your words!' Balram said, his voice rising.

Dush shrugged. 'The truth is the truth.'

'And what is the truth?'

'That scum should stay where they belong. Not try to be like us.'

Balram slapped him. The flat, hard sound of palm against cheek echoed across the akhada.

Bhim dropped the wooden club in his hands. Duri, who was doing press-ups with the neck weight, flopped on his elbows.

Balram was notorious for his temper, but in recent times, no one had seen it.

Duri removed the neck weight and rushed towards them.

'What happened, Bhaiyaji?' he asked, coming to stop before them.

'I will not tolerate such behaviour,' Balram said in his coldest voice.

'What did he do?' Duri persisted.

'Ask him yourself,' Balram said, glaring at Duri.

Dush's cheek bore his handprint. A slap from an older man is a physical reprimand and no more. By the time the marks fade, so should any ill feeling. But not with Dush. Not when he had been slapped in the presence of a girl, a Dholi. The sting continued to sear and blaze within him.

As the days passed, everyone got used to washing their hands every few minutes and being permanently masked. Revati insisted on wearing a mask even during sex. In all honesty, it did perk things up more than usual for both of them.

By mid-June, the lockdown had ceased to be as rigorous as it was in the beginning. The pehelwans returned, and in the open arena, they didn't have to worry about social distancing.

With the arrival of the others, the air between Duri and Bhim became even more taut with animosity. Balram could sense that the akhada was split in two factions. After giving it some thought, he decided that the best way to clear the air would be to let Duri and Bhim grapple with each other. When they had each pinned the other down for a few seconds, they would start respecting each other. He was certain of that.

Besides, there was some talk of a dangal to be organised by the WFI in December in Purvanchal, and he had to decide whom to send for the contest. Once he had seen them fight each other, he would know if it should be Bhim or Duri.

Instead of making it a contest between just the two of them, Balram announced a competition for the entire akhada that would take place on 15 September. The winner would take home fifteen thousand rupees and represent the akhada at the WFI dangal in December.

For the first time in a long long time, the monsoon arrived that year on 26 June. Twelve days early, and with such an abundance of rain that if he were a peacock, Balram thought he would have strutted around with his tail of feathers unfurled.

As the rain continued to fall, the land appeared satiated. Kanhaiya said it was because of the lockdown. The markets were empty, the factories were still, the roads deserted. It was as if nature had finally found a way to heal itself. Revati had said as much to him, but now that Kanhaiya was saying it, he realised it must be the truth.

Bhim helped prepare the soil for the planting. The other workers took care of the Kharif crops while Shyama and two women planted the corms.

Revati and Shyama had spent a great deal of time planning how to turn the field of flowers into a viable business. Shyama had found on the net someone who would buy the flowers straight from them. They wanted the large flower gladioli variety. So the corms had been sent for, and preparations began.

The maize fields alongside grew denser than ever, the stalks tall, the heads robust, and the leaves longer, wider and raspier. They were usually ready to harvest by September. But these weren't. They were heading for a bumper crop, but Balram knew he needed to be patient. You can't hurry the land, he told himself. He decided to wait until after the contest at the akhada.

Was he to blame? Or was it the virus that stopped the world and helped nature heal, so the rain fell longer and fuller than it had for several years, and the maize kernels grew plump and took longer to reach the point of harvest?

Shyama took to visiting the field of flowers earlier and earlier in the day. The maize fields drew petty thieves and she was afraid of them stomping all over the corms. He overheard Revati telling her that she should be careful going out so early on her own.

'Who's going to lay a finger on me, Bhabhiji?' she responded. 'Everyone knows that Bhim and I are to be married. Who would dare touch me?'

Four days before the contest, Balram decided to let Bhim and Duri wrestle each other for a full twelve minutes. It was evident that they were evenly matched. From the first time they stood face to face, he saw that neither would buckle to the other. There was more than just competitive zeal here. He could see some of the other pehelwans cheering Duri on. He hadn't realised the full extent of their resentment either.

Then someone from the other group called out, 'Bhim, what are you waiting for? If you don't squash Duri, Shyama will keep you dangling for the rest of your life.'

Balram frowned, wondering what he meant. Had Shyama laid down such a condition?

'I heard a rumour,' Kanhaiya said, when Balram turned to ask him. 'Shyama wants Bhim to win the dangal at the akhada.'

That he knew about. 'The prize of fifteen thousand rupees?'

Kanhaiya shook his head, his eyes fixed on the grappling men. 'Apparently, she wants to see Bhim sit astride Duri's back and grind his face into the mud,' he said under his breath.

Balram stared at him in shock. Why hadn't anyone told him this before? Why hadn't Kanhaiya? Perhaps he was afraid that Balram would cancel the contest. Or perhaps it was because he knew the futility of trying to change the course of destiny. It was something he often said to Balram, that one has little control over the consequences of one's actions.

Duri Suryavanshi had started coming to the akhada six years ago, when Shyama was thirteen years old. From the beginning, he had derived some perverse pleasure in troubling her. For some reason, he ignored her twin, but he would pull Shyama's braid and make jokes about her reedy legs and arms, and her complexion.

Once she began filling out in the right places, his ribbing had begun to border on the ribald, until Balram warned him to lay off. He did. But apparently, Shyama never forgot how much he had tormented her.

Balram hated to admit it to himself, but he wondered if Kanhaiya had spread the rumour himself. It was the kind of thing he did. In the interest of the greater good, is how he always justified it. This time, it was also personal. Bhim was his boy. Kanhaiya was only watching out for him.

Duri was a master of the move called dhobi paat, the shoulder throw. He knew exactly how to step, back step, level change, hold his stance with an outward thrust of the hip, and then hoist and throw his opponent over his shoulder. Like a dhobi slamming a piece of clothing on the washing stone.

Bhim went over in the sixth minute.

There was a shocked silence in the akhada. They hadn't expected this. Bhim had held his ground well until then. Balram had known that Duri was the superior wrestler, but no one would have believed him if he said so. Bhim gave him an imploring look. Balram sighed and said, 'We do this again, tomorrow.'

The next day, everything was different. Balram knew it the moment he saw Bhim clinch Duri's shoulders within two minutes of starting. His feet were light but firm on the ground. From the corner of his eye, Balram saw Shyama hovering behind a tree.

Duri and Bhim grappled fiercely, neither giving an inch. Then Bhim executed one of the most perfect takedowns Balram had seen—one that he hadn't taught him. There was a stunned silence as Duri lay on the raked-up mud face down. Then, as one, the pehelwans cheered. So did Balram. Behind them, Shyama's delighted laughter rose in the air.

Balram saw Duri's face and knew instantly that the mixture of anger and humiliation would goad him on to win the contest. He had needed this to shake him out of his complacency.

Later, Shyama whispered in Balram's ear, 'I showed him that move, Bhaiyaji. I found it on the net. A Russian wrestler whose father made him fight bears.'

'Is that so?' he asked, trying not to show his annoyance. He was becoming too much of a frog in a well, he told myself. He would have to start watching some of these videos on YouTube.

Shyama forgot to whisper as she added, 'Bhaiyaji, I am going to show him a few more videos this evening.'

Balram snorted. 'Are you planning to run the akhada for me now?'

Balram wanted the pehelwans to rest the day before the contest.

'Don't bother Bhim today,' he told Shyama, stopping his bike. He was on his way to the distillery. 'It's a big day for him tomorrow.'

Shyama was in the field. The corms had thrown up shoots and he saw her stoop to examine them, one by one.

She nodded. 'I know ... I won't. It's a big day for me too, Bhaiyaji.' She grinned before adding, 'I have decided, Bhaiyaji.'

'Decided what?'

'Whether Bhim wins the contest or not, I'll marry him after Diwali. As far as I am concerned, he won it yesterday when he rubbed Duri's face in the mud. I'll never forget that as long as I live.'

'And what about the fifteen thousand rupees in the bank?'

'Don't tell anyone I told you, but the Dalit Mandal plans to give him a cash prize of twenty thousand rupees. I am very practical, Bhaiyaji,' she laughed.

Balram shook his head. Shyama's eyes sparkled and her mouth was parted in an open smile. Around her, the field of flowers was a rippling sea of green, and the sky above a clear blue. The leaves on the row of mango trees abutting the road shimmered. The afternoon sun was a scorcher but Shyama didn't seem to notice it.

'Get out of the sun and go home, Shyama,' Balram said, revving up his Bullet.

'Don't worry about me Bhaiyaji ... I will be fine. I am strong enough to withstand anything.'

Balram woke up to a commotion outside the house. Revati came into the room, her face ashen. A wax mask of horror. As he listened to her repeating what she had been told, his limbs turned to stone. The hammering in his head kept time to a morbid chant: Ram naam satya hai.

A howl pushed its way out of his belly and became a roar. He wanted to break things. He wanted to smash somebody's head in.

There were four of them. Duri and Dush, and two others. They had waited for her in the maize field, knowing that she would reach the field of flowers before dawn. They ambushed her there.

Who slapped her first? Who threw her over his shoulder as if she were a bundle of dirty clothes? Who yanked away her dupatta and tore her kurta off? Who stripped her naked? Who raped her first as she lay there with her back broken, moaning in pain and terror? Who yanked her tongue out and sliced it off so her cries became blood? Who decided that they were done and left her to die?

Her mother found her. She had woken up and found Shyama missing. She knew the girl would be in the field and followed her there to give her an earful. She had no right to walk on the land as if she owned it. It was best she realised her place before someone else said or did something. 'Shyama, Shyama,' she called.

She heard a moan and wondered if it was an animal that had been hit by a speeding truck and crawled into the field to die. Instead, she discovered her nineteen-year-old daughter, a tangled mess of flesh and blood, barely breathing.

Kanhaiya was on his way to the house and had just turned off the road, on to the tractor track, when he heard the scream. He rushed towards Shyama's mother, then ran back to his car and pulled out a couple of gunny sacks from the boot. He draped them over Shyama so nobody would see her naked and battered body.

He asked Revati to break the news to Balram. He thought she would know how to handle his rage and pain.

Revati sat beside Balram, holding his hands tight. He could see she was in shock and hurting. They didn't speak.

When Revati finally left to attend to the children, Balram got up shakily. He opened his cupboard and pulled out a few things, and packed them in a duffel bag. He went down the stairs and slipped out of the side door. He started his bike and rode away. He didn't know what else to do. He couldn't bear to remain there, or to see Shyama. He knew that Duri and Dush would be arrested and then acquitted. They were men, and they belonged to the right caste.

But they were not the only ones to blame. Kanhaiya and he had both failed Shyama. Kanhaiya gave her a name and a piece of cloth to cover her nudity. And he had yoked her to a field of flowers and let her think she was more than a field labourer.

Balram knew that for as long as he lived, there would be no respite. Hell was no longer a distant realm. Hell was the world he inhabited now.

Balram sits up. Had he dozed off? He doesn't know. Asleep or awake, he can't stop thinking about Shyama.

So here he is, in this temple town, far away from his home and his people. Here he is, trying to find succour in a temple on a hill where the goddess is so powerful that male devotees are only allowed to gaze upon her from one side. A goddess who favours women and warriors. For she knows that to be a woman, she needs the resolve and courage of a warrior.

He glances at the clock on the wall. It is a little past four in the evening. He bathes and wears a fresh dhoti from the ironed pile that has been delivered to his room. He will go for the pooja at 4.30 p.m. at the mathrushala. He will sit there until it is time for the deeparadhana at sunset. When the lamp is lit and the priest holds it close to the goddess, she comes alive.

Every day, for more than a month now, Balram has waited for the goddess to give him a sign; a straw to cling to, something that will show him his torment is drawing to an end.

The goddess has still not looked his way.

TWIN BEDS

In fact, they had known what to expect.

They had both looked at the hotel room on the website. A splendid view of the Himalayas, snow-capped and seemingly at walking distance. The glistening wooden floor, as if someone had lovingly burnished it with expensive buttery-yellow face cream. The kind that cost a fortune and you would daub on your face carefully with the tip of your index finger. The furniture appeared to be more elegant than comfortable. It was exactly how Vasudha preferred a hotel room to be. One had the comfort of squishy pillows and favourite chairs at home. What one needed was a luxurious elegance that was someone else's responsibility to maintain.

As for the bathroom, it was vast and had a wall of louvred shutters that you could fling open to look out at the mountains while you sat on the pot or stood under the rain-shower or lolled in the free-standing bathtub. There was even a sliding wooden bath tray attached to the bathtub on which you could rest a glass of wine and a bowl of fruit as shown in the website photograph. It also had twin sinks so you didn't have to feel the quiver of distaste caused by spousal debris—toothpaste blobs and/or beard trimmings. It was the kind of hotel room that made you want to consider renewing your marriage vows or, at the least, stopped you from divorcing your spouse even if you had been considering it.

The bellboy led the way from the lobby, up the gracefully curved wooden staircase, to their room on the first floor. He opened the door and placed their bags in an alcove stand discreetly placed near the door. Tea kettles and battered suitcases were, after all, an unnecessary reminder of reality. Especially when you were meant to be in heaven on earth.

The bell boy pocketed his tip and smiled. 'Enjoy your stay,' he said, as if he really meant it.

She waited for him to leave with barely concealed impatience. One more hotel room. One more farce wrought out of late risings, sightseeing trips, cocktail hours, shopping sprees and a candlelight dinner on the penultimate night. Enough photographs to share on Instagram so everyone in their friend and work circles knew what a good time they had, year after year, at various exotic destinations.

The room was everything they had been promised. Except that, instead of the luxurious expanse of a king-size bed with its nest of bolsters and cushions were two immaculate twin beds with matching bedspreads and a solitary cushion propped against the headboard of each bed. For the first time in several hours, a smile came to her lips.

She waited for him to explode.

He was so used to having everything his way that he would take this as a personal slur to who he was. He had no patience for fools and the inept. Nobody messed with Akaash Deviah.

Vasudha couldn't remember when she had begun building a wall between them. It had grown from a steady disenchantment, a mental moue of distaste, and from those countless times her brows had wrinkled at his many grouses with the world. Mostly it grew from the knowledge that she was married to the most cynical man alive.

He felt her eyes on him as he frowned at the twin beds. 'Why have these idiots not given us a proper bed? It's like being in a hostel all over again.'

He didn't want her to know what he was thinking—that the twin beds were the best thing that could have happened. 'I am going down to the reception to give them an earful,' he said, grabbing his phone and his cigarette pack with a solitary cigarette left in it.

'You can't bear to be parted from your phone for even a minute?' she hurled at him as she went to stand by the window to gaze at the mountains. He frowned. What was she so tetchy about?

'What if there is a work call?'

'Aren't you supposed to be on holiday?'

'I am. The world isn't,' he said, slamming the door shut. If he stayed a moment longer, he was afraid he would hurl something at her instead of just wanting to. How did she produce that snide tone to order? He took the stairs down two at a time in his hurry to get away.

The reception clerk looked up as he approached the desk. He smiled at her and walked past into the long corridor leading towards the hotel doors. He stepped out into the freezing air and took a deep breath, then fumbled in his pocket for the cigarette pack. The doorman who looked like a high school student said, 'Excuse me sir, in Bhutan, you are not allowed to smoke outside.'

He shoved the pack into his pocket and went back into the hotel and paused at the reception.

'Good morning, sir, how can I help you?' A carefully made-up woman at the desk asked.

He wondered if he should ask about a room with a king or at least queen-size bed. But there were more pressing matters to attend to first.

'Is there a smoking section in the hotel?' He asked.

The clerk shook her head. 'No, we don't have any such place.'

He stared at her bewildered. 'Then where do I smoke?'

'In your room,' she said.

'Really?' He laughed. 'Is that alright?'

'Yes, of course,' the woman said, picking up the phone that had begun ringing.

He smiled to himself as he climbed the stairs to his room. Vasudha wasn't going to like it. She made such a production of it each time he lit a cigarette inside their flat in Noida. Flinging open the French windows, then an angry twist of the fan regulator followed by a five-minute lecture on passive smoking.

He knocked on the door. When she opened it, he saw that she had already showered and set some of her things out. He took a deep breath and asked, 'Why did you unpack? I told you I was going to fix it.'

Why did it bother him so much? On an obvious level, it seemed to suggest that she had no faith in his ability to 'fix things'. Or was it the suggestion that she didn't particularly want to share a bed with him? He felt a nasty little jolt; it upset his equilibrium more than anything else.

She stepped back into the bathroom where she had been laying out her creams and other stuff. 'Why? Have they given us another room?' she asked as she zipped up the grooming bag with a decided snap.

It broke his reverie as though someone had clicked their fingers in front of his face. 'Oh, what?' he stuttered.

'I asked if they changed our rooms?' She did not hide her impatience.

The peevish note in her voice smarted. 'No, not yet,' he said, deciding he wasn't going to even try. 'There's only one other room with this view. And it's occupied by a couple who've extended their holiday, apparently. An English couple in their seventies. They couldn't move them.' He wondered if he should give the couple names and add a description or two. He could almost see the man—a Polo t-shirt stretched over his belly—and smell Estee Lauder's White Linen on her wrinkled throat. 'They said they could give us another room but minus the view.'

'You should unpack your things,' she said.

'I will. But first I need a smoke,' he said.

'Are you going to smoke in here? Isn't this a non-smoking room?'

He shrugged. 'Apparently this is the only place you can.' He slid the window open. The cold cut through like a knife.

When he was done, he went to the bathroom and set out his toiletries one by one on the counter by the sink that he presumed she had allotted to him. Remind me, he told his reflection, why do I go on these holidays? Twenty-four hours of being in each other's face and hair. And not even a temporary exit area to retreat into. No, *I have run out of rolling papers.* No, *I need to take the car to the service station, it's making a strange noise.* No, *I am going out with the boys.* Not even, *I am stepping out for a goddamn walk.*

'The breakfast buffet will close in twenty minutes,' she said. 'We should get going. I really need to eat.'

He nodded. 'Give me five minutes.' And every fucking meal together, he mumbled under his breath. Why do I do this year after year?

The buffet spread wasn't as extensive or elaborate as the ones they were used to. Where was the bacon fried to a crisp?

Where were the plump doughnuts? The array of cut fruits? The creamy smoothies and disgusting vegetable juices? Where was the the opportunity to prevaricate between being greedy and sensible?

As if sensing their dissatisfaction, a hostess came to their table with a menu card. Breakfast was à la carte and included in their package, she told them. Vasudha beamed at her. For once she could order what she felt like eating. As if she didn't have enough of being sensible all the time at the school at which she worked.

'I am going to have the puri–aloo,' she said, 'and instant coffee.' Akaash's family were coffee planters and liked their coffee ground from their own beans and percolated in an old-fashioned filter.

'And I am going to have baked beans on toast, a cheese omelette and a pot of tea,' Akaash said, snapping shut the menu. Instant coffee, he shuddered. He would rather drink tea.

A few minutes later, Akaash broke the habitual silence that had crept between them. 'I've been thinking,' he said.

'What?' Vasudha said as she opened a WhatsApp forward.

'Shall we pretend we're two strangers meeting for the first time?'

She stared at him. There was a sparkle in her eyes, as if his suggestion was definitely more interesting than the video of a dog singing Blue Eyes at a talent show.

'Why?' she asked.

'You don't like the idea,' Akaash said, deflecting the need to say why. Where would he even begin if he were to start listing the many ways she got on his nerves? As they walked to the coffee shop, he had wondered how he could make her disappear.

The idea had suggested itself to him as they ordered breakfast. He had watched her ordering the greasiest breakfast on the menu and, for a moment, wondered who this stranger was. He couldn't remember the last time she had deviated from her daily oats porridge and boiled egg.

In the professional world of wealth management, he was considered a lateral thinker. The one who side-stepped the box and effected financial miracles. He had never had to use this talent in his personal life until now. 'There's a name for it. It's called role playing,' he said.

'So, how does it begin?' she asked slowly. 'Who are we? What are we?'

'Figure it out. If I have to tell you who we are, what's the point?' he said.

She stared at him puzzled. Usually, he liked to explain everything to her, whether it was how to peel onions or make a money transfer.

Her food arrived. She looked at the puffed out puris glistening with oil and the potato curry garnished with onion rings and a green chilli. He rose abruptly, the grating sound of the chair leg on the floor echoing his annoyance.

She watched him walk to the juice counter and speak to one of the stewards. They seemed to be sharing a joke. The man's smile was wide as he poured him a glass of canned pineapple juice.

Who was this Akaash Deviah?

By the time he returned to the table with his glass of juice, she had left. Her place had been cleared. He drank his juice slowly and started on his breakfast.

When he went back to the room, the twin beds stared at him with raised eyebrows: what now, Akaash?

He opened the window Vasudha had shut. He took out his rolling papers and the tobacco pouch. The sun had emerged, turning the bone-numbing chill to a more pleasant freshness that made him want to get out and explore. But first, a smoke, he decided. He cupped the flame as he held the matchstick to his cigarette. Then he inhaled deeply and stuck his head out of the window. A spiral of smoke rose to the skies that were an icy blue. He felt like a king surveying his kingdom.

The door opened. He sensed a movement in the room. But he continued to stand by the window without turning.

'Hey!' A familiar voice with a different cadence to it. 'I smelt cigarette smoke as I was going to my room and noticed the door was open.'

He turned.

'Hi,' she said. 'My name is Shona.'

'Hey,' he said, wondering what to call himself. Then he thought of how he had felt a moment ago. 'My name is Sultan.'

'Do you want a drag?' he asked.

She nodded. 'That's why I walked into your room. I am dying for a ciggie but I am not carrying any.'

He offered the cigarette to her silently. She placed it between her lips and drew on it deeply, her eyes closed. He thought it was the sexiest thing he had seen.

'Are you here on vacation?' he asked, fumbling for the words that would kickstart their story: strangers in the night.

The idea was his, but it seemed that she owned it already. Sultan. Just who was Sultan? What was the nature of the beast?

'You could call it that,' she smiled, handing him the cigarette. 'And you?'

'I am here to meet a client.'

She waited for him to elaborate. When he didn't, she glanced at her watch. 'Look, I have to go now. I should be back by seven. If you are free, why don't you come by to the bar at eight?' She went out of the room, closing the door gently behind her, while he watched bemused.

He sat on one of the twin beds feeling a little breathless. He didn't know if it was shock, anticipation or the altitude. He glanced at his watch. It was a quarter to eleven, What the hell was he going to do all day on his own?

She walked to the lobby. A thickset man wearing glasses peeled himself from one of the chairs in the lobby. 'Mrs Vasudha Deviah?' he asked.

She nodded. And then on a whim and because she was still being Shona, she stuck her hand out. He seemed startled but he shook it, saying, 'I am Ugyen, your chauffeur and guide for the day.'

Akaash, who disdained all things touristy, as he called it, had set it up with the tour operator. 'You can go to all the monasteries and nunneries you want. Leave me out of it,' he had told her.

She hadn't protested. By now she was used to discovering the tourist attractions of any place they went to on her own. She wasn't sure why she did it. It was almost a compulsion to tick a box: seen this, done that.

Ugyen led her to a small SUV. The back seat was swathed in fleece rugs. She took her jacket off and laid it on the back seat. 'Where would Madam like to sit?' Ugyen asked, watching her.

'In the front, of course,' she said. She knew that's what Shona would do.

He opened the car door for her. She sat down and adjusted the seat. A faint smell of incense clung to the insides of the car. 'Where shall we go?' he asked.

It was Shona who smiled and said, 'I have no idea. What would you suggest?' Shona asked. Vasudha would have known exactly where and when. She had her life mapped out. Whether it was her every day or holidays, she plotted it out with an iron hand.

'If you trust me, I'll show you what is really wonderful about Thimphu.'

He started the car, muttering under his breath. 'Is everything alright?' Vasudha popped out of Shona unbidden.

'I was just praying, madam. I hope you don't mind.'

Shona tilted at her head as she looked at him. 'Do you mind chanting a little louder so I can hear it too?'

Ugyen bent his head, his voice rising. The rhythm was of a chant. She didn't know what the words meant, but the cadence—as if they were words mined out of a deep, dark cave in the mountainside—filled her with an immense sense of awe.

She looked around, taking in the names of shops and buildings.

When he was done praying, she smiled at him and said, 'Are you a very religious person?'

'I wanted to be a monk. But I am the oldest son, and I have my responsibilities. I couldn't decide whether to give myself to what is beyond or what is around …' he said with a small smile.

Then he cleared his throat and asked, 'Where do you live in India?'

'Delhi,' she said. 'But I am from Karnataka. Have you heard of the state?'

Ugyen smiled. 'I know Kerala. We had Keralan teachers in the school I went to. And one of them had a son who was my classmate and best friend. He brought me a coconut once.'

Vasudha would have corrected him immediately: 'It's Malayali, not Keralan.' Shona didn't particularly care.

She thought of a coconut in the hands of a little Bhutanese boy. 'What did you make of the coconut?'

Ugyen's response was quick and light. 'It felt like I was holding something rare and incredible, like nothing I had known before.'

She took a deep breath; she knew that feeling. Vasudha had been handed something rare, incredible and unfamiliar when she found Shona.

They drove past the golf course and went up the road towards a building that looked understated compared to the photographs she had seen of other monasteries. Two young boys dressed in monk's robes were playing cricket in the courtyard. Around them, dogs with thick shaggy coats lay basking in the midday sun.

'This is the Zilukha Nunnery,' Ugyen said. He led her around the building, turning the prayer wheels as he went.

'This way,' he said, showing her how to turn the prayer wheel. 'Clockwise. And if you like, you could chant Om Mani Padme Hum.'

She did as he asked, the rhythm of the turning wheels and the chanting lulling her into a kind of calm that said, just be, just be … don't think about what comes next.

The room was in darkness when she entered. She took her shoes off and sat on the sofa with her feet on the table. Her feet and calves ached, but it was a sweet sort of ache. Of muscles that had stretched beyond their comfort zone. It had been a day spent outside her skin.

She shed her clothes and walked to the bathroom. Akaash had been here earlier, she realised when she saw the wet towel and the still moist floor of the shower cubicle.

She paused at the free-standing tub and opened the taps. Vasudha would have showered, not Shona. This woman was an unfurling bud, blooming petal by petal.

The management had left them a fruit basket. She placed a bunch of grapes on a plate and left it on the sliding tray fixed on the tub. Then she stepped into the pool of foam. The hot, fragrant water gathered her in its arms. She sighed in pleasure and rested her head against the edge of the tub. Was this for real? Was she in a movie? Was this a dream? All she knew was that within her was a sybarite who sat neck deep in a bubble bath eating jade-coloured grapes one by one while the water nudged open her pores and sloshed against the ceramic sides of the tub in tiny little waves.

She dried herself and carefully applied moisturiser on every inch of her skin. She lined her eyes with a kohl stick and put on a lipstick that was the colour of crushed mulberries. Then she slipped into a long t-shirt and went to the sofa by the window. It was ten to eight.

Akaash's cigarettes were on the table. She wondered how he was managing without being able to light up every few minutes. She opened the window just enough for the cold, sharp wind to enter the room.

She wondered where he was. Sultan, not Akaash. She picked up her phone and sent him a WhatsApp message: Hi.

Her phone beeped.

She smiled at the several question marks that looked back at her.

Feeling lazy. Not up to hanging at the bar. I am in room 125. Do you want to drop by for a drink? Have some local Bhutanese brew.

She added a wide-mouthed emoji.

Give me 15, he said.

It was Shona who pulled out the bottle of Ara from her bag. Ugyen had given it to her. He said it was brewed by his cousin.

Shona had asked to meet Ugyen's family and see his home on their way back to the hotel. Vasudha would have tipped him and forgotten all about the man who had spent his whole day with her.

She left the door open by an inch and went back to the sofa. A million butterflies rose from the pit of her stomach and fluttered through her.

When he walked in, the room was mostly in darkness. The bedside lamp was on, and a floor lamp by the sofa. She was bathed in a golden light. A bottle rested on the table alongside two glasses. He sat down on the sofa across from her. 'Didn't you think I would come?' he asked. She looked like she'd had an amazing day. Her eyes sparkled and her face was radiant.

He had had an unusual day himself. He had spent the first couple of hours not knowing what to do, and eventually decided on the Buddha Point. Just one place, no shuttling from point A to point B.

The cab driver had dropped him outside the gates. He had wandered in along with a group of tourists. An entire family—grandparents, couples and three apple-cheeked babies who looked like possible contenders for the role of

The Last Emperor. The serenity on the babies' faces made him pause and look at them carefully.

Vasudha would be astonished to learn that he had caressed a baby's cheek. The woman sitting across him wouldn't, he knew.

'Have you ordered a drink?' he asked, shrugging himself into his new avatar with the relief of a man who had found a seat in a crowded stadium.

'You can ask for a peach wine. Or a cocktail. I think I'll have the local tipple. Ara, courtesy my driver,' she said, gesturing to the bottle.

He schooled his features to hide his surprise. Vasudha only drank wine and never more than two glasses.

'I'll have the same,' he said, leaning forward to pour the Ara into their glasses.

'So, what do you do, Sultan?'

'So, what was your day like, Shona?'

They spoke at the same time.

She knocked down her drink in one swallow and stretched the glass towards him.

Akaash would have frowned and said, go easy, will you? This thing is potent. But not Sultan. He smiled at her and poured a shot into her glass.

The conversation flowed. She described her day to him; he told her about his.

They smoked, they drank some more and at some point, they called for food, both reluctant to leave the room and break the intimacy of the moment.

The level in the bottle dropped.

And then she said softly, 'Tell me something you've never told anyone before.'

He stared at her, taken aback. What was Vasudha up to? Then he remembered this wasn't her. Vasudha never probed beyond the surface. She seldom asked him why. But Shona was different. She wanted to know. She would listen.

Akaash looked at his drink for a long minute. 'More than ten years ago, in my previous workplace, I used to travel extensively all over India,' he began.

She didn't speak, just took a long sip of her drink. The taste of the alcohol drowned out what would have been Vasudha's waspish interjection: So, an affair then, is it?

Shona asked, 'Where?'

He shook his head. 'It doesn't matter. Just a tier-two city somewhere in this vast country.'

She remembered that one trip. He had returned withdrawn and surly. At first, she had put it down to exhaustion. But when, after days of monosyllabic responses or biting retorts, she had asked him if something was wrong, he had waved her concern away. 'Nothing is wrong. Just work stuff.'

When he moved into wealth management, she thought things would improve. It was what he had always wanted to do. But Akaash continued to be his distant self, and worse, turned into someone she didn't recognise anymore. Was it another woman?

His gaze was fixed on the night skies as he spoke. 'I went out for dinner to a restaurant that a colleague had recommended. He said the view and the food there were spectacular. It had been a long and gruelling day and I had a presentation to make the following morning, so I was carrying my laptop.'

The restaurant was on the roof of the city's tallest building. A young hostess escorted me to my table in a covered area. She must have been twenty or so.

When I asked to sit on the terrace, she shook her head. 'The terrace area has been reserved for a private party, sir.'

'It's just me,' I tried to convince her. 'I need a table where I can smoke. You can put me there.' I pointed to a table with an ashtray. It was close to the high parapet wall and hidden behind giant plants in tall pots. 'Your private party won't even notice me,' I added for good measure.

'Let me check with the manager, sir,' she said, and returned a few minutes later, smiling. 'It's sorted, sir. You can sit there. I just hope the party won't be too noisy.' She gestured to one of the stewards to lay the table.

The view from the rooftop was stunning. I sat nursing my drink and working.

About thirty minutes later, a local politician I recognised from hoardings and flex-boards across the city walked in with his all-men entourage. They were the private party the hostess had mentioned. Apparently, a celebration of some sort was taking place.

I didn't pay much attention. I had a meeting the next morning and a TBL to put together.

They were an unruly lot, and as the evening progressed, they got rowdier. I realised I was going to have to leave soon. Almost on cue, a steward arrived at my table and asked if I wanted my food served inside the restaurant. I shook my head, reluctant to move to another table and disrupt work.

I finished eating quickly, paid my bill and left. Just as I reached the lift, I realised that I had left my cigarettes and lighter on the table. I went back into the restaurant, which was strangely empty, and walked towards the French windows.

The young hostess was at the politician's table. I saw one of the men put his arm around her waist. I saw the girl push it away. I heard words. Angry words. The hostess's voice rose. One of the stewards rushed to her defence.

The men laughed. The man who had put his arm around her waist pulled her towards him. She turned and slapped him. She turned to the politician in his white kurta-pyjama and said something. I couldn't hear what she said but I saw his jaw clench.

He drank from the glass before him. Then he stood up. He picked up the girl and hurled her over the parapet wall. Eight floors down. He walked back to the table, poured himself a glass of water and drank it. None of his men spoke.

I left quickly and quietly.

The newspapers called it a suicide. End of story.

I witnessed a murder that night, Shona, and I did nothing to stop it from happening. Nor did I report the crime. I was too afraid to get involved.

Vasudha felt her breath strangle in her throat. She looked at him as he sat there with his head bent. Why hadn't he gone to the police? She didn't blame him. It would have been hushed up anyway, and the only thing that would have happened was a freak accident that sent Akaash straight to a mortuary table.

He had borne this alone for more than a decade now. His guilt and shame. And yet, he hadn't come to her. He hadn't trusted her enough to share with her the brutality he had witnessed.

What kind of a wife did that make her? All she had done these past years was jeer and pepper her conversation with condescension.

They had been through three parliamentary elections and she had never asked him once why he always voted None of the Above. She never asked him, 'Don't you believe India needs a change in governance?'

Instead, she had looked at him with a long suffering expression. 'Don't you see the sheer anarchy everywhere? The rampant corruption. The country is being fragmented into pockets of power. NOTA is not going to make it come together. All you do is find fault with the system. If you had voted, we may have had a better government in charge.'

She called him a bigot when he mocked the families in their apartment block for banging on plates to chase away the corona virus as per the prime minister's instructions. 'People are frightened. They don't know what to make of the virus. It's their desperation that's making them do it. By calling them names you are being as much of a bigot as you claim they are,' she had said.

When she had exclaimed at Rahul Gandhi's tenacity and strength during his padayatra, he had smirked, 'You think that's going to make a difference? A man walking across the country?'

'You need to believe in something,' she had snarled back.

'I have no faith in politicians. All of them are corrupt. Just the degree of it varies.'

'How can there be governance without a government?' she had tried to reason.

'I don't know. And I don't care.'

He felt her move to sit by his side. He felt her caress the line of his neck. The heaviness he had lived with for more than a decade felt less intense. He turned his face and looked at her.

'Something in me died that day. My faith in the right of law, democracy perhaps. This country is run by thugs. How do you fight it?' He paused.

He wasn't sure if it was Vasudha or Shona who took his hand in hers and placed her lips on the tips of his fingers.

He felt a tear trickle down his cheek. She brushed it away saying, 'Sultan, my Sultan, I can't even imagine what you must have gone through.'

He held her fingers and clung to them. Then he couldn't bear the storm in his chest anymore. He stood up abruptly. 'I have to go, Shona. I need to clear my head.'

She sat in the silence of the room for a few minutes. It was almost midnight. Where had Akaash gone? The Ara sloshed inside her. Almost on auto-pilot, she brushed her teeth and slid into one of the twin beds.

When she woke up, she realised that Akaash had come in at some point and gone to sleep, and she had a hangover. She showered and dressed as quietly as she could and left the room. Ugyen was already waiting for her.

'Give me twenty minutes,' she said. She headed to the restaurant for coffee and something that would alleviate the heaviness in her head.

More monasteries. A market. A souvenir shop. All Vasudha wanted to do was go back to the room, pull the drapes shut, get into bed and sleep away the fatigue. She wasn't sure if it was the Ara or if it was Akaash's unburdening that filled her with this queer listlessness. She went through the motions of playing tourist for as long as she could and then she asked Ugyen to drop her back to the hotel.

When she went up to the room, it was mercifully empty. She didn't know what to say to Akaash and she didn't have it in her to find the words.

Late in the evening, when she walked into the hotel bar, a young man was sitting on a stool in a corner of the bar strumming a guitar and singing the eternal favourite of hotel crooners: 'Killing Me Softly'. The steward led her to a cluster of sofas in the middle of the room. Single woman drinking on her own kind of seating. She looked at the menu. What would Shona drink?

And then a voice murmured, 'Hello, Shona.'

She turned. She would know Akaash's voice anywhere, but the timbre was unfamiliar. She had pinged him when she woke up from her nap, and set up to meet him at seven. 'Hello, Sultan,' she said. She could hear the softness in her own voice. 'I wasn't sure if I would see you,' she said, not quite meeting his eyes. Why was she feeling shy?

He sat down and raised his hand to click his fingers at the steward. He knew how much Vasudha hated it. He was certain Shona wouldn't approve either. The expression on her face said as much. He stopped himself and used the hand to brush his hair back in a convoluted movement.

Their eyes met across the table. 'I've always wanted to walk into a bar and seat myself on a bar stool. And brood into a drink,' she said with half a smile.

'And?' he asked.

'And start a conversation with a man seated alongside,' she giggled, replaying the countless times Hollywood used this particular scene.

He didn't speak. Then he stood up saying, 'I just a need a few minutes.'

She wondered if she had played it wrong. She gestured to the steward. 'I'll get my drink at the bar,' she said, rising. As if on cue, the crooner burst into 'Hallelujah'.

Leonard Cohen, she smiled to herself, the patron saint of crooners and lone women in bars. She hummed under her breath: *the minor fall, the major lift.*

The bar stool was like every bar stool she had seen in the movies. Tall, with a swivelling seat, so you hunched over the counter to speak to the bar man. And the barman was like every barman in the movies—muscular forearms, a tattoo that peeked beneath the half sleeves of the black t-shirt stretched tight across his broad chest and a leather thong wrapped several times around his wrist. This one had a granite jaw, cheekbones you could slice carrots with and narrow, slanting eyes. The tips of his hair glinted with russet highlights. Served on a plate alongside a slice of red velvet cake, he would win hands down.

She asked for a Margarita. He placed the drink on a coaster and moved it towards her with a sleek smile. She played with the swizzle stick and moved the slice of lime this way and that on the rim of her glass. 'Are you from around here?' she asked.

'That was meant to be my line to you,' a suede-sheathed voice growled in her ear.

She turned abruptly.

He stood there with a lopsided grin. 'I've always wanted to saunter into a bar and chat up a beautiful woman seated on a bar stool on her own,' he said, giving her a once-over.

Vasudha tugged at the hem of her top so it wouldn't pouch over her middle-aged waist. Did she need to shave her legs, she wondered, casting a covert glance at her calves draped on the rungs of the bar stool. She dropped her gaze, afraid of what he would see in her eyes.

'Oh my god, Shona, are you flustered?' The laugh accompanying the words was a little bark of exhilaration.

Blood rushed into her face. 'Where did you go?' she asked, taking a sip of her drink and hoping the ice in it would quell the heat singeing her skin.

He had stepped out to still his drumming heart. Who was this woman who lived within his wife of eighteen years? He had needed a moment to collect himself. When he came back, she was gone, and he had felt a moment of abject terror. *Where was she? Who had she gone away with?*

Then he had spotted her by the bar, and he knew the game was still on. He had rushed towards her only to hear her chatting up the barman, who would have belonged in the pages of *GQ* as if it were his home. Make your move now, Sultan, he had chided himself. You have a couple of hours at the most to swing it your way. Akaash Deviah would have to stay out of the picture until then.

'A drink for you, sir?' the barman asked.

'Surprise me,' he said.

'I had to make a call,' he said turning to her, 'and I didn't want to talk in the bar.'

She cocked her head at him like a curious bird.

'My wife,' he said, throwing his dice with a reckless hand. A silence tiptoed in between him.

She broke it with a clinking laugh. 'I am married too.'

Her dice had trounced him right down the ladder. Was she going to tell him about himself, he wondered.

'Is your husband here?' he asked, his eyes darting across the bar. A nerve began hammering at his temple.

'He is back tomorrow,' she said softly. 'He is touring Trashigang in the east,' she added.

'Oh,' he said, unable to stop the exclamation. 'I did wonder what you were doing on your own.'

She took another sip of her drink. The phrase was Dutch courage, she knew. The barman placed a drink before him.

'I am usually on my own,' she said with a small smile. 'Actually, aren't we all?' She raised her glass to clink it against his.

Here it comes, he told himself. Instead, she stole his swizzle stick.

'Hey, that's mine.' His voice rose a fraction in astonishment as he watched her slide the cherry off the stick into her mouth.

'I didn't think you're the kind who likes plumped up cherries,' she drawled, chewing slowly.

'Woman, woman, you know nothing about me,' Sultan whispered in her ear while a defeated Akaash Deviah skulked away with his tail between his legs to a dark corner behind the bar.

Vasudha took a sip of her drink, unable to comprehend what she had said and done. It was like she was acting in a movie that was being scripted even as the cameras were rolling. Back of her mind, she was waiting for an irate director to throw a fit and holler, 'Cut ... pack up!'

A steward placed a bowl of bar-mix on the counter between them. 'Should I get you the menu?' he asked.

Vasudha peered at him over the rim of her glass. 'What would you like for starters?'

He glanced at his watch. 'It's just half past seven. I am not really hungry.'

'Really? A man with a poor appetite, I see ...'

'Shona, I am hungry for many things, but not tandoori paneer or drums of heaven.'

A frisson of something; a forgotten feeling, or was it just the adrenalin surge of bantering with a stranger in a bar? He wasn't a stranger though. She knew everything about him: from how much milk he took in his tea to his favourite ghazal to the shirt brand he preferred to the expletives he mouthed while driving to the precise second when he would start a sneezing fit if he walked into a room with fresh-cut flowers.

'By the way, I got you something,' he said, groping in the inner pocket of his jacket. Her heart sank just a little. A silver Bhutanese design bracelet because she wore no gold. Or an expensive gee-gaw or in all probability a baby yak wool stole, for she had talked about that on their flight in. You couldn't accuse Akaash of not listening.

He pulled out a pinecone from his pocket. 'I found it on a mountain trail,' he said, touching the scales with the tip of his index finger and stroking it. It felt as if he was caressing the skin of her inner wrist. It felt as though this stranger, for this was not Akaash, had peeked inside her head and unearthed the pinecone from a secret chamber.

'It's exquisite,' she said quietly, wanting to stretch the moment with this man who looked like the man she was married to but whom she had never met before.

It lay in a heap of pine needles on the side of the mountain road that arced the Takin sanctuary. It had seemed like a miraculous find, a perfect pinecone with all its scales and prickles intact.

Vasudha often complained that he was a magnet for things that had no earthly use. A scarf that would be perfect for the tundra. Yachting shoes when he didn't even know anyone with a rowing boat. An antique clock that no one could fix. A glass block retrieved from a building site. A broken stone pestle. Possessions that lay around gathering neglect and dust. Waiting for the day when he would put them to use.

'Why don't you get rid of this junk?' *Or I will* was the underlying threat that he had learnt to not heed.

He didn't know how to explain to her what these things he acquired meant to him. In their own way, they added to the secret image of himself which was in daily danger of eroding. It was the only way he knew how to look beyond the image he had to confront each morning in the shaving mirror that magnified everything including the pathetic mediocrity of his existence.

Akaash Deviah may have it all in the eyes of the world. A lovely wife; two healthy super achievers for children who had neither acne nor attitude; a penthouse flat in Noida; an expensive car and a full partnership in a company that was racing ahead at full throttle. He had everything but himself.

It was all of this he wanted her to know when he offered her the weather-beaten but wholly intact pinecone. Vasudha would never get it. But Shona just might, he had thought. And it seemed she had, for she cradled it to her cheek as if it were an agate egg.

'A refill?' he asked, trying to erase the sadness that enveloped him.

'Why not?' She smiled. 'If I get plastered, will you see me to my room?' She doodled with her forefinger on the bar counter.

'Oh, you won't,' he laughed. 'But if you do, rest assured that I'll tuck you safely into bed.' He arched his eyebrow at her and he doodled his finger around hers, a finger waltz of sorts. Damn, he hadn't even known he could do this.

'Shall we move to one of the sofas?' he asked.

'I was hoping you would say that. The bar stool looks very nice in films but in real life, it's a pain in the ass.' She grinned.

He felt a growing admiration for her. Vasudha had retreated to a place where no one could trace her anymore. Instead, here was Shona, recklessly sassy and crackling like popcorn with life and insouciance.

The crooner adjusted his mic and began strumming the opening chords of 'Unchained Melody'. She slid off the stool and said, 'Dance with me.'

He stood with his hands stiff at his sides. 'I can't dance,' he said, almost adding: But you know that already!

'Neither can I, but this song begs to be danced to.' She stretched her hand out to him.

And there, in a little clearing between the bar and the sofa clusters, all the love stories that he had sneered at as products of a feverish imagination aided by lust, prodded him: What does it feel like now, Mister?

They held each other and swayed to the music. Her arms wrapped around his neck like they belonged there. His eyes smarted.

When the crooner switched the beat to the peppy 'Uptown Girl', and another couple joined them on the carpeted square she had assigned to be their dance floor, he took her arm and led her to an alcove the steward pointed out to him.

'Our drinks are here,' he said, groping through the bar-mix for a salted almond. He leaned forward and placed it between her lips. She nibbled at it, teasing the nut out of his fingers. As his fingers grazed the plump fleshiness of her inner lips, he wondered if she had done this before.

She read the question in his eyes. This was a dangerous game, she realised then. Turning fantasy into reality. There would be repercussions. Just what they would be remained to be seen.

It occurred to her then this was why married sex seldom deviated from the conventional. To allow a spouse to see you naked was one thing. But to allow a spouse to see the nudity and extent of your desire demanded courage and an unassailable position of self-worth.

Missionary was what your mother had done. And your mother's mother, and your aunt and your vegetable seller and your boss, she imagined. Everything else came with a subtext: where did you learn this? Who did you learn it from? Later, in the middle of the day, when you were doing the dishes or tallying your credit card statement with the bills or working on a project from home, a little red-nosed goblin would poke its head out and mutter, now that he has seen the extent of your appetite, will he still respect you?

But did Shona care about any of this?

Before she could answer her own question, the steward appeared with the food menu.

Vasudha would have insisted on Bhutanese cuisine. She sneered at people who went looking for Indian food on the streets of Milan and Paris. 'They should just stay at home and eat rasam and rice, the philistines!' Shona was different. She wasn't afraid to admit that she craved familiar food. She placed her order and he placed his and they weren't the same. Vasudha would have rebuked Akaash for the possible wastage of food. Shona knew there were plenty of dogs around who would be happy to receive a doggy bag.

When the steward left with their food order, she propped her elbow on the arm of the sofa, rested her chin on her wrist and gazed at him.

For a while, they both sat there in silence. Then Vasudha began telling him about the market she had gone to that day. She saw his eyes glaze. She realised that they were in danger of reverting to Vasudha and Akaash again.

The food arrived then.

'Tell you what,' she said with a grin, sitting up. 'You are going to answer one last question for me. A wise woman once said, the past is guaranteed to give you indigestion and heartburn. So, look to the future where hunger awaits.'

He stared at her for a moment and then laughed aloud. With surprise more than merriment.

'Tell me, if you had the chance to be born again, who would you be?' She nibbled on a fried wonton. She wasn't hungry anymore. At least, not for the whole array of starters she had ordered. Chicken lollipop and fried wontons, stir-fried broccoli and crackling spinach.

Akaash, or was it Sultan, reached for a chicken drumstick with an aluminium foil boot. He smiled. 'I've never thought about it. But I do dream of a life I wish I had.'

'Which is?'

'It's not one thing. It's many things. I would like to be a carpenter. And keep a goat farm. And fill the farm with dogs, cats, chickens, ducks and a couple of alpacas.'

She leaned forward, unable to help herself. She wanted to peer into his eyes and see if he really meant it or was shooting the breeze, as one of her senior students liked to phrase it.

She saw how his eyes gleamed. Like a fire lit from deep within. She was reminded of a Russian Babushka doll. Every doll opened to reveal another one. When had she stopped seeking what lay beneath the next layer? Or had she turned into a pernickety judge forever evaluating his guilt rather than innocence?

She reached for his hands and held them in hers. 'How wonderful! How utterly wonderful!'

'You don't think I'm being ludicrous,' he asked, almost hesitantly.

She shook her head. 'Not at all. What will you do for money though?'

'Live frugally. Live off what I make. If you are happy doing what you are doing, money can't be the driving force of existence.'

Thus spake a wealth manager who was caught in a trap of his own making. All his early adult life had been spent in the pursuit of a career that would make him rich. He had discovered that he understood money and its erratic temperament. So he had set about using the skill to make money grow for others. When did he forget what it was that first drew him to money? When did he forget that he had other dreams?

'And you, Shona? Who would you like to be if you were born again?' he asked, taking a large bite of his second chicken lollipop.

She toyed with a piece of broccoli and said, 'I don't think I want to be born again ...'

'But why?' He paused mid-bite.

She shrugged. 'If I am born again, I would like to study music and become a singer. Not a professional singer, mind you. I don't want to be subject to public scrutiny. Just to be able to disappear into myself as I sing.'

Vasudha couldn't hold a note. She was tone deaf. This was a test of some sort, he realised. 'Sounds wonderful. May I offer you a room in my farm where you can sing all day? The only ones to hear you will be my animals and I am yet to hear of a goat who is a music critic.'

She burst into laughter. And just like that, they sat there planning their next lives, eating their meal, drinking that one last drink that became 'definitely the last drink', stretching the evening as far as it would go, while all the time, their lives swung at the tip of a pendulum.

And then, because he couldn't bear it any longer, Akaash stood up and said, 'I am going to my room for a smoke. I'll be back in ten minutes.'

She watched him leave. He wasn't walking away from boredom or restlessness or because he actually needed a smoke. Soon, it would be time for Shona and Sultan to dissipate, and he couldn't bear the thought. She knew this because it was exactly how she felt.

She signed the bill and walked slowly up the staircase. The door was ajar. The room was mostly in darkness. He stood by the window, smoking and staring out at the night. She went to stand beside him.

He took the cigarette from his mouth and placed it between her lips. She inhaled deeply, then returned it to him.

They stood there in the silence, smoking. When they were done, they held hands and walked to the bathroom through the louvred shutters which they flung open with an exaggerated flourish. She ran the water, and he tipped the contents of the bubble bath that housekeeping seemed to have replenished while taking away wet towels and emptying the dustbin. They stood there watching the foam fill up the tub.

They undressed each other. Sultan and Shona. It was like they were seeing each other for the first time. A magic eraser caused lines, folds and politics to fade away, so that all they saw and felt was the moment, natural and perfect.

He stepped into the tub and sat down amidst the bubbles. 'Come,' he said softly.

She stepped into the water. He lay back against the curve of the bathtub. 'Here,' he said, opening his arm so she could snuggle into his shoulder.

She sank into the foam and rested her face against the side of his neck. The water swished, rocking them ever so gently. From deep within her, a memory shrugged its way out. Once, in a magic womb, she and he had felt secure, cherished, loved. He wrapped his arms around her.

They would make love that night. They would sleep in each other's arms in one of the twin beds without feeling that either was encroaching on the other's territory. They would be Shona and Sultan. Strangers who had discovered each other.

Who knows what tomorrow will bring?

THE LAND OF LOST CONTENT

The mirror reflected exactly who she wished to be: Urvashi, the successful social media influencer who gave her 323K followers the full female experience and then some.

Grey paisleys on a yellow chiffon sari #HouseofChiffon Boutique, a string of South Sea pearls #GNCJewels, the silver cuff that glinted a dull steel when she raised her hand to sweep back a strand of grey hair #jazzisalon, everything about Urvashi said: Look at me, isn't this who you want to be?

She fixed her phone on the gimbal and moved into position, then used the Bluetooth clicker to turn on the video. She walked a few steps towards the camera and did a slow pirouette till her sari became a yellow cloud. She flung the pallu over her left shoulder and adjusted the drape so she was all flowy grace and demure sexiness. She pinned the edge of the pallu to her plain, U-neck sleeveless blouse with a tiny brass safety pin. It had become such a fad to wear mismatching saris and blouses that wearing a regular choli was now a statement.

It was all part of the aura she had created. Or as Gen Z would say, she had great aura points. *Let us be the women we want to be. Not the superwomen we are expected to be.*

She smiled at the eye of the camera and spoke to the phone as if it were her best friend: Off to an art show, followed by lunch with the Grey Girls Group. We call ourselves that—GGG.

She tucked a strand of hair behind her ear, waved her signature two-finger goodbye and walked towards the door.

The first part of her reel for the day was done. It would be both a reel and a story. She could already see the hashtag: #GRWM 'GetReadyWithMe'. Being an influencer wasn't as easy as people presumed. So much planning and preparation went into content creation. She still blanched at the word 'content', but there was no escaping it.

Urvashi switched off the camera. The art show was at a new gallery in Hegde Nagar, not too far from home. I'll call for a cab in a few minutes, she decided, humming under her breath as she put the gimbal away in its case.

From the living room, she could hear the studied intonation of a podcast host—something about why the truth never works. She thought again of Mahesh's pretence of indifference to the way his professional standing had crumbled in the past few years. He probably didn't deserve what had happened, but it had anyway.

The Me Too allegations about his business partner had siphoned away several existing clients and the bad press had destroyed the possibility of new ones. Before long, the business had wrapped up for good. Mahesh was a man in mourning, and he had made it his life.

The divorce she had wanted was put on hold. You can't kick a man when he's down, she told herself. Fortunately, their apartment went for a princely sum. They would have to live off that and their savings until Mahesh could set up a new company. He said he was in discussions about it.

Meanwhile, they had rented a villa in a gated community at the other end of the city. A new home was a new start, he said.

Everything here was new. None of the neighbours knew that the Trapeze that had filled the newspapers and news sites had been Mahesh's. They saw them as yet another couple who had chosen to abandon the city life for the near bucolic bliss of a gated community replete with birds, bees and orderly lines of avenue trees.

Just when Urvashi had made up her mind to ask Mahesh for a divorce, a little virus had cast its giant shadow over the world. A divorce. A new life. All of it seemed insignificant when getting through each day felt momentous: I survived today.

During the lockdown, Urvashi and Mahesh had negotiated a new way of living that let them share a house, if not a life. It was around this time that Urvashi started creating content, and soon, the divorce no longer seemed important. Book reviews, movie ratings, gardening tips, cooking reels, sari drapes, wardrobe reveals ... It felt like a reinvention.

Once, Urvashi had been a journalist with a by-line that a certain kind of reader watched out for. But that was before journalists stopped being journalists and media houses turned into mouthpieces for plutocrats and their sycophants.

In this new avatar, Urvashi no longer sought stories. The world could turn on its own without her having to nudge it along. Wars, elections. Stock-market crashes, rapes, caste murders, corrupt politicians, bank scams—once, all of these would have found their way into her columns. But now, if she switched on the TV, it was to watch a film or a show on one of the OTT platforms. Almost as if reading her mind, the news feed on her phone threw up Bollywood gossip, propagation tips for hydrangeas, details of a sari Nita Ambani had worn to an event, reasons why you should never throw away your boarding passes, and so on.

Urvashi learnt to be several people so she would never have to look into the eyes of the woman who had fallen into a rut and didn't know how to escape it. It was simpler to be the gregarious social media influencer, the smiling friend, the aloof neighbour. And when that deep vault of sorrow threatened to fling its steel doors open, she learnt to summon the apostle of denial: I won't think about this, I won't. Sometimes, as she strolled through the gated community, she told herself, I have this at least: the city kept at arm's length, a home in an oasis of green where the trees grow quietly large.

She heard her mobile ring and glanced at the number. It wasn't one she recognised, but she took the call. The organisers of the art show, she assumed, to check if she was on her way.

A woman's voice. 'Is this Urvashi?'

She didn't recognise the voice but she recognised the almost impatient tone that ran like an undercurrent in calls from anyone who had anything to do with the government. She hoped it wasn't from the Income Tax Department. Her CA had said that the service tax issue from her influencer income had been sorted. So what could this be about?

'Yes, who is this?' she asked, mirroring the caller's impatience.

'Please hold while I transfer your call.'

'Who are you?' Urvashi demanded, but what she got in response was music. She went to sit in the chair by the large window that overlooked the front garden. Who chose the music for when they kept people on hold? Music that did nothing but fill the silence and was punctuated by a beat that seemed to promise immediate deliverance: a human voice.

A crow pheasant strutted across the tiny lawn. A rectangular patch of orderliness in a garden otherwise overwhelmed by her husband's plans for a wilderness. He would have taken over the lawn too, if she hadn't thrown a fit, as he called it. 'I need a patch of green, a *neat* piece of green for my videos. I can't stand in the middle of an untended garden and give my motivational spiel. They want my manicured life. They don't want to see your pampas grass or *Asystasia gangetica*. It's a dissonance that could make me lose followers. And we need my income to pay the bills, Mahesh,' she had said in a voice that didn't allow any further arguments.

The music stopped and another impatient voice came on. 'Madam, we are calling from Delhi Customs. There is a package with your name as the sender.'

Urvashi sighed. She received several packages from various brands. One of the perks that came with having 323K followers was how brands wooed you with freebies. So far, she had avoided obviously paid for partnerships lest it take away from her credibility. But she didn't send out anything. So what did the man mean? Why couldn't these fools check before calling her?

The man grunted and switched to Hindi. 'Is this your address?' he asked, reading out the full address.

'Yes,' she said, not bothering to hide her annoyance.

He continued in Hindi, 'You sent a parcel to an address in Malaysia.'

'I haven't sent anything to anyone. Besides, I don't know anyone in Malaysia.' Her voice rose, as she tried to find the words in Hindi, a language she had learnt in school and had no use for until she moved to Bengaluru. She had to dredge her memory to be able to speak to autorickshaw drivers and street vendors when they pretended not to understand Tamil or English. Over the years she had picked up a smattering of Kannada, making her Hindi even more garbled.

'The parcel has books in it. Hidden inside the books are fifteen ATM cards, seven expired passports and 25 grams of MDMA,' he said.

'What?'

'Do you know what MDMA is?' His voice was gentle. Before she could answer, he added, 'It's drugs. Illegal substance.'

'But I didn't send any package to anyone,' Urvashi said, certain she could sort this out with the simple truth.

'Did you use your Aadhaar card recently?' he asked in a voice that sounded weary.

'I'm sure I did. We all use it all the time, don't we? As ID proof. For travel. For hotel bookings. For Digiyatra.'

'Looks like a case of identity theft,' he said, sounding sympathetic. Then, as if to console her, he added, 'We see so many cases. Madam, I'm going to connect the call to the CBI desk attached to the Customs department. They will be handling this. But, madam, please be prepared to visit Delhi to sort this out.' She heard him pressing buttons and his voice murmuring to the person who came on about case #201/B2 320. 'Probable case of identity theft,' he said.

Urvashi rose from the chair. She glanced towards the living room, wondering whether she should call out to Mahesh.

Then she hesitated. There was no knowing what Mahesh would say or how he would react. It was quite likely he would tell her this was her ROI on time spent on social media. And who said returns on investment had to always be positive? He'd pause, flick his hair and grandstand: I know you think there will be no consequences to putting yourself out there, but there's always a consequence for every action.

Another voice came on, also impatient. Another man. Were there no female police officers? Urvashi glanced at the time. 11.40 a.m. She was already late.

The new man said he was Sub-Inspector Manish Sharma. Urvashi didn't know what to say. So she said hello.

He said brusquely, 'This is a serious offence. Smuggling drugs. It's best you be honest. Did you send this?'

Urvashi sighed. 'I told the other officer already. I have nothing to do with this package.'

There was silence from the other end. Then, 'Who else stays with you?'

'My husband.'

'Children?'

'We don't have children.'

'I see,' Manish Sharma sounded thoughtful. 'Have you used your ID proof recently? Aadhaar or passport?'

Urvashi frowned. She had travelled abroad on a sponsored trip to Zanzibar. It had involved travelling to Mumbai and a night's stay at a hotel before she boarded the Kenya Airways flight.

'Yes,' Urvashi said. 'I went to Zanzibar. That's an African country,' she added, unsure if Manish Sharma had ever heard of it. She didn't think he would have heard of Freddie Mercury either.

'On work or vacation?'

'Work,' Urvashi said, hoping he wouldn't ask about her line of work.

'What do you do?' Manish Sharma had switched to speaking in Hindi.

Urvashi fumbled for the word for journalist in Hindi. Eventually she mumbled, 'Patrakaar. And social media influencer.'

'So you have a public profile.' He had switched back to English.

'Yes, yes,' she said.

He sighed. 'You are an educated woman. You should have been more careful. Haven't you read about such cases of identity theft? Do you realise the seriousness of this matter?'

Urvashi felt a bead of sweat trickle down her back. She walked to the switchboard, cradling the phone between ear and shoulder, and turned the fan regulator to maximum speed. 'What do I do, Officer?' A friend of hers had said that it was best to call them officers, even if they were only constables. Makes them feel important and hence more easy to deal with, he had claimed.

'Hold on,' Manish Sharma said. 'We need to check if your identity has been used for anything else. You really should have been careful, Urvashiji.' She smiled. Her friend had been right. The 'officer' had worked its magic. She walked back to the chair.

The line crackled with static. Manish Sharma must be talking to someone in the control room. She got up again and walked to the mirror to check her face. Her makeup had already begun to run. She wondered if she should turn the air conditioning on. But this should be over soon, and she would have to leave immediately afterwards. She turned on the phone speaker and pulled the curtains shut. She would redo her face once the call was over.

'Madam,' her phone spat at her. She looked at it as if it were Manish Sharma.

'Yes, Officer,' she said, surprised at his change of tone from helpful public service official to custodian of law.

The 'officer' didn't work. Instead, he said, 'It's best if you tell me right now if you are involved in any criminal activity.'

What constitutes criminal activity? Smoking a joint? Getting into the swimming pool without showering? Pilfering a disposable toilet seat cover from Terminal 1 of Bengaluru airport?

'No, Officer. Not at all.' Urvashi was firm.

'That's not true. There's an FIR registered with your name as the accused.'

'I don't think that's right, sir,' she said, grinding out the 'sir' through clenched teeth. For a brief moment, she wondered if this was about Mahesh and his rants on LinkedIn because, though he disdained all social media, LinkedIn was different. It was a watering hole for corporates and professionals, he claimed.

'It's best you admit your involvement. You do know that we'll get to the truth and then there will be no way out.'

'No, sir,' Urvashi stuttered. 'What is the case, sir?'

'Human trafficking and money laundering,' he said. She could almost see his lips curl in disgust.

'What?' she yelped and then, strangely, she giggled—this was obviously a prank.

'This isn't a joke. Human trafficking is a very, very serious case, madam. As is money laundering.'

She took a deep breath to calm herself. What the fuck! 'Human trafficking and money laundering?' Her voice rose. 'Are you sure?'

'The FIR was registered by a woman whose husband has gone missing in Malaysia. Haven't you read about the case of twenty-three men who went to Malaysia on work and then disappeared? The wife of one of these men filed a missing case. The inquiry was transferred to the CBI by the Supreme Court. So once again, madam, it's best you admit to the truth. According to the case sheet, you and your team reached out to him and set up the job and also organised his travel.'

'I'm telling you I know nothing about this,' Urvashi snapped.

'Madam, India's population is three billion. Why is it that your name is in the FIR and not anyone else's?'

Urvashi heard the front door slam. Where was Mahesh going? Wait, she wanted to holler.

'I don't know, sir,' she said, suddenly realising this was for real. The allegation, the voice, the phone, the implication. 'Didn't you say that it could be a case of identity theft?'

'That's a different case. This is a CBI inquiry. And the way a CBI inquiry happens is quite different from a Customs investigation.'

'I know,' Urvashi said, trying to claw her way back into the unravelling narrative. 'I used to be a journalist.'

'I see,' Manish Sharma said. 'Then you know we're only doing our job and you need to answer some questions so I can take it to my senior officer.'

Urvashi didn't reply. What was she going to do? Whom could she call?

You can fight everything on your own: an uneasy marriage, an aborted career, wrinkles, greying hair, credit card disputes, surly staff, termites—anything but the system. How do you fight that on your own? How do you take on a system that could lock you in a cell and throw away the key?

'Yes, sir,' she mumbled, hating the sound of her meek voice.

'Urvashiji, I'm going to cut the call. I'll call you from our official WhatsApp number. It will be a video call. We have permission from WhatsApp to record this call,' he said, even as she opened her mouth to tell him that WhatsApp didn't let you record calls. 'Please connect your phone to a charger. It will be a long call. But first, tell me where you are.'

'I am at home,' Urvashi said.

'The address in your ID proof?'

'Yes.'

'Who's there with you?'

'No one, sir. I'm alone here.'

'Good,' he said. 'It's very important that you don't mention this to anyone. No relatives or friends. This is very confidential, and it's for your safety as well. But first, take down my name and designation, my badge number and your case number.'

Urvashi felt her clothes sticking to her. She sent a hasty message to the art gallery owner pleading a wrenched back. She copy-pasted the same message to the Grey Girls Group.

Oh no … how terrible, darling. Get well soon, will be thinking of you. The responses from the gallery owner and her friends were identical. She wondered if they were both using ChatGPT or if the world had been reduced to stock phrases. *At least I pleaded a bad back instead of a headache*, she thought with a wry smile.

She sent Mahesh a message. *Where are you? When will you be back?*

And then she remembered. Mahesh was gone until Tuesday evening. He was checking into a Vipassana retreat. 'You know what that means, don't you?' he had said, as if explaining it to a truculent three-year-old. 'I won't be reachable till Tuesday. I'll have to leave my phone at the reception when I check in. They give it back after the retreat is done.'

She wondered who she could reach out to. But just then, the phone rang. The long, persistent note of a WhatsApp call.

She picked up the phone and held it in front of her. The video came on, and for a fleeting moment, she saw a man in a police uniform in what seemed like an official looking space.

Urvashi felt her mouth go dry. What on earth was happening? Until now, it had seemed like a misunderstanding. Something that could be cleared up in a few minutes. But no longer.

The man disappeared from the screen and was replaced by the official CBI insignia.

'Urvashiji, once again, please note down my details. I am Sub-Inspector Manish Sharma. I'm sending a picture of my ID card to your WhatsApp number.

'Please connect your phone to a charger. This is being recorded and in your own best interest, please speak the truth and don't hide anything from us. We'll find every little detail even if you don't tell us,' the disembodied voice continued.

Urvashi moved to the chair by the window and plugged the charger into the switchboard. She had a power bank lying around somewhere. But for now, she was shackled to a wire.

As she turned her attention back to the video call, a bizarre image struck her between the eyes: a prisoner manacled to a chain suspended from a wall—dishevelled hair, dirt-crusted fingernails, torn clothes. The prisoner had her face.

Urvashi felt a shooting pain along the length of her left leg. Sciatica, her old foe had appeared again.

The condition had settled once they moved out of their old apartment and put behind them the judgemental glances and muttered exclamations of, 'Disgusting. If his partner was pouncing on young girls, he must have been doing it too.' But here it was, having resurfaced in a more vicious form.

In the next hour and a half, Manish Sharma asked her a hundred questions, if not more. She stopped counting after the first ten. Every once in a while, he would crack the whip. 'Please state only the truth. We'll find it even if you hide it from us.'

'No, Officer,' she would protest, the fight having leeched out of her long ago. 'I have nothing to hide. I'm innocent.' She said it again and again.

Name. Age. Number of bank accounts. What is the balance in each of them? Why do you have a State Bank of India account when you only have a minimum balance in it? Cooking gas subsidy? But the subsidy isn't being paid these days and you still have the account?

Number of properties owned. Nil? What about the house you are living in? Husband's name, age, bank accounts. What do you mean you don't know how many bank accounts he has?

Number of vehicles owned. Year of purchase. Do you own a car registered in someone else's name?

She was filled with fatigue. Her mouth had run dry with all the affirmations and denials. She hadn't stopped sweating since the officer had sent her his identity card. Urvashi wished she could curl up in bed, pull the cover over her head and fall asleep to wake up and find it was all a bad dream.

But Manish Sharma wasn't going everywhere. She glanced at the clock. Almost half past one. The clock was fifteen minutes behind, and no matter how many times it was set, it slowed down by fifteen minutes. She had been on the phone for almost two hours now.

'The preliminary investigation is over. I'm going to take your file to my senior officer. He'll decide what to do next,' he said abruptly.

'I would like to call my lawyer now,' she said.

Manish Sharma's sigh was long and impatient. 'I told you, madam, that you can't speak about this to anyone. I have sent you a confidentiality statement which states that this is an ongoing investigation and a matter of national security.'

'I understand,' she said quietly. Her arms and legs felt leaden. An excruciating pain ran down her back, along her left thigh, to her ankle.

He must have seen her wince, for he asked, 'Are you alright?'

'Yes, yes,' she said quickly.

'Urvashiji, I am going to take this to the additional director, Anil Kumar Yadav. I can see that you have been implicated wrongly. The AD who handles serious crimes is a very experienced man. If anyone can help you, it's him. He has been in a meeting all morning. If the stars are in your favour, he will be in his office. Please cooperate with him, madam, so the investigation can be closed and your name cleared at the earliest. Do you understand?'

She heard static in the distance. A crackling of the wireless. She imagined Manish Sharma walking down a long corridor speckled with people of all shapes and sizes. She saw him pause outside a brown door. Slung from the adjacent wall was a wooden board. White letters spelt out: Anil Kumar Yadav, Additional Director.

Manish Sharma suddenly muttered in her ear, 'Urvashiji, please cooperate with the investigation like you have done until now. I hope your phone is attached to the charger. And please be polite. These big officers have egos bigger than the rooms they sit in.'

She heard him knock on the door. Heard the door creak as he pushed it open. Heard him say, 'Jai Hind, sir.'

She heard a low-voiced grunt in response.

Manish Sharma rattled off a case number and the details of the case in brief. 'Looks like identity theft, sir. Urvashiji has been very cooperative with us until now,' he finished.

He seemed to be handing over his phone to his senior. 'Good afternoon, Ms Urvashi. I am Anil Kumar Yadav, Additional Director, Serious Crimes Division. Tell me ...'

Something about the even timbre of his deep voice, the choice of words and his educated accent, the quiet authority of his tone—all of it filled her with reassurance. She was finally talking to someone who was on her social level, not some cog in the wheel. Urvashi almost sighed in relief but caught her breath in time.

She cleared her throat and began, 'Good afternoon, sir ...' The old clock on the wall chimed two.

'My name is Urvashi Varma. I am a journalist, and I received a call this morning ...' She narrated a summary of her conversation with the Customs person followed by Manish Sharma.

'I see,' Anil Kumar Yadav said in a voice devoid of emotion.

In the ensuing silence, Urvashi rushed to establish her credentials. 'I'm a journalist, though I have now moved to the world of social media. I used to write for *India Today* and the *Times of India* and then I went freelance.'

'Ms Urvashi, I thought I recognised your name,' he interrupted. 'So, I did a quick search on you even as we were talking, and I must confess I am truly embarrassed to be interrogating you.'

Once again, Urvashi knew relief; she was talking to someone who could see the impossibility of what she had been accused of. 'Thank you, sir, for saying that,' she responded around the lump in her throat.

'You do realise the charges against you are very serious. And I don't mean the contents of the parcel; I can deal with that easily. In fact, I'm doing it right now. I'll have the scanned image with me in a few minutes and send it to you.'

Urvashi could hear him mumble in Hindi. 'But this other case, those are serious criminal offences and a threat to national security,' he continued. 'I've sent you the rejection notice. You can take a look at it and call me back. But right away, you understand?'

When he cut the call, Urvashi opened her WhatsApp to find a new message from an unknown number. A PDF attachment with a message beneath:

This is my official number. Call me via WhatsApp.

Urvashi opened the attachment. It was from the office of the Commissioner of Customs (Airport & General), IGI Airport, Terminal 3. A case report, including the contents of the parcel, the recipient's name and address, a transaction ID. And there it was, her name, Aadhaar number and mobile number.

The notice was on an official letterhead with the insignia on top as well as a watermark on the sheet. A red seal stated: 'Rejected'.

Urvashi called the number. He picked up almost instantly. 'Hello, Ms Urvashi,' he said. 'As a matter of information, this call is being recorded. Please switch to the video call so you are visible.'

Urvashi's mouth was dry. 'Are you certain it's me and not some other Urvashi Varma?' She couldn't control the wobble in her voice.

'I know how hard this must be for you, Ms Urvashi. Unfortunately, the case has already been registered. I'm going to send you the Supreme Court website link and guide you on how to find the details of your case. Don't disconnect the phone. You can do it while talking to me.'

Urvashi mumbled her assent, feeling numb. A link popped up in her WhatsApp inbox.

'Click on the link you've just received,' he said. 'Now go to "Cases". I'm going to repeat your case number; you'll need to enter it there.'

She did as he asked. The Supreme Court website opened. She looked for the tabs—there it was, Cases. She clicked on that and he repeated the case number for her so she could enter it.

A drop of sweat fell on the phone screen. She mopped it quietly with the end of her sari, then daubed her brow.

'It isn't opening, sir,' she said.

Somewhere, a tiny matchstick flare of hope that this was all a ghastly mistake.

'You may have missed a digit. Let me say it again,' Anil Kumar Yadav said. His voice was gentle, his tone patient.

This time, the page opened and there it was, the details of her case. The petitioner, the crime, the details, her name in full and her ID.

Her eyes glazed as she read it again. This was for real. As it could get. She felt her face crumple.

A long time ago, a biscuit baron had been incarcerated and died within a year. He had been denied bail and medical assistance even though he was a rich and connected man. More recently, an aged priest with Parkinson's who had been accused of involvement in terrorism had languished in prison, denied a sipper or even a straw so he could drink water without spilling it. His medical bail had been rejected, and he had died in prison. A trade union and human rights lawyer accused of involvement in a conspiracy to kill the PM had been lodged in prison for three years and three months. A Delhi University professor, wheelchair bound, had spent a decade in jail over his alleged Maoist links. His release by a lower court had been overturned by the Supreme Court just a month ago. A young student activist accused of sedition four years ago was still in jail, awaiting trial, and had been denied bail again and again.

There was no higher appeal than the Supreme Court, and it was there that her name was listed as the prime accused in a case.

'What do I do, sir?' Her voice dropped to a whisper.

'Ms Urvashi, I can see this has shaken you. Trust me, any of us law-abiding citizens would feel the same. We believe in the law, but we also know that the law doesn't address grey areas. I can see you are innocent. I know it for a fact, but that isn't enough. We need to go through the process of investigation to prove you are innocent.

'I suppose Manish Sharma has already sent you the confidentiality agreement.'

'Yes,' Urvashi said, feeling her shoulder slump. The sciatic nerve twinged. That crippling, shooting pain ran up her leg once again. She felt her lower back spasm.

'Now I'm going to send you something that is just for your information. Please don't share it with anyone. Which means, please don't speak to anyone at all. Someone like you must have lawyer friends and connections in the police department, but you can't reach out to anyone. A journalist of your calibre must know that there is a nexus in which politicians, police officers and even judges are involved.

'Look at point one of the confidentiality agreement. It's as much for your protection as for the investigation. You may not leave the country and not even your residence without permission.

'The thing is, we do not know who is watching you. It's truly fortunate that the Customs case popped up and that Manish Sharma had the good sense to bring it to me immediately.'

There was a long pause.

'Look at what I sent you now,' Anil Yadav said.

Urvashi opened the PDF and gasped. It was a warrant of arrest issued by a first-class judicial magistrate. Once again, the details of the case were mentioned: stands charged with offences under 359, 360, 364A, 370, 390, 400, 411, 413 and 414 of IPC, concerned with human trafficking and money laundering.

'What am I going to do, sir?' she whispered.

Sweat ran down her face and back. Needles pricked the soles of her feet. What karmic sin was she paying for? And from which past birth? She twisted the end of her pallu with nervous fingers and then suddenly remembered that she was visible to Anil Kumar Yadav.

'Ms Urvashi, please wipe the sweat off. I can understand how tense you are. I'm going to help you get out of this. I promise. Please go drink a glass of cold water. Not water from the fridge, you should add ice cubes instead. That will cool you without causing any further shock to your system.'

Urvashi got up and went to the kitchen. She could hear the thumping of her heart in her ears.

She did as he had asked. Wiped her face and neck. Poured a glass of water and added ice cubes to it. She gulped it down thirstily.

She poured another glass and added more ice. She picked up the glass and a kitchen paper roll and went back to where Anil Kumar Yadav waited, watching her every move.

'You should turn the AC on,' he said.

She did as he asked: pulled the windows shut, turned the air conditioner on, then went back to the chair by the charging point.

'Feeling better?' The solicitous tone made her eyes prickle.

'Yes, sir. And thank you for being so considerate,' she replied.

'Ms Urvashi, I know that like everybody else you must think the police are a heartless bunch of scoundrels. But not all of us are. And it's not just you, I would do the same for anyone I know is innocent. I'm truly sorry for what you're going through.'

Urvashi took a sip of water. The air conditioner had cooled the room, but she could still feel the heat under her skin.

'We need to see what we can do because there is also an asset seizure order in your name. Again, issued by the court. I've sent it to you. Take a look at it.'

An asset seizure order to prevent fraudulent removal or concealment of property. The words blurred, then swam into focus. 'Sir, should I call my lawyer?' A friend's son was a lawyer in Delhi. A bright young man who could be counted on.

'No, no,' he said. 'Not yet. You'll need to call your lawyer at some point, but not right now. It would complicate matters. What we need to do is get everything notarised so it's legal,' Anil Kumar Yadav said, sounding vexed with her.

'But how do I do that without a lawyer?' Her voice rose above the whisper that had become her speaking voice for more than three hours now. As if to make amends, she said, 'I wouldn't even know where to begin, sir.'

He was silent, then asked, 'You are right now in Bengaluru?'

'Yes, sir.'

'You need to come to Delhi first thing Monday morning. So all of it can be done here.'

'I can do that, sir.'

'Good. But first, we need to do an estimate of assets. So, you have to share all details. Bank accounts with the current balance; any fixed deposits, RBI bonds, stocks and shares, immovable properties, vehicle registration numbers and details of jewellery you own. It's best if you share statements, property documents, vehicle RC books and bills for jewellery. I will do the estimate myself for you, Ms Urvashi. As I said earlier, I'm very embarrassed to have to interrogate you, but it has to be done. I'll try and make it as painless as possible.'

'Thank you, sir,' Urvashi whispered. The raging woman within her had been asked to shut the fuck up and stay put in its place.

'It's my duty. Once we start, we won't be able to stop for a couple of hours at least. So, if you need to use the washroom, please do it now. Leave the phone on and be back in five minutes.'

Grateful for the respite, Urvashi rushed to her bedroom. She unwound her sari and flung it on the bed, then removed the jewellery that felt like restraints. She pulled on a pair of track pants and a t-shirt and went into the bathroom to wash her face. For a long moment, she stared at herself in the mirror. The face of a fugitive stared back at her. She wondered if this was how it felt when you had your face injected with Botox. Like a rabbit caught in the headlights of a car. She giggled, then slapped herself hard on the face once, and then again, to quell the gathering hysteria. She had to stay calm. She had to hold herself together until this ended.

She washed her face again and briskly applied serum to soothe the stinging. Some concealer to hide the marks of her fingers. Lip balm to conceal the rawness of lips gnawed on since the morning.

As she walked out, she saw her laptop. Should she send Mahesh a quick SOS? It wasn't going to be of much use. If she was a fugitive from the law, Mahesh was busy being a fugitive from reality. That was how he had described his Vipassana retreat.

'You're late,' Anil Kumar Yadav barked.

'I'm sorry,' Urvashi apologised.

'Did you call someone when you went out of the room?'

'No, sir. I only have this phone.'

'What about email? I'm sure you have a laptop.'

'I do, but no, I didn't send an email to anyone.' Surely he could see that she was speaking the truth.

'Ms Urvashi, I'm making an exception for you here. I don't usually handle such clerical work. It's only because I feel sorry to see you in this position. But please don't make me regret it.'

'No, sir. I'm sorry, sir,' Urvashi stammered. 'I'm truly grateful. It's just that I feel like my body and mind have turned into a block of steel. I can't move or think.' The words rushed out garbled.

'It's fine,' he said. 'I understand what you must be going through. Please be cooperative and we can try and sort this out ASAP. So, shall we start the listing?' His gentleness was like a clasp of hands: Don't worry, I'm here.

She heard a bell ring. She heard Anil Kumar Yadav say: 'Paani lao.' And then he continued in Hindi, 'I am on a very important call. No visitors until I say so.'

Urvashi took a deep breath and tried to relax. Then he was back. 'Well, Ms Urvashi, let's begin with the bank accounts. How many bank accounts do you have?'

She had already told Manish Sharma everything. For a moment she debated telling him this, then changed her mind. He was going out on a limb for her and it was in her best interest to cooperate.

She detailed the two bank accounts she used. 'Sir, I also have a State Bank of India account. But I don't use it at all. I used it only to receive the cooking gas subsidy the PM had promised when the prices went up.'

'Hmm. What is the balance in both accounts?'

'I have forty thousand rupees in one account and ninety-two thousand five hundred and three rupees in the other.'

'The first thing we need to do is notarise the balances. Please bring your laptop.'

When she brought the laptop, he said, 'Now keep it facing the phone so I can monitor it. How much is the minimum balance required?'

'Twenty-five thousand, sir. Both accounts.'

'I see. Please retain the minimum balance and transfer the rest to the account details I am sending you. I'll send you the receipt in an hour's time. Once the investigation is over and we establish that you have been wrongly accused, you can produce the receipt and the court will reverse the sum to your account.'

Urvashi opened her laptop and logged into the net banking website of one of the accounts. She transferred the balance to her other account.

'Good,' he said, when she told him it was done. 'Now transfer the ninety-two thousand five hundred and three rupees to the details sent in Form 5.'

Urvashi opened the PDF. It was from the Reserve Bank of India and was an application for fund legalisation issued by the New Delhi Notary Public Office bearing the watermark of Ashoka's lions and the legend Satya Meva Jayate. Truth shall prevail.

Truth would prevail, Urvashi told herself as she transferred the money to the account number provided in the document.

'It's done, sir. I've sent the receipt to myself on WhatsApp and am forwarding it to you,' Urvashi said. Surely, he could see for himself that she had nothing to hide.

'What deposits, bonds and shares do you hold?'

'I don't have any fixed deposits or RBI bonds sir. And my portfolio is managed by a wealth manager. I don't remember the details.'

'I see. What is the value of your portfolio?'

Urvashi gnawed on her lips. 'It's a family portfolio. So, it includes both my husband's and mine. I don't know the full value of the portfolio as I receive statements only for mine, which is about forty-five lakh, sir.'

'I see. You will have to call your wealth manager and ask him to transfer the funds to you. The stock market is closed on Saturdays. I suggest you speak to him later today and start the process on Monday. Have you booked your flight to Delhi?'

Urvashi wondered what Mahesh would say to her pulling out her share of the money received from the sale of their apartment. It was her entire life's earnings. But it wasn't as if she had a choice.

'Yes, sir, I'll speak to him. And I'll book the tickets once we finish here.'

'Good. Let's now move to the properties you hold.'

'Nothing in my name. We don't own any property. We live in a rented house.'

'Inherited property?'

'Nothing, sir. What I had was sold when we bought our apartment. And we sold that two years ago and moved into the house we live in.'

'Tell me a bit about your husband and what he does,' Anil Kumar Yadav asked after a pause.

Where do I begin, she wanted to say.

'He has retired now, and we lead a very quiet life,' she said.

'What about jewellery?'

'I have some jewellery. What my parents gave me at my wedding. And what I bought myself,' Urvashi said, her mind sorting through the contents of the safe in their bedroom where the jewellery was kept.

'I suppose you have a bill for every item.'

'Not for what my parents gave me,' Urvashi said, the heaviness in her chest intensifying. Would those heavy pieces be seen as unaccounted wealth?

'You have your wedding photo, don't you? Send me that as well as the bills for everything else at the earliest.'

'Yes, sir,' Urvashi said, wondering where she was going to locate them.

'So, Ms Urvashi, we'll stop for now. But you are going to have to follow certain rules.

'First, you can't leave your residence without informing me. We have placed you under digital arrest. Any deviation, and your local station will pay you a visit. And you don't need me to tell you what that will be like. And the effect on your neighbours.'

'No, sir, I'm not stepping out,' Urvashi interrupted hastily. She didn't think she could survive another round of neighbourly scrutiny.

'You can't call or email anyone. Your phone and email will be monitored. I hate to admit it, but now that the investigation has begun, the criminals involved in this would also have understood and they'll be watching you as well. In fact, I'm quite certain that your phone is being tapped as well. Which is why we are using WhatsApp for the questioning.'

'Oh.' Urvashi's hand flew to her mouth. 'Oh my god!'

'Don't worry. We're here to make sure nothing happens to you. But sometimes people don't understand the danger they are in and do stupid things. Like throwing their SIM card away or leaving town. These days, anyone can be traced. It's just a matter of time. So, please follow what I say carefully and diligently.'

'Sure, sir, I understand. I really do.'

'You need to call me every hour. Make it a voice call, and when I tell you to, you can turn the video on. I've held back the look-out notice in your name. But if you fail to report at any point, I'll have to release it. Also, you need to book your ticket to Delhi and send me the details. Meanwhile, start sending me the jewellery bills. I've just sent you the acknowledgement for the amount that was notarised. That's it for now. Trust me, Ms Urvashi, we'll sort this out. And remember I expect you to answer each time I call, no matter what time of the day or night. It's 15:30 hrs now. I will expect your first call at 17:00 hrs.'

The phone went dead.

I won't think about it now. I'm just going to do my chores and get on with my day, Urvashi told herself over and over again. She detached the charger cable from her phone. She turned off the AC and went to the kitchen. She held onto the kitchen counter and tried to take deep breaths. Instagram gurus advocated multiple ways to calm down, but all she could remember was what her mother used to tell her when she was a little girl. Drink a glass of water and count backwards from ten to one. She took a bottle of water and drank it in one continuous stream until it went up her nose and she spluttered and retched.

She rushed to the bathroom and hurled into the toilet bowl. When her stomach was emptied, the retching began again; a dry retching that almost tore her throat with its ferocity. Eventually, it stopped.

Urvashi rinsed her mouth and began cleaning the bathroom. She scrubbed the floor. It was something to do.

Her arms ached, but she started on the tiles on the walls next. When there was nothing left to scrub and clean, she pulled her clothes off and stood under the shower. The water was warm from the day's heat, but she was shivering.

She dried herself and pulled on a kaftan. She hadn't had anything to eat since dinner. It was her day for intermittent fasting, and her stomach growled. The thought of making and eating food, any sort of food, felt overwhelming. But she needed to eat.

There was some leftover rice in the fridge. She heated it and added curd to it. A while ago, on one of her journalistic assignments, she had spoken to a mahout. They were talking about elephants running amok at the temple festivals in Kerala, and he told her about his secret recipe that was guaranteed to lull an elephant into a soporific calm: hot rice with curd. 'I don't know why the animal is always much calmer after eating it,' he had grinned, 'but it works each time. And none of the elephants in my care have ever created any trouble.'

The hot rice and curd tasted like chalk. She forced herself to eat a few mouthfuls and tipped the rest into the wet-waste bin.

Perhaps a cup of tea will help, she thought, putting a saucepan of water on the hob. She made the tea strong and sweet, and drank it slowly. Then she went to the bathroom and vomited again.

Just as she had finished rinsing her mouth and crept into bed, the alarm rang. She had to message Anil Kumar Yadav. She picked up her phone.

His response was almost immediate.

–Have you booked your ticket to Delhi?–

–Just about to, sir– she texted back. She had put off booking the flight in the hope that this would all go away somehow, that there would be no need to travel, after all.

–Where will you be staying?–

–My friend in Saket. He is a journalist.–

–No, you can't stay with friends or family. Check into a hotel. Send me the details of the hotel booking.–

Urvashi put the phone down. She would do everything he asked her to, and only that.

She started looking for a flight. The cheapest ones were late in the night. That wouldn't work. She needed a clear head for her Monday morning meeting with Anil Kumar Yadav. By the time she booked a mid-morning flight and found an affordable hotel, her time was up.

She messaged Anil Kumar Yadav. She used the word he had used when he instructed her. –Reporting sir.–

A moment later, the piercing WhatsApp call.

'Good evening, Ms Urvashi, where are you now?' His voice cordial, but flat as always.

'I am at home, sir,' she said.

'Have you booked your ticket?'

'Yes, sir.' She sent him her flight details and the hotel booking acknowledgement.

'Good,' he said.

Urvashi felt a burst of happiness. She was a child again, joyful and filled with a sense of validation by the five gold stars her teacher had stuck on her homework.

'Have you started sorting the bills and documents?'

'I'll start once this call is over.'

'Very well.'

When he cut the call, she felt bereft. As long as he was speaking to her, she could believe that she would emerge from this nightmare. With him at her side, she would surmount every problem.

She started with the jewellery receipts. And then, because she had always been the sort of child who worked on her school projects with an almost manic alacrity, she took pictures of every piece of jewellery mentioned in each bill.

7 p.m. –Reporting sir.–

–Good.–

8 p.m. –Reporting sir.–

–(Thumbs up emoji) Who is there at home?–

–No one sir. I told you my husband is away.–

–I hope you haven't invited anyone home. That would break the conditions of the digital arrest.–

–No sir. I remember what you said–

9 p.m. –Reporting sir.–

–(Thumbs up emoji)–

Urvashi wondered if she was expected to ping through the night. At a quarter to ten, Anil Kumar Yadav called. 'Hello, Ms Urvashi. Have you had dinner yet?'

'No, sir.'

'Why not? Not your dinner time yet? Or not hungry?'

'Not hungry, sir. As you can understand.'

'Ms Urvashi, what you are going through is unfortunate. But trust me, we'll get you out of this. So please don't starve. You are going to need your strength in the days to come.'

'Yes, sir. Thank you,' she said. She wondered if she was crossing a line but couldn't help asking, 'Have you had dinner, sir?'

He chuckled. A low, throaty chuckle. She understood it to be ironical when he said, 'I am still in office. I usually leave by ten.'

'Oh.'

'You know what they say: with power comes responsibility. Anyway, you don't need to text me anymore tonight. I'll expect the next one at 6 a.m. Please continue to cooperate as you've done until now and this will be over quickly.'

'Yes, sir,' she said.

'Well, Ms Urvashi, good night. Please eat something and try and get some sleep.'

Urvashi had three food delivery apps on her phone, but she didn't bother scrolling. She ordered Chinese, but when it came, she didn't feel like eating. She went back to photographing the receipts and the jewellery. When that was done, all she wanted to do was sleep. But she had to pack. In her head Anil Kumar Yadav murmured in his low baritone: You must eat. You need to be strong, Ms Urvashi.

So Urvashi forced herself to eat a quarter of the mixed American Chop Suey. The prawn and chicken tasted like plumped up thermocol.

She pulled out a suitcase and stared at it. How many days should she pack for? She wished she had asked Anil Kumar Yadav, but she'd been fearful of irritating him.

Almost as if he were telepathic, her phone beeped: –Please prepare to stay for 4–5 days at least.–

She packed her suitcase and took it to the living room. The wall clock chimed eleven. She should go to bed now, she told herself, even though she knew she wouldn't be able to sleep.

She went through her bedtime rituals meticulously. As long as she had things to do, her thoughts wouldn't stray to that sword of Damocles that swayed over her head by a thread: what if even Anil Kumar Yadav couldn't help her?

The bathroom still bore a faint stench of vomit. Or was it the stench of distress? She no longer had the strength to resume cleaning the bathroom. In the bathroom cabinet was an aerosol that promised the fragrance of an ocean breeze. She sprayed it across the bathroom. In the mirror, the woman's eyes had a maniacal gleam.

She brushed her teeth. One by one, she dealt with each tooth. Then she flossed. Tasted blood. She was doing it all wrong, but it was something to do.

She daubed cream on her face and neck and moisturised her hands. She got into her oldest nightie. Time and hundreds of spin cycles had washed out all resistance from the fabric, so it felt like a second skin.

She checked the doors and windows. That's when she saw a car parked near her gate. At a discreet distance, but not too far away. Who could it be? The gated community she lived in had a multi-layered security protocol. In a neighbourhood where all the cars were high-end, an ordinary sedan was conspicuous.

She pinged Anil Kumar Yadav. –Sir, there is a car parked near my gate. Should I worry? Should I call the police?–

–No need to call the police. I organised it for your safety. Please don't worry. We just want to ensure you are safe. Good night, Ms Urvashi–

Urvashi got into bed prepared for a long and sleepless night. When the alarm rang, she woke up instantly. For a moment, she stretched her limbs, feeling remarkably refreshed. Then she remembered the happenings of the day before.

She sat up abruptly and checked her phone. She would need to shower, dress and leave for the airport by 6.30 a.m. Before that, at 6 a.m., she had to report to Anil Kumar Yadav. But first, she would drink tea in the biggest cup she could find. She wished Mahesh hadn't given up smoking. There would have been cigarettes at home then.

The night before, she had done a quick search of the CBI website. There was a photograph of Anil Kumar Yadav with a mention of his IPS batch and details of his police career in the Madhya Pradesh cadre before he was transferred to the Central Bureau of Investigation. He had led some high-profile investigations. She had studied the man's face. The fleshy clean-shaven face, the hooked nose, the narrow eyes, the beginnings of a receding hairline. His face matched his voice. An amicable and no-nonsense man. She had felt reassured that this was the man who was watching out for her safety and wellbeing.

At six, she pinged him and received a thumbs-up almost instantly.

7 a.m. –Reporting sir. On my way to the airport. Should be there in 15 minutes–

Anil Kumar Yadav called. She accepted the video call.

'You are on your way to the airport?'

'Yes, sir, my flight is at 9.30 a.m.'

'I know,' he said. 'Ms Urvashi, I have some good news for you.'

'Yes, sir.'

'I have managed to get the court's approval to conduct a remote investigation in your case. I had appealed to the judge last evening, but he issued the order only late last night and it just dropped into my mailbox. I am going to be personally in charge of the investigation. So you can cancel the flight and return home. I hope you are feeling a little relieved now. Message me when you are back home. We have a lot of work to do.'

The cab driver looked at her strangely when she beamed at him. 'My trip is cancelled. Could you please turn back?'

He didn't say anything, merely took a U-turn at the next junction. He was used to passengers snarling or becoming dejected when their travel plans were cancelled. But this woman was smiling as if she had won the lottery.

Urvashi hadn't known it was possible to feel this way. Ridiculously happy but also apprehensive. A child who has been given a rainbow to hold. The feeling persisted until she walked into her house and put her suitcase away. She would unpack later.

She pulled out her charger and plugged it near the chair that had suddenly become her favourite spot in the living room. Then she poured herself a tall glass of water. It was only a little past eight, but the heat was already pressing down from a cloudless blue sky.

She had been part of the agitation, both as a journalist and citizen, in the pre-pandemic days when the state government had decided to go ahead with building a nearly 7 km–long steel bridge. It would cost 1,800 crore rupees and entail cutting down 800 trees. Urvashi had stood on the roadside with a placard that said 'Steel Bridge Beda'. Although the National Green Tribunal had since ordered the suspension of all such plans, the threat still loomed.

'Cut a few more trees, assholes,' she muttered as she turned on the AC. 'And turn this into a furnace from hell, fucking bastards!' The epithets dripped from her mouth with a felicity that surprised her. It felt cathartic, made her feel in control. So, she said a few more fuck yous, took a sip of water and called Anil Kumar Yadav.

He didn't pick up. He was probably in the bathroom, she told herself. She messaged him.

–Reached home sir. Tried calling you.–

There was no response. Where was he? He had asked her to call him. So why wasn't he picking up her call or responding to her message? Her stomach began churning again.

She walked to the window and stared at the lawn unseeingly. A group of raucous mynas were parading on it. She turned her gaze to avoid the lone 'one for sorrow' myna and sought out a pair or three. There they were. Two for joy. Three for a letter.

Her phone rang. She felt her heart lift when she saw it was Anil Kumar Yadav.

'I was at the ministry. We had an emergency meeting. Which is why I couldn't respond to your call or message,' he said. Not being apologetic, just matter of fact.

'On a Sunday?'

'National security doesn't know weekdays or Sundays, madam.'

'Yes, of course,' she said hastily, afraid that she had offended him.

'Well, let's get started. Have you taken photocopies of the jewellery bills?'

'I've got pictures of the receipts on my phone. I was going to get them printed in Delhi, sir,' she said. 'Also, I've added a photograph of each piece of jewellery to support the bills I have.'

'I see. Just WhatsApp me the bills and photos. I'll have them printed here and add them to your file. The asset legalisation we did yesterday will also be part of the file. We'll need to do an asset legalisation of the jewellery as well.'

'What does that mean, sir?'

'You'll have to sell the jewellery and have the amount notarised like we did with the balance in your savings account.'

Urvashi bit her lip and tasted blood. 'Sir, I don't have bills for every piece of jewellery. I had mentioned earlier that some of it was from my parents.'

'Yes, I remember.' He sounded displeased. A moment later, he said, 'I had asked you to add a wedding photo to the jewellery pictures.'

'I can do that,' Urvashi said, relieved. Mahesh was meticulous about his possessions from a box of pencils pilfered by his father from the Steel Works he had worked at, to his own first international boarding pass. There would definitely be a photo of their wedding.

'And what about the details of your stocks and shares?' he asked, breaking into her thoughts.

'I'll call my portfolio manager first thing in the morning.'

'All right, but make sure you don't delay. Also, send me the latest statements.'

After he cut the call with a reminder to start on the hourly reports, she remained slumped in the chair exhausted at the thought of everything that needed to be done.

10 a.m. –Reporting sir.–

–Thumbs-up emoji–

11 a.m. –Reporting sir. Sending photos of jewellery+bills. Also wedding photo–

She had found the wedding photo in an envelope marked '1997'. Behind the photograph Mahesh had written: Van Heusen trousers; Arrow shirt. LV Belt. Hugo Boss shoes. Armani watch. Urvashi: Kanjeevaram silk sari; jewellery–20 sovereigns. For once, she was glad that he was so meticulous about his possessions.

Anil Kumar Yadav responded almost instantly.

–Good. Let me go through them. Where is the statement?–

–Sending it right away, sir.–

Urvashi heard the clock chime half past twelve. She still had fifteen minutes to message him. She went back to the window.

The car was back and parked not too far from her gate. A man was leaning against it and looking at his phone. He looked like a policeman in his off-white half-sleeved shirt and fawn trousers. His haircut was a dead giveaway, she thought. Her phone rang.

'Hello, madam.' The low measured tone. Urvashi wondered what his heart rate was. Probably fifty-something.

'Hello, sir, I was just about to message you.'

'I thought let me surprise you.'

'Oh.'

'How are you feeling?'

'Very shaken, sir.'

'Still shaken? I thought you would be less stressed now that we are conducting a remote investigation.'

'I'm thankful for everything you are doing, sir. But each time I think of the arrest warrant or the case details on the Supreme Court website, I start trembling. I can't help it.'

'I can understand. But we'll get this sorted. I hope you haven't spoken to anyone about it.'

'No, sir.'

'What about your husband?'

'He's at a Vipassana retreat. They would have taken his phone away.'

'I see. When does he return?'

'Tuesday.'

'By the way, I kept thinking, you resemble someone.'

'Oh.'

'I'll send you a photo. Take a look and you'll see it for yourself. Alright then.'

1 p.m. –Reporting sir.–

–Thumbs-up emoji–

2 p.m. –Reporting sir.–

–Thumbs-up. Have you had lunch?–

–Yes sir.–

She had an apple for lunch. The crisp, juicy flesh tasted of nothing. It suddenly occurred to her that since her parents' passing, no one had ever asked her if she had eaten or slept. Her health and happiness had become her own responsibility. And here was a total stranger checking on her every hour. Someone who seemed invested in her wellbeing. She felt a wave of affection for the faceless man.

Urvashi drank from a bottle of water as she walked to the bedroom. She got into bed riding on the rose cloud of a stranger's kindness. She checked her inbox. He had sent a photograph of a Bollywood actress from the nineties. She didn't think she looked anything like her. Nevertheless, she messaged him.

–I can see the resemblance, sir.–

If he'd said she looked like Arnold Schwarzenegger, she would have agreed.

Urvashi and her phone watched the day turn into night.

At 8.45 p.m. Anil Kumar Yadav called. 'Have you had dinner, Ms Urvashi?'

'Not yet, sir. And you?'

'I'll have mine a little later. I've come to a colleague's home with my family.'

She thought of his wife and children with a stab of jealousy, almost resentful of the time he spent with them.

'Please eat something. There is no point in going off food or staying awake at night. We have a long day tomorrow. And don't forget to speak to your portfolio manager in the morning. We shouldn't delay the asset legalisation, or all your assets will be frozen.'

'Yes, sir, I understand. I've already messaged him saying we need to speak at eight o'clock.'

'What will you tell him?'

'The truth. That it's required for asset legalisation.'

'No, no, don't do that,' Anil Kumar Yadav cut in. 'Just tell him it's a family emergency.'

'Alright sir, I'll do that.'

'It's best you don't mention the investigation to anyone. Which is why I said you can't even call your lawyer. Remember the confidentiality clause you have agreed to. Goodnight, Ms Urvashi. You don't have to report any more tonight. But first thing tomorrow, please report to me at 6 a.m.'

'I will. And goodnight, sir.'

Urvashi woke up a little past five after a night of tossing and turning in bed. She sat up and stared at the sky through the window. There was a hum in her head. Like cicadas. A constant note that refused to pause. She went to the bathroom, peeled off her nightie and stood under the shower. The humming wouldn't stop, even through the cascading jets of water. This couldn't be right. This couldn't be right.

She made a cup of tea and took it with her to the chair by the window. She took a notepad and made a list of things to do:

- Call portfolio manager
- Ask A.K.Y if I can have the maid come over.
- Check with A.K.Y if I can go to the supermarket
- Remind A.K.Y to send the updated court order with sanction for remote investigation.

6 a.m. –Reporting sir.–
–Thumbs up–

7 a.m. –Reporting sir.–
–Thumbs up–

8 a.m. –Reporting sir.–
–Thumbs up–

Urvashi filled a bowl with muesli, chopped a banana and poured milk into the bowl. Her movements were sluggish. It was as if she couldn't summon her body or her mind to do her bidding. The humming in her head continued. She forced herself to eat the last spoonful. She had worried she would throw up, but surprisingly, she felt more like herself.

Her phone rang. 'Good morning, Ms Urvashi.'

'Good morning, sir.'

'I hope you slept well. Have you had breakfast?'

'I did. Thank you for asking.' His concern felt like a gentle caress. 'Sir, I wanted to check a few things with you.' She went through her list.

He heard her out, then said, 'You can ask the maid to come. But send her off after one hour. I don't want her hanging around. No visiting the supermarket. Don't you have a delivery app? The court order with the revised date will be issued today.' His tone had become brusque, official. 'Let me know when you have an update from your portfolio manager.' He sounded annoyed as he cut the call.

Urvashi began gnawing on her lip. What had made him sound so brusque? She glanced at the wall clock. It was almost nine. Surely Harsh Rao ought to be at work now. She called him. But the phone went unanswered.

9 a.m. –Reporting sir. Tried calling the portfolio manager. But no response.–

Urvashi waited for his customary thumbs up. But none appeared. She felt her legs go hollow. He was well and truly pissed off. The only person who had her back was upset with her.

She called Harsh Rao again. This time, he picked up. In the background, she heard a pressure cooker hiss. Why the fuck wasn't he at work? She held the phone away from her ear and pressed the record button. It was best that Anil heard what she said. That should convince him that she was doing her best to cooperate.

'Harsh, I need to pull out funds from my portfolio.'

'Yes, of course. How much?'

'All of it. I mean, all of my share.'

She could hear the frown in his voice when he asked, 'Isn't this rather sudden?'

'Family issues. And I need it right away.'

'Sure, let me start the paperwork. But it will take at least three or four days for it to reflect in your account.' Unable to hide his concern, he asked, 'Are you certain? It's a lot of money—forty-five lakh rupees. And that's your entire corpus, if I understand it right.'

'Yes, I'm certain,' she said.

Urvashi didn't wait for ten o'clock. She messaged Anil Kumar Yadav as soon as she cut the call.

–Have spoken to the portfolio manager. Sending you the recording so you can verify for yourself what I said.–

He called her immediately. 'Ms Urvashi, that's excellent news,' he said, his voice different from its usual blandness. 'And it's good that you are pulling out the entire amount. Your willingness to cooperate is going to help with the case immensely.'

'I am glad, sir.' She basked in the warmth of his voice. 'I don't want you to think I'm not doing my best.'

'No, no, I know you are. Once the funds come in, let me know and I'll tell you how to notarise it. Also, try and get him to have the funds released today itself.'

'I'll try, sir,' she said. 'But it could take three or four days. Sir, do you think I can see you for just a moment? We've been talking continuously for two days now. It's weird that I don't know what you look like.'

'I can't do that as we are in the middle of the investigation. But once this is over, we will certainly meet. I'll be in touch soon,' he replied. 'Take care, Ms Urvashi.'

The maid was pleased that she didn't have to put in a full day's work. 'Are you going somewhere?' she asked.

'Yes,' Urvashi said, hurrying her along.

In less than an hour, Jayanthi was done. 'I still haven't done the dusting,' she said, taking in Urvashi's grim expression.

'You can do it tomorrow,' Urvashi replied, then followed Jayanthi to the gate to make sure she wasn't planning to lurk around.

As she drew closer to the gate, she noticed the car that had been parked outside the last two days cruising slowly up the lane. She waited to see if the driver would park nearby. Instead, he slowed as he reached the third house down the road from hers and stopped. The driver's side opened and a man emerged. He walked to the passenger's side and opened the door. An elderly woman stepped out, then another.

'Parvathi Madam has guests visiting from Mangalore. Her mother and aunt,' Jayanthi informed her. 'She's getting a knee replacement. They have been here for two days now.'

Urvashi couldn't speak. She clutched the gate to hold herself steady. She heard Anil Kumar Yadav's voice in her head saying, 'It's for your safety.'

Then she remembered how, during their last conversation, his low, measured tone had been replaced by a high note of excitement—or was it elation?

She stood there recollecting all that they had said to each other, one conversation after another. The red flags popped up like mushrooms after a thunderstorm. Every piece of paperwork had seemed legitimate, but what did she know of what was legitimate and what wasn't?

Fuck. Fuck. Fuck. Fuck. Fuck. Had she been played? Had she been scammed? Had she been fucked over? How could she have been such a fool?

Urvashi took a deep breath. She walked back into the house and picked up her phone.

Anil Kumar Yadav had messaged. –Any updates?–

She looked at the phone with revulsion, as if it were a grotesque creature with suckers oozing mucus. What if she was wrong? What if he was for real? The humming in her head returned. Intensified. This couldn't be right. This couldn't be right.

Her phone rang. Anil Kumar Yadav. She steeled herself to not answer the call. After a while, the phone went silent. She heard the ping of the message notification. A few seconds later, it rang again. She silenced the call.

White-hot rage replaced the fear she had been living with. It made her clench her fists and narrow her eyes. It erased the overwhelming anxiety that whispered at the back of her mind: what if you are wrong, what if it's for real? It made her pick up the phone and block the number. Rage was better, infinitely better.

She paced the room, back and forth, back and forth. Then she picked up the phone and looked at her contacts list. She would have to take the chance.

The call was answered on the third ring, 'Hello, you have reached Naveen Nagarjuna's law chambers.'

ACKNOWLEDGEMENTS

Were it not for Suromita Roy, who commissioned the audio stories and then encouraged me to pursue the line of thought, these state-of-the-nation stories wouldn't have found form or expression.

Were it not for the brilliant actor Prakash Raaj, who voice-acted two of the stories with a deep-felt commitment towards the theme, I wouldn't have found the tone I wanted to set for the book.

Were it not for my first readers, journalist Jayanth Kodkani and my long-time editor Karthika V.K., and their belief in the stories that made me want to push boundaries, I wouldn't have had the courage to follow my heart.

ALSO READ